TV
SAFE

TV SAFE

A STONEY WINSTON MYSTERY

Jim Stinson

Charles Scribner's Sons / New York

Maxwell Macmillan Canada / Toronto

Maxwell Macmillan International
New York   Oxford   Singapore   Sydney

Charles Scribner's Sons   Maxwell Macmillan Canada, Inc.
Macmillan Publishing Company   1200 Eglinton Avenue East, Suite 200
866 Third Avenue   Don Mills, Ontario M3C 3N1
New York, NY 10022

Macmillan Publishing Company is part of the Maxwell Communication Group
of Companies.

Library of Congress Cataloging-in-Publication Data
Stinson, Jim.
    TV safe : a Stoney Winston mystery / Jim Stinson.
      p.   cm.
    ISBN 0-684-19225-X
    I. Title.
PS3569.T53T88   1991
813'.54—dc20   91-569

DESIGN BY CHRIS WELCH

10 9 8 7 6 5 4 3 2 1

Printed in the United States of America

For Sue, as always,
and for Violet Wilkinson,
who for eighty-three years thought of others first

Special thanks to Randy Neece, a professional
and a gentleman

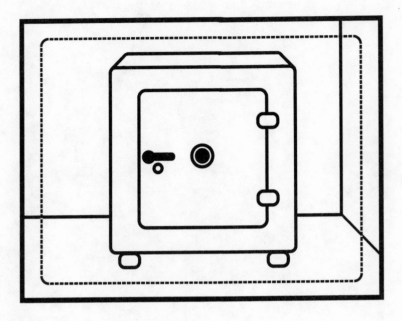

When a film is photographed "TV-safe," the shots
are composed so that all essential information is
confined within the area displayed on TV screens,
which cut off the edges of the original picture.

TV
SAFE

1

*T*he sound stage flashed like a giant zircon with each fake facet twinkling in the lights, and the transparent, Plexiglas, stage-center safe glittered the brightest of all. Its own special key, fill, and kicker lights kissed it as sweetly as if the safe and the visible cash piles within it were Bette Davis in closeup.

The same lights lacquered the game show host, Smilin' Jack Kilparrow in his thousand-dollar jacket and two-thousand-dollar hairpiece. Ambient radiance splashed off the set and glazed the first rows of audience, mesmerized by this certified celebrity who was propping his elbow on one million manifest bucks.

Smilin' Jack patted the safe and twinkled at camera five, which stayed on him throughout the show. "We still have time to learn whether any contestant will get a chance to say the magic words . . ." pat, pat, pat on the transparent plastic ". . . *Oh-Pun Sesame!*" As he said the show's name, a ten-foot neon OH-PUN SESAME blinked wildly in sync with the APPLAUSE signs and the dutiful audience waxed ecstatic. "Okay, contestants, the category is still Movies. Whaddya call a ten-thousand-pound gorilla with indigestion?" The contestants depicted Heavy Thought, then the bubbly blonde stabbed at her buzzer. "Dulcy!"

But the blonde couldn't quite dredge it up: "Uh, uh, ooh-ooh-ooh, oh, oh . . ."

"A ten-thousand-pound gorilla with indigestion?"

BUZZZ!

"Amber!"

After what looked like the windup to a low-grade orgasm, the chic Oriental woman yelled, "Kong with the Wind!" a sound tech punched up the Right Answer music, and Kilparrow brayed, "Right again, Amber, for five hundred dollars!" The APPLAUSE lights went frantic, the floor manager cheered and whistled in case the audience forgot its lines, and I whimpered silently at the depth to which my career had sunk.

The writers' table stood between the set and the audience, and as the most junior scribbler, I was down at the far end. That's why the voice was right at my side: "Stoney!" I turned to confront the producer, Marcia Barker. She jerked a thumb toward the studio door. "Chop chop, Winston!"

Ms. Barker looked like an apple-cheeked granny and ran the show like a Mafia capo, so everyone called her Ma Barker.

But not to her face. "Yes'm."

Ma stomped away, still talking. "I got news for you. What? Later." She waved off an assistant who'd proffered a clipboard. "Talk in my office. Such a goddam zoo around here, I can't concentrate. Cactus!" The floor manager glanced our way. "Three minutes, not one minute more, not one goddam second. Don't hold that door, Winston." She rumbled out into the studio hallway. "I'm not a goddam queen."

"Ma" was a feeble nickname. She should have been Mother Goddam.

KLPP, a sad independent channel half-crippled by a license renewal challenge, was only too happy to rent us its one big stage, especially on weekends when it ran only canned shows.

Ma Barker bivouacked in the program director's office. The carpet stank of cigarettes and the walls were paved with framed awards from as late as 1970.

But Attila's mom was indifferent to decor. "We got trouble." Ma jerked a thumb at the office monitor, where Amber Sung Li was beaming and clapping soundlessly. "That goddam Chink is still winning."

Her prejudices seemed to have seized up fifty years back, but I said only, "Somebody has to."

"Not the million bucks, Buster. That's impossible."

My Lieutenant Spock eyebrow: "Oh?"

She shook her head impatiently. "Hell, the show's not fixed." Ma vacuumed in smoke from a Marlboro. "You think we'd risk that with S and P peering up our nose?" The Standards and Practices people kept us pure of heart and clean of mouth, though for this syndicated show they were outside contractors rather than network drones.

"Then why shouldn't Amber win?"

"Because the odds favor the house and the questions keep getting harder."

"I know. I write the goddam things." Now I was doing it.

She stubbed out the butt with more care than required. "Yeah, we got to talk about that." An ominous note. "Anyway, the top three question levels are so tough an Einstein couldn't get them."

"But Amber's nearly at level two. Why don't you want her to win?"

"Economics, Sonny. This shit—mercy sakes, what *am* I saying? This *class-act family entertainment* costs twenty-five grand a show, above *and* below the line. At that rate, the big payoff would eat the budget for *forty shows*."

How sad. The shows sold for four times their budget, so an extra million in costs would just *slash* annual profits to a pitiful 250-plus percent. Aloud, I said, "Nonetheless, Amber's winning. How?"

Ma's shrug said it was obvious. "Somebody's feeding her answers."

"Who?"

"Nobody. It's impossible. The head writer gives me the questions and I stick 'em in the database. Forty minutes before taping, the goddam computer spits out questions *at random*. I personally pick half of them, also at random. Nobody else has access."

"Until you feed them to the floor when we tape." She nodded.

"The floor" included the onstage monitors of Smilin' Jack and Kelli Dengham, the show's juicy bimbo and comic relief. The only other monitors were on the table of the

writing staff and the special crew who typed the questions
on the Chyron Character Generator that superimposed
question and answer text on the video.

"The Chyron crew must get them early."

"Yeah, but they're up in their goddam penthouse."

"So Amber can't be cheating."

Ma sucked on a second Marlboro. "Correct."

"But Amber can't be winning."

"You're two for two."

"What're you planning?"

"That's bad news and good news. First the bad: as of
now, you're off the writing staff."

"I'm fired?" Time for the old stone face.

"You are." The old stone face must have crumbled a bit,
because Ma frowned and smashed out the half-smoked butt.
"Goddammit, Winston, you aren't delivering usable gags!"
She swept up a page of copy so near at hand that she must
have prepared for this interview. "Look at this: 'Medicine:
What do you call a morbid fear of education? Answer: *Scoliosis.*'"

"I sort of liked . . ."

"Who the hell knows from scoliosis?"

"You said the questions got harder . . ."

"You still don't get it. No matter how hard the questions,
the answers have to be obvious when you see them. The
yokels at home have to think, *Hey, I could have answered
that.*"

"Fine. On my way out you can tell me the *good* news."

She chose to ignore my icy tone. "You're not out, because
I personally saved your buns. As of now you're assistant to
the producer, me."

I couldn't believe she was making a job to keep me employed, not Ms. Attila. "You already have assistants."

"You're going to find out how Amber Sung Li is cheating."

"You just said she *couldn't* be cheating."

Ma Barker rolled right over that: "You write crappy gags, Winston, but you got overall smarts, I can tell. You got a funny mind."

"But not funny enough."

"Not *funny* funny, original. I know you can do this for me."

"I think you need a professional."

"Just what I goddam *don't* need! Look . . ."

I missed half the rest of it, bemused by the sign that'd gone nova two feet from my face: YOU WRITE CRAPPY, WINSTON! It was flashing like the show's neon logo: CRAPPY! CRAPPY! I caught only the gist of Ma Barker's problem: She wouldn't risk a real investigation because (a) the least public whiff of scandal could kill the show, and (b) if Amber Sung Li was *not*, in fact, cheating, then snooping around her could be grounds for a lawsuit. Ma's attitude seemed paranoid, even downright craven, but that's the way TV producers think.

Whatever the case, I didn't need charity. I smiled politely. "I would prefer not to."

And Ma smiled politely back. "Then collect your pay and get off the show." She plucked the half-glasses riding her bosom and set them smartly on her nose.

Ah, pay: a thousand a week. I'd never earned money like that before. A second neon sign blinked on: *$1,000, $1,000.*

"Um, same salary?" She nodded. "I'll think about it."

• • •

That took almost thirty seconds of meditation on my bank account, which, after only five weeks on this show, was not yet off life support. I had no real choice, though being bounced from a quiz show writing team was like being fired from a whorehouse. Nothing to do but darn my fishnet stockings, polish my plastic purse, and go find a flattering street light. Not for the first time, I wondered how long I could keep on doing this.

I was back at the foot of the writers' table for my final trick with my brothel mates, taping the rest of show three. To save money, we shot a week's five shows on Saturday and Sunday. Since the cast and contestants changed clothes between tapings, the resulting five programs looked "live" when aired Monday through Friday. A typical TV deception.

Smilin' Jack glanced at the tiny screen concealed in his lectern. "Okay, contestants, the category is Automobile Parts. For two hundred dollars," pause, "whaddya call a guy who yells insults at other freeway drivers?"

The sound booth punched up Question Countdown music, and the contestants mimed cogitation by jiggling or squinting or flapping their hands, but nobody sounded a buzzer.

Ah-OOH-gah!

"Awww, sorry, folks." The host turned upstage toward the lissome blond vision poised at her own lectern next to the safe. "Kelli?" Kelli Dengham propped a small fist on one cocked hip, delivered a wiggle that set her sequins winking, and frowned in comic concentration. "Kelli, whaddya call a guy who yells insults at other freeway drivers?"

Then Kelli showed why she earned ten thousand a week and why this low-rent syndicated show was expunging its network competition. Her big blue eyes went round and blank as Orphan Annie's. "Aahh . . . aaaaahh . . . um . . ." Her performance was nothing but *shtick*, but somehow Kelli transformed it with her blend of little-girl innocence, scorching sexuality, and simple, goofy joy. "Aaaaaaaaaaaahhhhhhhh . . ." pause, giggle, pause, ". . . would you repeat the question?" (Appreciative yocks from the audience.)

Though Smilin' Jack hated her guts and bones for stealing his show from under him, he played to her expertly. With fatherly patience, "A *guy* who *yells* at *freeway drivers.*"

"Oh!" Her perky face lit up. "A car-berater." As the audience groaned on cue, Kelli did Stan Laurel Confronting a Thought. "I don't get it." They snickered and she wheeled on them with drop-dead timing. "I just *read* this stuff, y'know!"

As the audience howled, I shook my head yet again at the talent coiled in that seemingly empty head. Delivering gags in her odd, scratchy voice, Kelli Dengham could milk laughs from a phone book.

2

*H*alf an hour later I strolled out the artists' entrance (dream on, Winston) and into the studio parking lot. Pleasantly shocked by the glaring January sun, I unlocked my

'63 Beetle and climbed in, careful of snagging my pants on
a seat spring.

Though B. Bumble's outsides were as leprous as ever,
its guts were all nearly brand-new. My beloved landlady'd
surprised me with this refit while I'd been away knitting
two cracked ribs a while back. Sally'd wickedly added a
sporty muffler, so I surged through the gate with a roar
that snapped the guard's head around, and then warbled
due west on DeLongpre through a Hollywood stupid with
Saturday sun.

Arlo Bracken, the contestant coordinator, had supplied
Ms. Sung Li's address in a Westside district penned in by
the Santa Monica and San Diego freeways. She'd also disclosed that Amber was twenty-seven, single, and an un-
employed oral hygienist—which sounded as if she censored
foul language. Hey, maybe I could use that . . .

But I wasn't a gag writer anymore, just a glorified gofer.
That kind of job was getting old fast and so was I: a full
decade since film school and two since my mother'd yanked
me from England to sunny L.A. Thirty-five's not as dis-
maying as forty, but it meant I was half through my three
score and ten. And with sod-all to show for it.

I burbled down La Brea to the Santa Monica westbound.
Freeway traffic was rolling at sixty—which nowadays happens almost monthly—and I found sour comfort in out-
running pricey hardware with my sportscar disguised as a
dumpster.

I'd taken this job on my Sally's advice. She'd said stop
doing low-rent stints as an editor, cameraman, writer, or
manager, so that nobody knew *which* I was. Writers, at
least, were "above-the-line" talent, so I'd promoted this

job from Ma Barker, who had used me at times in the past.

I finessed a clod in a Cadillac coupe and rolled down the Overland off ramp, which lay between Metro and Fox. So near and yet so far.

But this writing job was another dead end, since I hadn't the knack for exploiting it. I was trained to make films, not connections.

Amber's address was a garden apartment, a fifties confection redeemed by four decades of planting and pruning. I sat a spell in the hot winter sun and reviewed why I'd come here. Only a show staff member could feed someone answers, and with thirty-odd staffers but only one Amber, checking her out was less work. Not a brilliant rationale, but right now I just didn't care.

So let's get it over with.

My story was that since Amber was likely to win the big prize, we were gathering more background on her for publicity. This fiction worked only too well when I tried it on the apartment manager, who beamed at me through his granny glasses, swept his screen door wide, and practically dragged me into his living room.

"Hear that, Alice? We're local color." Alice nodded her mouse-gray head without looking up from her magazine. The man was dressed in a T-shirt and rubber sandals and ten-gallon shorts that almost encompassed his twelve-gallon paunch. "Publicity. I want to know how that works. That's the big secret: know everything." He pointed to his forehead.

"Always a sound plan."

"I'm in training myself, you know; going to be a

contestant—hey, not on your show; your show's just puns
and puns are the lowest form of humor, right, Alice?" The
mouse-colored head nodded.

"Some people seem to like . . ."

"I'm going for *Jeopardy*; *Jeopardy*'s class. I'm in training
myself: watch every show, read everything I can, don't I,
Alice?" (Nod, nod.) "You know the big secret? *Buzzers!*"

"Oh-ho."

"That's right, buzzers! Doesn't matter if you know the
answer if someone else beats you to the buzzer. I'm in
training myself: I practice on Nintendo; it's all in the
thumb."

"Same as hitchhiking."

"Last month I sprained my thumb, you know, taking a
toilet out of 12C and I thought, Oh God, I'm out of action:
that's my buzzer thumb. But it's okay now, you think so,
Alice?" Alice nodded and turned a page.

"About Amber Sung Li . . ."

"Local color, right! Uh, lessee: nice and quiet, no visitors,
no loud music." Lowering his voice, "Great set a . . ." He
snapped a glance toward Alice, then cupped his own ap-
preciable breasts. "Uhhhh, hm. Trouble is, she just moved
in three weeks ago."

"Oh?"

"A suitcase and a couple books; 10A's furnished, y'know."

"She give a previous address?"

"Yeah. Santa Monica, Alice?"

(Nod.) "Yucca Street—1423." Alice spoke without looking up.

"Isn't she amazing? Memory like hers, *she* oughtta be
the contestant. Trouble is, I'm the one with the personality,

right, Alice?" Alice didn't nod for once, but the manager wasn't looking at her.

I eased the front door open again. "Well, thanks for your help."

"No problem. Y'know, I got ideas for game shows myself. How about this . . ."

"Thanks, we'll call you." I beat a rapid retreat to the sidewalk.

When I found the place I stared at the building while Beetle Bumble rumbled under me, wondering if Amber Sung Li had given a phony former address. This seedy old pile resembled a warehouse: a windowless, one-story tan stucco block with a peeling front door and a sign that said ARNESEN EYE. I killed the motor and went to look at it. Smaller type below the name explained, *Warren Arnesen: Commercial and Industrial Photography*. I pushed the buzzer, waited a full minute, then banged on the scabby door. Still nothing, so I turned the knob: unlocked. I pushed through into a hallway faked with a Sheetrock partition half the height of the sixteen-foot ceiling. I stuck my head through an open doorway: an improvised apartment with primitive kitchen area and living space furnished in Good Will Revival. Framed photos dappled the walls, most of them showing a plump, bearded man festooned with cameras, posing with trade show models, TV bit players, and similar would-be celebrities. The football-style jacket he wore was embroidered *Warren Arnesen*.

"*Hello!*" My yell bounced around the roof trusses overhead. Then silence.

Back in the hallway I strolled past eighteen-by-twenty-four framed color prints: on one side a series of slick, empty product shots, on the other a slave market parade of erotic nudes—pose after pose of pouting Kimberleys, Candies, Staceys, and Bambis in bad imitations of every style from David Hamilton fog to *Hustler* magazine meat. The nudes looked just like the product shots, and so, in fact, they were. The next-to-last print was a boudoir scene with a striking Oriental model, none other than Amber Sung Li. That seemed to be progress of some sort.

Thirty feet from the outside door the hallway opened into a studio littered with light stands, strobe equipment, diffusion boxes, and seamless paper backing rolls, in a thick confusion made worse by the feeble work light dangling from the high, curved roof.

"Anybody home?" Hardly waiting for an answer now, I groped across this shadowy barn toward the opposite wall, where the chemical smell from the left-hand door announced a darkroom and the light through the right-hand doorway revealed an office beyond it.

Inside, a bare-bones work room of used slab doors laid across low file cabinets to form work tables. In fact, file cabinets claimed so much room that there was barely space for the overturned chair . . .

. . . and the body tangled around it. Drunk, drugged, hurt? I hustled toward it.

Hurt, yes, until he'd passed beyond pain: his head had been pounded to spoiled ground pork, gray and pink and what had been red before it had dried and blackened— some time ago, it appeared. He still sat in the cheap office chair, ruined head on the concrete floor, slack legs bent by the front seat edge, which now pointed up at the roof. The beating had left him some of his face—white, mid-thirties, curly brown beard paving overweight cheeks—the photographer in those pictures: Warren Arnesen.

Was this a burglary? Except for the capsized chair, the office looked normal if somewhat untidy. What did you steal from a photographer?

Pictures, of course. I opened a file drawer and sure enough: page upon page of transparency strips snuggled in clear plastic sleeve-pages. I looked around: over thirty drawers in all those cabinets. It'd take half a day to check them all. I studied the drawer faces helplessly.

One drawer protruded half an inch, as if it had been shut carelessly. I pulled it open and scanned the names on the hanging file folder tags. It was the Bimbo Bin: I'd found Kimberley, Candy, Stacey, and Bambi.

Uh-oh, and *Kelli* as well. The name on the label read Kelli Dengham, as in *Oh-Pun Sesame*.

But the file folder was empty. Stolen? I thought about it. Maybe just being used—say, next door in the darkroom. I scuttled in there, now tiptoeing absurdly, and snapped on the white work light.

No, all the bimbo shots were in color, but the darkroom lacked the temperature-controlled drums and what-not required for color processing. Besides, the counters showed no visible work in progress.

Except maybe that Nikon on the enlarger base. In place of a lens, it was fitted with an optical system for copying film frames. A short piece of 35mm film emerged from each side of the copy rig. I aimed the camera at the ceiling light and peered through the finder.

Kelli Dengham all right, and as lushly nude as a peach

on a tree. The basic equation, at least, seemed clear: Arnesen plus Amber plus Kelli plus naked pictures equaled blackmail, with the payoff in quiz show answers. Yes, but subtract one murdered Arnesen and . . .

I suddenly stopped and cursed myself. I'd found a homicide linked to two people on my show, with the bludgeoned corpse in the next room, but I was bumbling about on the site of the murder, fingering doors and drawers and cameras. Time to saddle up, Pilgrim!

On a shelf, a box of Photowipes, essentially lintless paper towels. I snapped open the copier gate, pulled out the short strip of film, folded it into a wipe, and pocketed the package. I cracked the camera back: no copy film inside. Using a second wipe, I cleaned the camera, copy attachment, darkroom door and light switch, office file drawer handles, living area door, and . . .

A sudden thought, then back to the phone in the office and dialing 911, thinking at mach three. When the call was picked up, I put on my very best Mexican voice: "Hey, like I may dis deliv'ry for da pizza, jou know? An' dere som dead guy in here . . . No name, lady, I don't got no papersss, okay? Oh! Hey, lady? I takin' a pizza back too; he don' wannit." I hung up, knowing that the 911 system had locked on this phone line and displayed its address.

Which gave me maybe five minutes. Wipe phone, sprint to door, open door *slowly* with paper towel, check street —good: deserted—grab outside knob with towel, close door, wipe same, pocket towel, saunter *slowly* to Beetle, start up, rumble sedately away.

I'd driven four blocks when it finally hit. Too shaky to steer, I pulled over and just sat there staring at nothing, dry-washing cold hands like Pontius Pilate, trying and failing to deal with a smashed-in head on a concrete floor and the dead meat inside it where a person had lived. The winter sun was as bright as ever, but its warmth had somehow leaked away like the blood on Arnesen's office floor.

3

That night Sally stayed me with flagons and comforted me with Sally, and by morning I felt better. Now I was standing in my darkroom, staring down at Kelli Dengham reclining nude on a satin chaise. She gazed back with unsettling directness. To see better, I pushed my enlarger head to the top of its column so that the slide image filled my printing easel. But there was little more to see: a seamless backing, prop furnishings, and Kelli's slender roundness presented with classic calm.

Sally stood beside me. "Where have I seen that pose before?"

"He's quoting Manet, Titian, Giorgione—you name it. Seems a bit self-conscious."

Matter-of-factly, "But *she* doesn't. She's beautiful."

Kelli was indeed, from dainty toes to softly sweeping hip to sassy little breasts and perky face. "In a delicate sort of way." The opposite of Sally, who, at five-feet-nine and 160 pounds, was an essay in measured extravagance. I called her my thoroughbred Clydesdale. "You're more my type."

"I'm not *your* type; I'm *mine*."

"A thousand pardons." When would I learn to watch my mouth? Sally bridled at the merest hint of possessiveness.

I pulled the film and inspected it. "Hm. Fujichrome, original camera stock."

She pointed at the two frames. "Why identical pictures?"

"One's half a stop lighter. Photographers bracket exposures."

"Whatever that means. Why was Arnesen copying this slide?"

"Or was Arnesen doing the copying?" I snapped off the enlarger light and removed the film from its holder. "Only one thing we can count on: there's at least two sets of Kelli nudes." I waved the strip. "Originals like these and dupes made in Arnesen's copy rig." As I talked I wandered out of the darkroom. "Question is, who has them?"

My apartment was more like an office now that I was eating and sleeping upstairs. The main floor of Sally's house perched high above Laurel Canyon, its front door barely at grade level. The downstairs flat she leased me was really her basement, with three walls of water stains to only one of windows. I'd christened it Mildew Manor. But now those windows were ablaze with morning light, and the joint didn't look half bad if you ignored the smog of dust motes in the sun rays.

Sally came up beside me and snaked an arm around my waist. "I'm glad my type is your type." For Sally, that mumbled line was a peace offering. I looked at this amazing person whose life I'd blundered into. When I caught her eye, she withdrew her arm abruptly. "Enough of this mush. Let's go back upstairs."

I followed her out my door and around to the flight of
steps at the side of the house. Sally started up them, talking
as she went. The stairs were so steep that my eye level
matched her Wagnerian rump, and for twelve steps I ogled
deplorably, backsliding wretch that I am.

"It doesn't add up, Stoney. I mean naked-shmaked. If
Kelli's pose was any tamer, they could run it in *Good House-
keeping*. How could you extort quiz show answers with
pictures like *that*?"

"Because the show's producer is terrified of scandal—
she as much as said so yesterday. She's not rational
about it."

"It still doesn't figure."

True, but it was all I could think of.

Another superb winter day as I rumbled east on Hollywood Boulevard through the heartbreaking tropical light
that sometimes reminds L.A. of what we discarded for cars.
I didn't have to go to work until noon because Sunday meant
only two shows to tape.

Two rounds that Amber would probably win. Then semi-
finals next Saturday and jackpot time on Sunday. Exactly
one week to learn how Kelli was feeding Amber the answers.

Impossible: Kelli didn't even *see* the answers until both
of them were onstage, in public.

And yet Arnesen had shot nudes of both Amber and Kelli
and Arnesen had been killed and Kelli's slides were missing.

I stopped at the World Book and News Co. on Cahuenga
to pick up an *L.A. Times*. Even this early, the sidewalk

was sprinkled with hookers, gawkers, punkers, bums, and teenagers down from Pacoima—the Hollywood *boulevardiers*. Crazy George was prancing along his usual beat: six-feet-six of Watusi warrior in yellow miniskirt, spike heels, and Dynel wig.

"Yo, George. Beautiful day."

"Praise be to God, Stoney!" He threw up his arms like Judy Garland in concert and ankled away in his lime-green panty hose. As a feminine vision, George did his bit to promote the ethnic slur about skinny legs.

Arnesen had been killed at an address Amber'd listed as her own. Better tell Ma Barker her contestant was linked to a murder.

Better *not* tell Ma Barker. As the only soul who knew the questions ahead of the taping, she was a logical suspect herself—except that she was the one who'd put me onto this in the first place.

Around and around, going nowhere.

The KLPP lot was half empty when I roared in, slapped the mighty B. into a parking slot, and got out. Wait a minute, one group did get the questions in advance: the Chyron crew who turned them into titles.

They were indeed exiled to what Ma Barker'd called "their goddam penthouse," an enclosed wooden platform hung against one sound stage wall ten feet above the floor and reachable only by a single flight of steps. That way, no one could plausibly wander through their booth and just happen to see the show's questions and answers.

The head of the Chyron crew was Ronald N. Tolkis, nerd deluxe, right down to his horn rims, adam's apple, dandruff, and negligent dress. All he lacked to complete the cliché

was a pocket protector and pens. He punched a short code
on his keyboard and the *Oh-Pun Sesame* logo pulsed blood-
red on his screen.

As it happens, I like nerds. They tend to be quirky,
bright, and obsessed with one thing or another; and in this
world of opportunists and timeservers, true passion is only
too rare. I walked up behind him. "Rockin' Ron!"

He peered at his work. "Isn't that wuv-wie? Hehehe-
hehheh." Ron's true passion was Warner cartoons, and his
Elmer Fudd voice was flawless. I envied it.

"Got a minute?"

"Sure." He revolved in his posture chair. "What's up,
Doc?"

"I'm working for Ma Barker now . . ."

"Yeah, she told me."

". . . and she wants me to check security."

He squinted up at me anxiously. "Something wrong,
Stoney?"

Time for a small fiction: "No, no, Ma just thinks I should
know how it works." Tolkis still looked worried, so I added,
"And she said you knew more about the system than anybody."

I'd offered the opening no nerd can resist. "Damn right;
I designed it!" Ron leaped to his sneakered feet, inflated
visibly, and launched a detailed exegesis of the system.

It boiled down to this: he'd fitted Ma Barker's computer
database with an algorhythm that picked thirty questions
at random, from which Ma selected fifteen. She printed
her choices and hand-carried the printout directly to Ron
in this booth.

"You're not linked electronically?"

"Just sneakernet; her 386 is a standalone."

Which meant that no hacker could tap it remotely. "Could someone get at the computer itself?"

"Let 'em; I used full DES encryption. Only Ma has the password." I nodded as wisely as if I knew what DES meant.

"How does security work after you get the questions?"

"We just don't leave this booth, do we, Sondra?"

His assistant turned to peer at us through thick spectacles. She nodded. "I'll tell ya, babe, you learn to take a leak in advance, 'cause when you're here, you're here."

Ron resumed his lecture. As for the Chyron procedure, he and his crew typed the questions and answers on the system, numbering and storing each one. No one else saw a question until Ron put it on screen, at a cue from the director.

"Then your phone goes to the booth." He could see and hear the show on his monitor, but speak only to the director. Hm.

I swept the gloomy little cave with an admiring look. "You've really done a beautiful job."

"Son, you have artic—, ah say, articulated a *maothfull!*" His Foghorn Leghorn voice needed work: it wobbled off into vintage Kingfish.

I nodded and smiled and went out. Everyone in the director's booth could see the questions in advance. Maybe wander back there and check it out.

The windowless master control room reminded me of why I prefer the simpler technology of film. Scrunched in a canvas chair at the back, I counted ten telephones and twenty-three monitors, plus switching panels, patching cables, knobs, buttons, sliders, and rack after rack of obscure electronic equipment. In the hyper-cooled gloom of this tight metal shell I expected the director to snap, "Down periscope; dive, dive!"

Ah-OOH-gah!

As if on cue, Audio Control next door punched in the "time's up" klaxon effect, and Smilin' Jack's image said, "Sorry, folks; Kelli?"

"Ready, three . . . *three.*" At the director's command, the tech director put Kelli Dengham's camera on line. Her sequins today were blue.

"Five."

Smilin' Jack was back on screen. "The category is Magazines. Kelli, whaddya call guys who fix your car right the first time?"

"Three." While Kelli went through her routine, I checked the monitors. The question was supered over the line picture—the image recorded on tape—and appeared by itself on the Chyron monitor: *People who fix your car right the first time.*

"Um, *Popular Mechanics!*" and the answer flashed on the screens below the question. Well, so much for that idea: the booth didn't see the answer until everyone else did. While a sound man sweetened the audience reaction with canned groans and hisses, I threaded my way out.

Interesting, though: Amber Sung Li was not giving *all* the right answers.

4

*E*verything about Arlene Bracken screamed, *"Butch,* and what's it to you, Jack?"* Black shoe-brush hair with polish still clinging to it, equally shiny black cycle boots, black pegged pants, and a black vinyl shirt with more buckles than Bogart's trenchcoat. Small, wary eyes in a truculent face that relaxed when she spotted me. "Hey, Winston."

"Hey, Arlo." I guess she'd realized that I couldn't care less about her lifestyle, I didn't do macho numbers, and I valued her brains and energy. Arlo'd accepted me promptly. She was propping her short, chunky form on a standup desk as she lacquered her nails, one black, one silver, one black.

I recycled the line that had worked with Ron Tolkis: "Ma Barker made me her assistant."

"The old bitch found your level of incompetence."

As a gag writer, yes. "You don't sound partial to Ma."

"She was to *me.* She hit on me once, but I brushed her off. Too *old,* man." She dipped the small brush in liquid moonlight and silvered another nail. "Since then she's been on my case."

"Ah. Well, she wanted me to see how you run your department." Arlo was contestant coordinator.

"Bullshit, Winston, you just like to watch girls—but, hey, I can empathize." By unspoken policy, most contest-

ants were young, attractive, and female, and they hid themselves here in the dingy Green Room before and between
show tapings.

"How do you 'coordinate' contestants?"

Lips pursed, she blow-dried the nail, then, "Screen 'em,
pick 'em, rehearse 'em."

"What are you doing right now—aside from exterior dec-
orating?"

"Just babysitting—and check their hair and makeup. You
know."

I leaned an elbow on her desk. "Mind if I hang out a
while?"

"Off the furniture, Winston!" When I snapped erect,
looking surprised, Arlo's face softened. She waggled a brush
at the pots of polish. "That crap's twenty bucks a bottle."

"Sorry."

"You spill it, I'll make you lick it up." Arlo seemed to
sense that this amiable jocosity didn't quite lighten the
tone, so she smiled and added, "Go ahead and hang out—
but there's really nothing to see."

"Thanks." I backed my skinny six-feet-two against a wall
beside her, wondering why Arlo made such a production
of her preference. Nowadays folk went to bed with the
other sex, the same sex, both sexes—or, for all I knew,
with Michelin inner tubes—and without this aggressive
display.

But then, Dr. Ruth Westheimer I wasn't.

Little to see indeed, except three very nervous contestants. Dulcy the bubbly blonde perched with a mirror in
one hand and a book in the other, reading, checking
makeup, reading, checking hairdo, reading. The lone male

contestant paced like a prisoner. At every fifth step he snapped on a grin and as quickly snapped it off again, as if he were rehearsing.

Amber Sung Li draped herself on a couch, showing elegant legs to advantage. Her face appeared calm, but she swilled compulsively from a two-liter bottle of Coke.

A few minutes passed and then Kelli swept in, her arm around Smilin' Jack's corseted waist. He said something and she giggled appreciatively, raising one spike-heeled foot behind her like a forties actress stretching for a kiss. Kilparrow squeezed her small waist, then his hand drifted to her blue-sequined buttock and cupped it.

Arlo muttered, "That's how he shows he despises her, the prick." She started painting her second hand.

Kilparrow and Kelli went off, he to his dressing room on the left, she to hers in the center.

The feeling of tension persisted. Dulcy primped and read, the male paced faster, and Amber sucked at her half-empty bottle. She set it down, uncoiled gracefully, and went off to the women's rest room.

I wasn't surprised. "Ms. Sung Li sure knocks back the Coke."

Arlo nodded. "Believe it. She goes through two of those bottles a day. Says the caffeine keeps her alert."

"And commuting to the john."

Another nod as Arlo anointed a cuticle.

A long, dead pause while I soaked up the tension in the room, and then Ma Barker came in, knocked on Kelli Dengham's door, was admitted. Interesting: she carried a sheet of paper.

"What's Ma doing with Kelli?"

"Dunno. Maybe psyching her up for the show or some-thing. Kelli's such a ditz."

Super-casual: "Ma always do that?"

"Mm-hmh. Think I'll paint the last one silver."

"Two nails in a row?"

Arlo raised her spike-haired head. "Don't get hung up on symmetry, Winston, it makes your head too tight."

I wandered back to the set, where the troops were idling in strict segregation: stagehands at a table concealed from the audience by freestanding flats, cue card crew way off to one side, writers trading snappies at their table, the fans in their bleachers, as patient as cows.

Ma went to Kelli's dressing room with a piece of paper, and she did so before every show. Why?

Puzzled by this, I ambled toward the camera crew near the Chapman crane. Within this one crew were yet more class distinctions: the cable pullers, all female, wore mesh-backed driving gloves to announce their profession and sneakers to keep their feet silent. The cameramen, male, sported sneakers as well, except for debonair Josue Martinez, who commanded the crane in cowboy boots because *his* feet did not touch the floor.

They were squeezed around Cactus Pomeroy, the floor manager, who was holding an open magazine. He glanced up and said, "Winston! Hey, check this out!" The knot of people unraveled enough to let me through and I looked at the magazine, a copy of *Raunch*. "Come inna mail yesterday; I subscribe."

Knowing Cactus, he would. *Raunch* was a rag for the macho redneck: a cesspit of scatological japes, repellant cartoons about black sex equipment, and articles written with very short words—all divided by spread after slick photo spread of flesh from the view of a purblind midwife. Detestable stuff.

And there, across four glossy pages, were the rest of Kelli's nude photos. Like the shot I'd discovered, the pictures were tame, especially for "readers" of *Raunch*: Kelli odalisque, Kelli facing the camera with hands on her hips, Kelli smiling and lifting her cloud of backlit blond hair. Though her delicate legs and round hips were delicious, her sexual punch really came from her face, with its wicked blue eyes and moist mouth.

Another choice theory shot down: if anyone wanted to blackmail Kelli, they were only a tiny bit late.

I brooded on things through the second taping, and by the time the show called it a wrap I was ready to do the same with this job. Arnesen was indeed dead, and both Amber and Kelli had links to him. But beyond that I had only a woolly extortion theory—now half unraveled by *Raunch*—to explain allegations of cheating made solely by Ma, who alone had the answers to cheat with and who visited Kelli before every show. A game was in progress, no question about it, but I had been told the wrong game. So here I stood with my Ping-Pong ball in the midst of a football scrimmage, and the giant thugs thundering down on me would cause serious pain upon impact.

But how do you punt a Ping-Pong ball? I'd tried three times to speak to Ma Barker and each time she'd curtly brushed me away. When I spotted her now in the parking lot I gave it my final shot. "Ms. Barker!"

She unlocked the door of her classic Jaguar. "Not now, goddammit; see me in my office tomorrow."

I planted myself a scant foot from her nose. "*Now*, goddammit. This. Goddam. *Minute*."

Her complexion acquired an interesting tint and her eyeballs popped like a lizard's. "You . . ."

"Don't bully me, *Ma*, I'm not your flunky." Surprise tinged her choleric look. "I've resigned."

"What . . . ?"

"But before I get my severance check I owe you a report. The man Amber lived with until three weeks ago was just beaten to death. See you around." I stalked away toward Beetle Bumble.

She yelled, "What do you mean?"

I called back, "That's the report, Ma."

Her face froze like a computer screen when its processor's crunching big numbers, and for much the same reason. Finally, "Okay." She glanced around the lot and then jerked her head toward her car. "Uh, you better get in."

"I have wheels."

She approached with a weary, thick-ankled gait that suddenly signaled her age. "Just drive around a few minutes. I can't talk to you here." Her face looked tired as well.

I nodded.

Ma's Jag was a '53 XK150 coupe—or rather, a glass fiber replica shoehorned onto a Mustang frame. We tooled up La Brea and into the hills while I told her what I'd learned. She nodded when I explained how I'd informed the police without involving myself, and when I pointed out that they would certainly question Amber because she'd lived with the murder victim, Ma Barker just shrugged. "The media won't pick up on that—not 'til it's too late to hurt us."

"But the media picked up on Kelli: those pictures of her are all over the new issue of *Raunch* magazine."

Another shrug. "I knew that months ago. I helped set up the sale. How's she look?"

Her nonchalance took me aback. "You don't care?"

"I care about free publicity, Charlie."

"You want *Raunch* readers for viewers?"

"I want *anybody*, but that's not the goddam point."

We drove through the winter dark in silence while I digested this. Ma surged over the crown of a hill and picked up the road that corkscrews northward down to Little Cahuenga Boulevard. She spotted a scenic view turnout, jerked the car into it, and squealed to a stop two feet from the night sky twinkling over Hollywood, which twinkled determinedly back.

Ma scowled at the view and explained with weary patience, "Naughty bimbos who show their boobies in redneck magazines are gossip items." Her broad face brightened at the thought. "We're getting calls all the way from *People* down to *The National Insider*."

"I thought you wanted to avoid scandal."

Impatiently, "Cheating is *bad* scandal, pussy is *good* scandal—in fact, the best kind of all. Don't be dumber than you need to, Winston."

I suddenly recalled that I'd quit this job. "Smart enough to know you go to Kelli's dressing room just before every show."

"So?"

"What's on the piece of paper you carry?"

"The show questions and answers."

She said it without a pause or a flicker of expression. Nonplussed, I could only ask, "Why?"

Only then did Ma hesitate. Finally, "I have to. Kelli's —whaddaya call it?—dyslexic. She can't sight-read off a monitor worth diddly, so before each show I rehearse her. If I didn't she'd screw up the tapings."

Well, maybe. "Why didn't you tell me?"

"Like I said, there's good gossip and bad gossip. Adults who can't read are dummies, right?"

"Dyslexics are not at all stupid."

She waved it away. "Whatever. Besides, Kelli doesn't leave her dressing room 'til I personally take her to the floor."

"She's still the logical suspect."

"Why?"

"Something to do with those pictures." But I couldn't think what, so I stared at the carpet of lights down below while I followed a different idea. "Look, you say Kelli's photo spread makes a good scandal. But what if they shot more explicit stuff too, maybe with a partner, maybe hard core? Would publishing that still be 'good' scandal?"

Ma's turn to think now, and her peevish expression shaded into worry. "How do we find out?"

One way was obvious: "Ask Kelli."

"You don't know our million-dollar Twinky, Bub. In case you didn't notice, that darling child—and I mean *child*— is already flaky as a bucket of bran. If she's scared enough to give away answers, you don't want to accuse her of it. She'd go right through the goddam roof."

"Star temperament. They recover."

"Yeah, *eventually.* Look: when we started the show Kilparrow got the only dressing room suite—I mean, he was
the star, after all. When Kelli found out—well, talk about
your tantrums and tears and calling in 'sick.' We lost two
weeks' production, had to switch the goddam dressing
rooms so Kilparrow's walking a mile to the john, which
makes him a treat to live with too. No, don't talk to Kelli."
Ma put the car in gear, reversed out of the turnout, and
aimed us down hill.

"Well then . . . ?"

Ma didn't answer until we were halfway back to the
studio. "Drenko. Ernie Drenko's her agent. He sold those
pictures to *Raunch.*"

"Will he talk to me?"

"I'll have my girl set it up."

Hold it: somehow I'd tacitly signed on again. "After we
clear the air, Ma. I told you I won't be your flunky."

The car swerved slightly as she fumbled a Marlboro out
of her purse. When she lit it the flare of her Bic showed a
face more tired than ever. "We're all flunkies for someone,
Sonny, so why are you any different?"

"I think I made my point, Ma."

"Yeah." She nursed on her Marlboro, then, "Why're you
calling me 'Ma'?"

"It must be your matronly warmth."

"You got a mouth, Winston; that I'll give you." And
Attila's sweet mom swung her phony Jaguar into the studio
lot.

Sally jackknifed at the hips to reach a shirt out of the
clothes dryer, deftly installed a hanger, and slapped it on

a door hook. "Okay, your producer's afraid the show will suffer if cheating or blackmailing or whatever gets out. Why is that important to you?"

"The job's important." I paved the washer drum with wet panty hose, careful to keep them clear of the agitator.

She plucked out a shimmering blouse. "You're out of work about once a month. You always get more."

"I wouldn't mind changing that pattern." I fished her bras from their dishpan of rinse water and deposited two in the washer drum. "How can you go through so many bras?"

"Because you didn't wash them last week. Stoney, ol' buddy, you can't change your employment pattern until you change your line of work. After ten years, haven't you figured that out?"

That stung me to a dirty answer: "Easy advice from a coupon-clipper."

"And how do you think I got the money to buy the coupons?" She slammed the dryer door harder than necessary.

She was right: Sally'd sold enough mainframes, before they'd gone soft, to build up a fund for mad, impetuous flings at investing. But the more she flung, the more the market flung back; and now, with a phone, a PC, and a modem, she made more in a week than I did in a month.

I disentangled two more bras and added the pair to my load while I searched for the real reason that this was important. "Fact is, there's something dangerous there—I can feel it. A man is dead, people are playing nasty games, and Kelli Dengham's wandering around in all that like a toddler on a freeway."

"Uh-huh, and Lolita appeals to the pederast in you."

"That's kind of rough, isn't it?"

"I dunno. Who appointed you her protector?"

Damn hooks. Whatever its effect in the bedroom, female underwear was a pest in the laundry. "I guess I did."

"Hmpf."

Untangling this bird's nest of sopping bras, I reflected that cup size was an unneeded measurement. Just label the damn things two-hook, three-hook, or four-hook—or with Sally's bras, kilo-hook. Impatiently, I dumped in the clot of tangled snuggies, punched the fast button, and started the spin cycle. "What's for supper?"

"Why should I know any more than you do?" She snatched the hanging clothes with one powerful hand and stomped away toward the bedroom. Oh great: now Sally was peeved about something or other.

The perfect end to a peachy day.

5

*M*onday morning was, well, Monday morning, as I grumbled downhill from Laurel Canyon all the way to Wilshire and headed west toward Beverly Hills and a chat with Kelli's agent.

The Ernest L. Drenko Agency wasn't a factory crawling with smoothies taking meetings, giving phone, doing lunch, carving deals, and otherwise herding bankable talent

through the holy labyrinth to the secret center where the
Go Projects lurked. Nor was it a hole in the wall where
one hustling agent wheedled bit parts for wannabes and
cameos for has-beens. Drenko's large flock of supporting
actors worked often, and collectively they earned enough
to finance his Rodeo Drive taste—to employ that oxymo-
ron.

Rodeo was just a brisk walk from his office on South
Robertson in a typical fifties office block done in Car Hop
Futuresque. I climbed foyer stairs to the second floor, entered the reception room, and explained myself to the delicious young man at the desk, who phoned in my name
and languidly waved me to a seat.

I watched him fussing with things on his desk. Young
Golden Delicious could flounce sitting down, and for
the second time in as many days I wondered why some
homosexuals made a production of it. Most of my gay or
lesbian friends did whatever they did in the hay and
otherwise got on with life like the rest of us. But what
could I possibly know of the pressures that shaped gay
behavior?

He whickered into his phone again and then beckoned
me into the sanctum.

Drenko's lair was a showroom of yuppie toys: spindly
halogen lamps on the desk competed for space with an
exotic phone/fax/copy rig that bristled with buttons like
black M&M's. A wall-hung oak and brass weather station
reported a climate that never changed and a massive video/
audio system filled an alcove like a cathedral chapel.

Drenko was in the opposite corner, Laocoöned in a fit-
ness machine the size and price of a small sedan. He flexed

and extended for thirty more seconds, then powered down, extracted himself from his chromium maiden, and thudded toward me, a tall, bulky man with a gray spade beard. His sweat shirt said NO STRAIN, NO TRUSS in crimson letters, and his eyes said nothing at all. As he extended a meaty hand to shake, cordiality washed into his face as if dialed up by a dimmer knob.

"Winston? Call me Ernie. What is it you do again?"

"I'm Marcia Barker's assistant."

Drenko yanked the towel from his shoulders and mopped his face. "To be right up front about this, I don't get it. When I deal with Marcia, I deal with *Marcia*, no offense." He threw the towel on the floor.

"We're not dealing, Ernie; we're putting out a fire."

"Kinda fire?"

"Hot enough to burn down *Oh-Pun Sesame*, Kelli Dengham and all."

Drenko padded around his desk and plonked into a leather chair originally designed for race cars. "In that case I *only* talk to Marcia."

"She doesn't know the details."

"You do?"

I nodded and poured banana oil: "She thinks you're important enough to get them firsthand—and firsthand, in this case, is me."

Drenko stared at me, then nodded back and waved me to a chair. "Makes sense." He punched a button and his chair reclined until he could contemplate his ceiling.

I covered Amber's cheating and her connection with Kelli through Arnesen, omitting the trifling detail of the photographer's murder.

Still inspecting the ceiling, "To be honest, I take offense. My Kelli wouldn't do that."

"How do you know?"

"I *know*."

Time to get down to it: "Suppose Amber got hold of the pictures shot for *Raunch*."

"So?"

"Were there any other pictures—rougher stuff?"

That sat him up again. "You mean like going down on some jerk? N.O., *no*."

"Sure?"

"I was at the session—I set the whole thing up. And I saw everything they shot."

"Could there've been other sessions?"

"Not without me." Drenko leaned back again, perceived that his seat was still supine, and powered it up to meet him halfway. "Look, Winston, I manage that kid; I run her career. She's a gorgeous lady but, to speak candidly, maybe not Einstein, okay? She doesn't make move one without my input."

I kept my tone neutral. "You've made her what she is today."

He took it as a compliment. "Who'd have figured? A nice kid, I guess, but no ball of fire, and this town's so fulla bimbos they gotta wear numbers. Marcia needed some tits in sequins—like all the other game shows—so I sent Kelli over."

"She does have talent, though."

Drenko poured something bubbly from a high-tech desk decanter, sipped it, and contradicted himself: "I'll tell you

the truth: I saw that right away—a special kind of spark—
not like the others."

"How long she been with you?"

Pause. "Year maybe."

"Before that? Where'd she come from?"

Another pause, then, "Where they all come from: some
place in flyover country." Despite the offhand tone, a faint
wariness filmed Drenko's thick face.

"So you don't know much about her background."

He tacked away from the topic: "I know she wouldn't
throw the show."

"All right." I stood up. "But *someone* is, and if that gets
out, we're dead in the water—Kelli too."

Drenko dialed up the good cheer again. "To be frank,
I'm as concerned as you, but what can I do?"

"I'd find out if someone's holding her up."

Stubbornly, "Impossible."

I looked at him intently, but Drenko just stared back
through the eyeholes in his genial mask. Time for Plan B:
"Okay, I'll take your word for it."

He nodded. "Like I said, I'm all up front." And so was
a back-lot facade.

I pretended to think of something, then pulled a binder
out of my little briefcase. "Almost forgot: I'm supposed to
deliver these show notes to Kelli." Drenko's shrug asked
what that had to do with him. "Can I drop them off at her
place?" This time the shrug said *whatever*. "Can I get the
address from your secretary?"

Drenko nodded and picked up his Flash Gordon phone.

● ● ●

Conejo Canyon's laid out to repel boarders, with dinky
lanes that curl away from the main road like vines, writh-
ing back on themselves, changing names, and snaking
up the hillsides into blind dead ends. The elect who can
afford it here like it that way. If you belong, you already
know where you're going, and if you don't, you shouldn't
be here anyway in your crummy old Beetle. The houses
along my baffling route ranged from Moonlight in Madrid
to Merchant Builder Baroque—and everywhere in between.

Kelli's home might be listed as *Cape Cod Charmer*, *2br*,
2ba, *frplce*, *spa*—a small, gabled house painted chalky
gray-blue, on a tiny lot carved from the hillside. I parked
in the steep driveway, praying that my emergency brake
cable wouldn't snap yet again, and climbed ten steps to the
white front door.

Kelli answered my ring. "Hi." She sparkled today in a
lime-colored turtleneck and sloppy yellow slacks.

"Morning, Kelli. I'm Stoney Winston—from the show?"

After her patented grimace of goofy thought, she brightened. "A writer. Hi!" Giggle. "I said that, didn't I? C'min."
I was struck again by her comical voice: the odd, husky
rasp of a little girl with a sore throat.

I stepped into a hallway papered in teensy-weensy flowers and hung with a dozen needlepoints of herbs in oval
frames. "Did you make these?"

"Waiting in my dressing room. Something to do. C'mon;
I'm out in the kitchen." She walked away, still talking: "I
look at you at the writers' table while we tape."

"Well . . ." Was it just my usual prurience or was she
overdoing the Mae West wobble?

"You're the only one who isn't fat or bald."

I did Margaret Hamilton: "All in good time," and followed her into a kitchen that looked like a magazine cover: used-brick walls and wood-veneer appliance fronts and hanging copper pots and pans that no one ever cooked with. The other decoration was Siamese cats: one on the slate-black Corian counter, two more prowling a thicket of chair legs, a fourth peering down from a cabinet top with that wacky cross-eyed stare that Siamese give you. "Graaahh," said the cat in the voice of an elderly parrot.

"That's Cheddar; she's the sharp one." Kelli buried her nose in the countertop cat so that gold curls splashed palomino fur. "And this is Velveeta: all softy." The cat ignored her, not with normal feline disdain, but as if it were too stoned to notice. "Jack's under the table with Zola—being bad, I bet."

"Cheddar, Jack, Velveeta—and *Zola*?"

"Mm-hmh, Gorgonzola." She resumed cutting white meat off a cold chicken carcass and tossing the bits into four pet bowls. "What's up?"

I settled in a chair. "Nothing much. Kelli, maybe you can help us with a problem."

She poked at the chicken corpse with timid fingers. "I'm not real good at problems."

"You know Amber Sung Li, the contestant?"

"Sure: the smart one. Willya give me a *minute*?" The two floor cats had joined Velveeta on the counter and were eyeing the fowl with psychotic glee.

"Maybe *too* smart, Kelli. We're pretty sure she's cheating."

Kelli still frowned at the chicken. "You're kidding!"

"It's hard to explain, but the questions are just too tough for her to get all of them."

"She doesn't. Shoo-shoo-shoo!" But the cats kept up their demented stares.

"Well, Amber gets enough answers to keep winning. I just wondered—you see her down in the Green Room between shows. Does she ever do anything funny?"

Kelli mimed industrial-strength thought while I fought to keep a straight face at her droll expression. At length she shook her curls. "She just sits there."

I tried a different route: "You know, Amber used to live with the man who took that photo spread of you."

"No kidding. Wimpy guy like him?" She sucked her fingers like a child licking icing.

"And I wondered if she got hold of some of the pictures."

Kelli looked puzzled. "What for? Unless she digs girls."

"Pictures you wouldn't want people to see."

For just an instant her face flickered, and then she nodded elaborately. "Oh, *those* pictures!"

Bingo! But I kept it dead-neutral: "Mm-hmh."

Kelli pouted. "*I* thought it was real cute. I did my hair in these little pigtails?—and put on this real short skirt, you know?—but I mean no panties and all, and no top, and I held these books in my arm like I was going to school."

Maybe not bingo after all. "Ah?"

"Well, Ernie said I looked about twelve that way and you can't use pictures like that 'cause you're like a molester or something." One of her giggles. "Or like vice versa, I guess."

"Ah." In a schoolgirl skirt with her knickers down she might look a little gamy, but not enough for blackmail. I tilted my ladderback chair on two legs, trying to seem casual. "But nothing else?"

Her face grew a look of little-girl guilt, then she twinkled. "I *was* sucking a Popsicle."

"Ah."

"It was banana."

I was searching for a variant of *ah* when fifteen pounds of ballistic cat, launched from the cabinet top behind me, WHOMPED onto my shoulder and sprang forward toward the counter while I saluted Isaac Newton with an equal and opposite arc to the floor. I crashed onto my back, still in the chair, and Kelli just creased herself laughing. Her mockingbird trill was so infectious that I started laughing too—until the thought hit that I'd found Arnesen dead in exactly the same position, chair and all.

As I spiraled down the coiling road that unscrewed me from the Canyon, I pondered why I disliked Siamese cats. In most ways they were the *essence* of cat, distilled almost to parody: sleek bundles of lazy energy, negligent beauty, unshakable self-regard. But their crossed blue eyes were grotesquely droll, like Marilyn Monroe with buck teeth, and their whiskey voices were comically wrong for their lithe and elegant bodies. Their impulsive antics were funny too, but they whispered freezing hints of dementia. Maybe that was it: Siamese cats made me laugh at pathology, then made me ashamed of my laughter.

Uh-huh, or perhaps I disliked them because one had just knocked me flat on my kiester and made me a buffoon in front of the most beautiful lady in Conejo Canyon. Come on, Winston, don't take it out on the cats.

6

I roared up to the house about five P.M., berthed the Bumble by Sally's blue Supra, and set off in search of my landlady. She was out on the deck, boiling her munificence in the hot tub while she studied *The Wall Street Journal* under the twelve-volt garden lights.

"How do you keep the paper dry?"

"Eventually I don't." She laid it on the deck beside her iced tea. "Hi, Stoney; hop in."

I was tempted, since Sally was sleek as a dolphin and just as bare; but I was chasing an idea, and Sally in Eve's condition was reliably fatal to thought. "In a minute. I'm working something out and hot water wrinkles my brain."

"Okay, then hop in but don't sit down."

"Wacka-wacka."

Her rumbling chuckle. "My ray of sunshine returns. What's wrong?"

"Four days 'til we tape again and I'm nowhere."

She patted the *Journal* with dripping fingers. "I picked up ten K today; sold the Rockwell shares."

An idea coalesced. "After all that punishing labor you need diversion."

She arched her back and stretched, which lowered the levels of the water and my resistance. "Make me an offer."

I focused doggedly. "How'd you like to be a contestant?"

"On *Oh-Pun Sesame*? Surely you jest."

I tugged off my sneakers abstractedly. "I've been think-ing." Peeling socks. "Amber has to get the answers just before each show, but I can't figure out how she does it." I stripped off my rugby jersey. "And I can't stake out the Green Room without letting her know something's up."

Sally finger-combed her sopping cornsilk hair. "But I could."

Concentrate, Winston. "As a contestant." I undid my scrimshaw belt buckle and pushed down my Monkey Ward jeans.

"I don't think I have the talent."

"Oh, you're plenty smart, but you couldn't be allowed on the show anyway." I went on husking clothes. "You have a 'personal relationship' with a staff member. No, just go through the screening and coaching."

"What would that do?"

I eased down into the warm, dark buoyancy of this ma-hogany womb. "Let you hang around during the week when I've no reason to be there."

Sally stood up. "I don't know, Winston, you have a way of attracting trouble."

Look who was talking. I wrapped my arms around her and Sally returned the favor, adding, "That's the reason I like you." She sank down onto her seat again and pulled me along.

"The only reason?"

"I'm open to suggestion."

As predicted, my train of thought promptly derailed.

• • •

The next day I sold my idea to Ma Barker, who god-
dammed me for spilling show secrets to Sally but was clearly
impressed by her presence and brains. So on Tuesday
through Friday Sally underwent screening sessions; took
coaching from Arlo in squealing, smiling, and acting perky;
and competed in a simulated taping, where her answers,
which had been fed her by Ma, were more than enough
to qualify her for the real thing. It didn't hurt either that
Sally lit up a monitor like a phosphorus bomb.

"That's a goddam sexy lady." Ms. Attila stared at Sally's
image on her desktop TV with what seemed more than
professional interest.

I interposed a distraction: "I reached a dead end on Kelli.
A year ago she just showed up."

A puzzled frown. "You lost me."

"If Kelli's telling the truth, those slides aren't good
enough for blackmail."

"You mean *bad* enough. So?"

"So I wondered if Amber might have something else on
Kelli, something—I don't know—from her past."

"That's really reaching, Bucky." Ma shook her gray head.
"But I'll bite: whadja find in her past?"

"She hasn't *got* a past. No friends, no love life, no former
addresses, no background at all."

A shrug. "In this goddam town, she wouldn't be the first
one."

"Her agent Drenko couldn't tell me much either—or
wouldn't."

"Or maybe she's not our boy after all."

I stared sourly at the gaudy prints on Ma's office wall.

The production company's headquarters on Melrose was far more cheerful than the studio, but today that gloomy old barn would have better matched my mood. "I'll keep looking," I said, and sighed.

But to little effect, and by Saturday I'd only confirmed that Kelli Dengham had no past or present outside life that I could discover with my amateur skills and resources. As I watched her image while we taped the first Saturday show, I got the eerie feeling that Kelli was an invented being like Daffy Duck, created within her screen medium and unable to breathe outside it. The difference was that the material Daffy was a stack of painted plastic sheets, but the material Kelli was a human being who lived in the actual world—at least nominally. Or maybe she wasn't a Toon after all, but a leftover Rod Serling vision.

"Our contestants don't have the answer." Smilin' Jack was now on the monitor screen. "So *Kelli Dengham rides again!*" Flash of Kelli; back to Jack: "Astronomy, Kelli. Whaddya call lovemaking that's only average?"

Kelli's goofy stare. *"Parsecs!"* Freeze. Frown. "You want to explain that t'me?" Audience roar.

Jack: "You don't understand lovemaking that's only average?"

"Not by experience." Her innocent little-girl-bullfrog voice made her comeback suggestive and funny.

But for once Kilparrow managed to top her. He froze for two perfect beats, then looked straight at his camera:

"Moving *right* along . . ." The audience went bananas, and I wandered off toward the Green Room shaking my head.

I found Arlo Bracken in black punk chic again, glaring

across the seedy room at Sally, who sat with a book that I knew she was only pretending to read. "She shouldn't be here today."

" 'S'matter, Arlo?"

Arlo dipped her head to point inky hair spikes at Sally. "That Helmer. She's *next* week. I already got backup contestants." I encouraged her with a puzzled frown. "Two weeks to screen and train, *then* they get on the show. That's my system. But Ma Barker says bring her in now. I go why? She says we need more backup. I go why? She says *do it*. Well, shit!" Arlo pounded her standup desk and Sally raised her head, smiled brightly, and returned to her book. Arlo jerked around in disgust. "Someone's gotta be in her pants."

"Hm. I'd like to talk to her."

Arlo snorted. "You too, huh?"

Me *only*, as far as I knew, but I just smiled and walked away toward Sally. Until I could write Arlo off as a suspect, I couldn't tell her the truth. I hoped the contestant coordinator wouldn't take it out on Sally, but then reflected that *no one* took anything out on Sally. I said, just loudly enough. "Ms. Helmer? I'm Stoney Winston," and put out my hand.

Sally shook it sitting down. "Hi."

I sat, faced away from Arlo, and lowered my voice. "Spot anything yet?"

Sitting where Arlo could see her, Sally kept her face socially pleasant and murmured. "Just a bunch of nervous people. That man paces like a cat in a cage. The redhead plays with her fingers." The male contestant was back this week, but low-scoring Dulcy had been replaced by a cheer-

ful young woman with green eyes and freckles and strawberry hair.

"What about Amber?"

Sally's face looked as if I'd asked about the weather as
she muttered. "Just what you said: she sits on that couch
and drinks Coke. Never goes anywhere but the can."

Without moving my head I shifted my gaze until I could
see the adjacent wall: Kilparrow's dressing room on the
left, the women's room on the right, and Kelli's suite between them. "Listen, Sally, the first show's about to wrap.
When the troops come down here, notice who goes in
which room and *exactly* when."

"Okay, why?"

"We're talking too long already here, but I'll tell you
when we break." I stood up and raised my voice a notch.
"Great, Sally; I'll see you at lunch, then."

As I walked past her, Arlo snarled, "Fast moving, Winston."

That seemed childish, even for Arlo. I wondered what
she was on about.

The "lunch room" was just a much smaller studio, fitted
with folding tables and chairs. The food was the usual thrift
shop chic, meaning seventeen kinds of pasta, and the amen-
ities stopped at plastic forks that snapped when you used
them and napkins made from Bulgarian toilet paper. Probably recycled. No wonder the show earned such an obscene
return on investment.

The troops were as clannish as ever, with camera jockeys
at one table, control room cowboys at another, and stagehands nowhere to be seen—unless you ate lunch in the

saloon across the street. The contestants were grazing together too, except for Sally, who sat off to one side, communing with Arlo Bracken.

That was a problem. I crossed to Ma Barker, who was vainly attempting to wind spaghettini on a fork that kept bending in half, and leaned close to her ear. "Can you distract Arlo Bracken a minute? I need to check in with our mole."

She threw down the fork in disgust. "I should just shove my face in the plate and suck." Sighing, Ma creaked to her swollen feet and trudged off toward Arlo and Sally.

I filled a plate while Ma got Arlo out of the room on some pretext, then ambled across to my landlady. "Hi. What was that all about?"

Sally's liquid chuckle. "Arlo seemed to resent me at first, but she's suddenly peaches and cream." She twinkled at me as I sat down. "I think she's beating your time, Stoney."

Not knowing what to say, I found a topic on Sally's plate. "You're not eating much."

"Any wonder? Besides, my stomach's a bit upset."

My turn to twinkle. "Butterflies? You're really getting into this contestant role." Sally flashed an unamused look, so I changed the subject. "Got any news for me?"

She pulled a piece of paper out of the book she'd been using as a prop and handed it to me. On it, in Sally's bold scrawl:

12:04: Kelli goes into her dressing room.
12:06: Producer follows her—has paper in hand.
12:15: Producer leaves—still has paper.
12:20: Sung Li goes to rest room.

12:30: Producer returns, announces show 2 starting.
Sung Li leaves rest room. Producer/Kelli leave together.

Something Ma Barker had said: . . . *had to switch the
goddam dressing rooms so Kilparrow's walking a mile to
the john* . . .
"Tell you anything?" Sally asked.
"Yup: Kelli's getting the answers into that rest room
somehow."
Sally stared at the sheet thoughtfully, then nodded.
"From twelve-fifteen to twelve-twenty, Kelli's writing
down the answers and feeding them into the bathroom."
"And it takes Amber ten minutes more to memorize them
and flush away the paper—if it *is* a paper."
Sally nodded again. "You don't need ten minutes to get
rid of a Coke." She put the paper away. "But how do they
do it?"
"We need to check the two rooms."
"Show three starts in ten minutes."
I shook my head. "But Arlo stays in the Green Room,
and I can't be sure she isn't part of it. We'll wait 'til the
end of the day."
At that point, Arlo herself reappeared, thunked into her
chair, and resumed shoveling pasta. "Barker bitch gives me
fits."
"Yo, Arlo."
Ignoring me, she turned to Sally. "Know what she
wanted? Did you have a change of clothes for show three."
Arlo clutched at her spiky hair. "Who cares? You weren't
in the first shows anyway."

Sally smiled sympathetically and I stood up. "Well, nice talking to you, Sally."

She nodded absently, still focused on Arlo. As I stepped back from the table, Arlo glanced up at me and grinned triumphantly.

While I threaded my way through the browsing herd, I tried to sort out what was bothering me. Arlo's flirting with Sally was harmless enough; and anyway, a man prone to jealousy would go bats loving Sally. Without trying or even caring, she made men bellow and rattle their antlers. I'd learned to take that in stride. But this time the snorting, turf-pawing buck was a female. That made me feel queasy—which made me feel guilty. Could it be that my ever-so-modern beliefs were only complacent cant? Stoney Winston: *closet homophobe*.

The two words together were funny enough but the idea behind them was not.

7

*K*ilparrow stood in his favorite pose, embracing the transparent, cash-packed safe—prop cash, in fact, that we didn't guard, since the actual jackpot was stashed in a bank. "Will tomorrow's prize be a million dollars? We'll find out *today* as we play . . . *Oh-Pun Sesame*! Okay, contestants, the category is Computers! Whaddya call transferring a patient to a new mental hospital?

BUZZ!

"A DIP-switch!"

Hm: the redheaded woman got that one. I eased up to the edge of the set. The writers sat rapt at the writers' table, the makeup crew stood transfixed, and even the stagehands had dropped their card game to peer from the opposite side of the set. The Tension/Suspense theme from Audio Control was unneeded: the entire sound stage was snapping with it.

Even Kilparrow was jacked up three notches—if that was possible: "All right, for another *thousand* dollars," he dropped into Bugs Bunny Brooklynese, "Stocks an' Bonds! Whaddya coll dem guys dat never get in da boll-games?"

BUZZZZ! *"Debentures!"*

"Right again, Amber, for *one thousand bucks!!!!*"

Ma Barker, by now, would be having a stroke. As I went off to find the producer I realized how Amber made it look honest: she responded to only half the questions, letting other players get the easier, low-paying ones while she supplied only the big-money answers and piled up most of the points. Very cute.

By the time I found Ma in her dingy office, the show was into its final round and Ma was into a scorching rage. She stood quivering behind her desk, her pale eyes glued to the monitor, bellowing, "The bitch is gonna win, god-dammit, the bitch is gonna WIN!"

"Um, Ms. Barker . . ."

Her eyes never left the screen. "Shut up! She's gonna win! One lousy question to go and her total's up to twenty-five thousand bucks! And you know what that means? It means tomorrow, she gets a shot at one *million* bucks!"

"I . . ."

"ShutupshutupSHUTUP! Wait!"

Smilin' Jack boomed from the stereo speakers, "So this is it, contestants! For a bonus award of *two. Thousand. DOLLARS!*" (Fanfare.) "The category is . . ." (Drum roll.) ". . . *Science!*" (Audience groan at this killer topic.) "Science: Whaddya call the Soviet Union's rationale for *collective farming?!*" (Tick-tock, tick-tock, tick-tock.)

No wonder the audience groaned. Half of them wouldn't know what "rationale" meant. The question was clearly impossible. I moved to where I could see the screen, quick-cutting among the contestants. The man appeared desperate, the redhead looked sandbagged, but Amber Sung Li mimed intense concentration.

Cut to Jack: "Ten seconds, contestants. *Science: Whaddya call the Soviet Union's rationale for collective farming?*" BUZZZ! "Amber!"

"Augh!" from Ma Barker.

"The Unified Field Theory!"

"Auuuggghhh!"

"Correct!" Kilparrow's roar was no louder than Ma's. "Amber Sung Li, that brings your total to: *Twenty. Five. THOUUUUSANDDOLLARS!*"

The screen pandemonium looked like a Democratic convention, right down to the rain of balloons and the sound blaring "Happy Days Are Here Again." Ma stabbed at the off-button, sank into her chair in the suddenly deafening silence, and held her gray head in her hands. "Ohgod, ohmygod, ohgoddam." She was practically whispering.

"It's not as bad as you . . ."

"Ohmy . . ." She broke off, glanced up at me, saw who I was, and her sagging face set in the crazy leer of a vintage Walt Disney witch. "Wiiiinnn-ston," she crooned like the summons of Death, "you blew it, you screwed it up. I saved your skinny, miserable ass, I kept you on this show when you couldn't write a gag worth shit. And all I asked you to do was stop that goddam Chink, not a big thing, no big deal, just *stop* her somehow." She gathered momentum like a Rossini overture: "So you screwed around for a solid week, doing nothing. Zilch! Zippo! You failed me, *failed* me!" This sweet old lady was screeching now. "And today she topped twenty-five K and tomorrow she'll win *one million bucks* because you were too goddam incompetent to find out *how the fuck she was doing it!!*"

I took two quick strides to the front of her desk, then stabbed a finger almost up her nose. *"That's enough!"*

She jerked and stopped dead, though her mouth still gaped in her purplish face.

"One: I can still stop Amber because I did find out how she does it."

"How?"

"Two: I will not tell you how she does it, and I hope that 'Chink,' as you so sensitively call her, walks away with that one million dollars and leaves you dressed in a barrel!"

"What?"

"You cannot pay me enough to submit to this kind of abuse."

"I . . ." As she stared at me, I could almost see her calculating whether stopping Amber was worth backing down. At length she mumbled, "Okay, I got a short fuse."

"You've got something far, far blacker than that, Ma, something that makes you squirt bile in quarts. Whatever your devils, I'm sorry about them, but I am not standing out in your acid rain."

Her face didn't crumple—faces don't do that—but the muscles and blood walked out on it, leaving it dead, flabby dough.

I just stood there, waiting.

She took off her glasses, twiddled them in pudgy fingers, stuck them back on her nose. "Okay." Glasses off again. "I'm sorry, okay?"

I kept silent.

"You gonna help me, or what?"

I nodded grimly. "Kelli *is* feeding Amber the answers."

"I don't believe it."

"Believe it. In the Green Room john." Ma gaped again. "Now listen: get Arlo Bracken out of that room so that Sally and I can check it." She sat like a boulder. "Can you manage that, *Ma?*"

This time she registered on her nickname. Her jowls tensed and her eyes glittered again. "Goddammit, don't call me Ma! Of *course* I can do it." I raised a furious eyebrow, and she moderated her tone: "What're you going to do?"

"With luck, I'll get your evidence and save *your* ass, which, unlike mine, is anything but skinny."

After a pause she nodded. "Okay, and bring what you find to the production office. I'll be over there."

"No. I'll tell you tomorrow, on company time."

"You're gonna leave me all night to worry?"

"With considerable pleasure."

8

I couldn't recall when I'd last felt that furious, but by the time the captains and kings had departed and Sally and I were alone in the Green Room, my rage had burnt down to coals and then ashes of self-reproach.

"Don't worry about it." Sally looked around the dismal room. "You have to call a bully's bluff; they don't understand anything else."

"By being a bully myself. I still don't like it."

"My sensitive boy. C'mon, let's get busy. What are we looking for?"

"Some link with the ladies' room."

"*Women's* room."

"Sorry. Go look in Kelli's . . . no, you take the *women's* room."

Sally walked away, chuckling. "It's only a toilet, Stoney; the sign on the door doesn't make it taboo." She entered the rest room and I hustled toward Kelli's suite.

Inside, a typical windowless dressing room with makeup table and padded stool, an easy chair, a wardrobe rack. Door on the left a closet: empty. Door on the right. . . . Aha: a bathroom. It would be back-to-back with the women's room next door.

Maybe Kelli could talk to Amber. I said in a low voice, "Sally?" No answer. Louder: *"Hey, Sally?"*

A muffled "Yo" from the other side.

No good: if Kelli spoke loudly enough to be heard, she'd be audible in the Green Room too. "Never mind." What, then, a CB radio? In the clinging outfits that Amber favored, that would be hard to conceal. "Does Amber carry a purse?"

"Just a little clutch bag."

Hm. Then an air duct, perhaps. I looked at the ceiling but saw only an exhaust fan that switched on with the light. No easy way to get past it.

Maybe a simple hole in the wall. Nothing visible, though . . .

Wait a minute: instead of a commercial-style chrome valve and handle, this toilet had a conventional tank. And people didn't look under toilet tanks. So I did, and down where someone would have to kneel to spot it was a nickel-size hole with light from the women's room visible through it. It was recent enough so that plaster snow still dusted the top of the floor molding below, where the janitor's mop didn't reach. "I got it!"

"Why is your voice coming out of the toilet?"

"Look at the wall underneath the tank."

A pause, then, "I see it, but how could you push a paper through that?"

"Rolled up. C'mon over."

A scratch pad sat on the makeup table, and by the time Sally'd joined me I'd rolled a piece of paper into a tube. But when I pushed the tube into the hole, it proved to short to reach.

"We need to find something to guide it." I opened the makeup table's drawer: nothing but dead mascara pots and the usual harvest of lint. No, there was also a jumble of small rubber bands. Bands that could wrap a paper tube —or maybe tie it to something . . .

"Coat hanger." I opened the closet door and found three or four on the bar inside. But then I spotted something better: hidden away in the darkest corner stood a hanger that someone had unbent into a long, straight rod. I carried it to the makeup table, rolled the paper sheet tightly around one end, and secured it with a rubber band. The result was a much smaller tube with a handle attached.

"Let's try it out, and this time, *I'll* take the women's room."

"Stout fellow," Sally said, smiling.

I sat on the toilet and called, "Go ahead," and after a pause and a few faint *bonks*, the paper and rod eased out of the wall behind me.

"Okay, reel it in. And put everything back where we found it, okay?"

As I stood up, I noticed some kind of wall dispenser. Oh: bags for sanitary gear. DO NOT DISPOSE IN TOILET, etc. Hm, Sally was right: I felt a powerful social taboo in here that made me distinctly uncomfortable.

Nonsense! As if to defy my feelings, I lifted the toilet seat and relieved myself before going back out to the Green Room.

Sally was waiting there, chuckling again. "You gave me a turn."

"What?"

"The walls aren't soundproof, as you well know, and male noises coming out of a women's room are just a little surprising."

Embarrassed at feeling embarrassed, I turned a bit huffy. "Aren't we too old for bathroom jokes?"

Her smile became condescending. "Women don't like scatological humor; haven't you noticed that? We can't afford to snigger at physical functions; we have to accept them."

Before I could answer, a memory surfaced. As a boy, I would always aim my pee above the waterline to avoid splashing noises. I had to admit she was right again.

Sally said in a placating tone, "But you did put the seat back down, like the gentleman you are."

A Victorian gentleman too, it appeared.

Even in dinnertime darkness, the balmy air on Sally's deck had the vibrancy that tricks local daffodils into blooming in January and then, betrayed by a climate they never were bred for, dying off long before Spring.

Sally was blooming herself as she set out the wine on the patio table. "Jug chablis better go with this game hen; it's all we got. Good: you lit the candles." In their soft yellow light she looked even shinier, sleeker, than usual.

My John Gielgud voice: "You rival their glow, madam."

"Must be the hot kitchen." But she smiled down at the Cornish hen as she transferred the bird from the serving cart.

I resented this underachieving chicken. I'd have to butcher it to serve it, half-destroying it in the process. Then I'd have to dissect it for meat that, however delicious, came away one gram at a time. This exercise burned more calories than it supplied.

Sally avoided the problem by picking the pieces up and gnawing. "Not bad, Stoney."

"Oh, it's delicious!" And it was, what there was of it.

She wagged a diminutive drumstick. "I meant today. We proved Amber's motive, means, and opportunity."

"All we proved is that, theoretically, somebody *could* push notes through that wall." I bludgeoned my way through the tiny breast, wishing I had an X-Acto knife.

"That's enough to hit her with."

I shook my head. "If we confront Amber and blow her off the show, we make giant problems."

A nod. "Since you can't prove anything, she could claim you made it up as a phony reason to keep her from the big prize."

"And sue our suspenders off."

Sally smiled at my finicky surgery. "Why don't you just pick it up?"

"Too messy. And if we *could* kick Amber off, we'd have to scrap every show she was in, or else tell viewers why she quit when she was winning."

" 'Too messy'! You see what I mean? Males are just naturally squeamish."

I pretended I hadn't heard that. "But the biggest problem is, Amber could still blackmail Kelli—or maybe sell those slides to someone. Kelli claims they're innocuous, but I don't believe her. She was just a little too shifty about them."

Sally scrubbed long fingers with a paper napkin. "I got it: feed Amber the wrong set of answers and just let her lose. Then she's dropped from the show but she can't complain."

"Then what would she do to Kelli for giving her phony answers?"

"Kelli wouldn't know they were fake."

"Would Amber believe that?"

Sally communed with her wine for a moment while I gazed at her with an astonishment that two years hadn't blunted. At thirty-three she was stunning inside and out. How would she seem in twenty years more?

Thou wouldst still be adored, as this moment thou art,
Let thy loveliness fade as it will . . .

"Stoney!" She was grinning now. "You're mooning again."

"Hey, I don't even have my pants down—yet."

"Eat your veggies." But the grin relaxed to a quiet smile, and her blue Delft eyes hinted at thoughts that were maybe not all that unpleasant.

9

*T*he trouble with Sally's idea was that if we switched questions on Amber, she'd know she'd been blind-sided. But suppose it looked accidental. How? As I drifted toward sleep against the softness of Sally's roller coaster contours, I almost, but not quite, had the answer.

The epiphany came as I cooked Sunday breakfast. Leaving Sally to skipper the stove, I phoned Ma Barker and asked her to meet me at the studio a few minutes before crew call. And now we were locked in her weekend office, slurping cardboard coffee from a vending machine.

Before I could explain my plan, Ma launched her own agenda: "We got more troubles, Jocky."

"*Now* what?"

"Mash notes. Some goddam crazy A-rab's writing dirty threats to Kelli." Ma snatched two packs of NutraSweet, ripped them open with her teeth, and dumped them in her coffee. "We got three so far, addressed to the production office."

"What do they say?"

"The usual. The jerk is gonna shtup her socks off and she's gonna love it or else." Slurp.

"How serious is it?"

"Who knows? Celebrities get these things all the time."

I thought about that. "Any connection with Amber, I wonder?"

Ma's look suggested that was feebleminded. "Anyway, I'm renting her protection. We're meeting on it tomorrow morning. I want you there." She swilled more asphalt coffee. "Now, what's your big idea for Amber?"

As I laid it out Ma's pouchy eyes grew worried, and by the time I'd finished she was shaking her head. "What if Sung Li decides to use the goddam pictures some other way?"

"Until we know what's in those slides, we can't tell how dangerous they are. We *have* to get Kelli to talk to us."

She set her jaw like a pike on a hook. "Not a chance, Jocko. If we put the screws on Kelli now, she'll be too upset to perform, and that'll tip Amber that something's up."

I shrugged. "Then we'll have to fly blind."

"That makes my stomach hurt." She tamped a Marlboro on a Chinese red thumbnail and lit it. "Besides, how's Kelli going to read the goddam answers if she can't rehearse them? She'll screw up the whole taping."

"Shoot pickups of her later and cut them into the show. We do it all the time."

"Yeah, but she won't be as spontaneous." She exhaled a clot of smoke big enough to hide in.

"Ma, it's executive decision time."

That snapped her to. "I need you to tell me?" But hired producers love risky decisions as much as they love being canceled. A long silence while Ma's little eyes darted between her cigarette and the Compaq luggable computer on the desk, and then she sighed. "Let her win and get rid of her." She smashed the butt.

I shook my head. "You don't get rid of blackmailers; they always hit you for more."

"Goddam you, Winston!"

"Don't kill the messenger, Ma."

Another reluctant pause, then, "Okay, okay."

"Okay what?"

"Okay *do* it" She shook a fat finger in my direction. "But I hate this, Winston, and I won't forget it."

It was all my fault, of course.

As I made my way toward the shooting stage, I thought about those threatening notes. An *Arab*? Well, one crisis at a time.

• • •

"Anybody here from outta state? All right! Where? Let's hear it for North Dakota! Anyone from overseas? You, sir? Aus-*trial*-ya! Well, g'die!" Smilin' Jack did his own audience warmup, to get himself up to speed for the show, he claimed.

As Kilparrow finished the warmup and walked off the set, I checked out the audience: handholding couples, a gaggle of Girl Scouts, the usual quota of sportshirted tourists. High up on the audience risers near me, a woman caught my eye: more formally dressed than the others, she looked around alertly, as if studying the situation.

Out on the floor, Cactus Pomeroy started his chant. ". . . five, four, three, two, one . . ."

The APPLAUSE lights flashed, the audience roared reliably, and the hidden announcer boomed into his mike, "You've come to the place where punny funnies win you monies! It's time for . . . *Oh-Pun SESAME!!!*"

Too nervous to stand still, I wandered away from the opening hoopla toward Master Control at the rear of the stage. If my plan worked, Amber wouldn't know we were mousetrapping her, so she couldn't blame Kelli. If it worked. As far as I knew, we were ready. Ma had fed Kelli a set of fake answers, and I had enlisted Ron Tolkis by telling him we had to get Amber off the show quietly because she was cheating. When he asked how she did it, I just said I didn't know. When I explained what I wanted him to do with the Chyron system, his eyes turned wicked behind his horn rims and he set to work with gleeful gusto.

I arrived in the booth as Kilparrow's image was introducing contestants. ". . . and our third player and current champion is Amber Sung Li, from Los Angeles!"

"Six." Amber's closeup came on line, smiling and miming *aw gosh, it weren't nothin', folks.*

As Kilparrow continued his opening hype, I glanced around Master Control: Ma looking grim in her canvas chair, Chyron monitor high on the left, Amber's face on monitor six, whose camera stayed on her doggedly.

"Pull, six." At the director's command, Amber's image widened to waist shot.

"Kill the announcer to the floor." Cutting the announcer's voice from the studio loudspeakers meant he was about to whisper the first question to the home audience.

Sure enough, Kilparrow said, "Astronomy. For two hundred dollars, players, whaddya call a preacher who drives a Ferrari?"

Amber'd been given the answer by Kelli, but as always, she passed on this low-paying question. As the countdown music ticked and contestants grimaced and slapped palms to foreheads, I glanced at the Chyron monitor: *Astronomy: A preacher who drives a Ferrari.* So far so good.

At the Time's Up klaxon, Jack fed the question to Kelli. I ignored her usual comic bit while I switched between the Chyron monitor and Amber's image.

"Ummmmm, the answer is . . ."

"WHAT THE FUCK IS *THAT*?" the announcer's yelp rattled the booth speakers and drowned Kelli out. Expecting

to read the answer off his screen, he had seen the same
thing we all saw:

ASTRONOMY: *A preacher who drives a Ferrari:*
FARDELGLUP!

The director, a handsome blond man in his early forties,
said, "Cut!" With a quiet sigh, he pushed a key on his
console. "Chyron? What's up?"
"*I dunno, Randy . . .*"
I already knew what was up, so I watched the action
unfold in the Argus-eyed booth.

During the next ten minutes Ma Barker moved around
the set to reassure cast and contestants, and Ron Tolkis, as
I'd told him to, filled the Chyron display with line after
line of whimsical nonsense.
At length, Ma trudged to a spot where both cast and
audience could see her. "Seems like the computer ate the
questions, folks, and we can't get 'em back. But don't worry:
we'll feed it some new ones and start again right away."
Ma nodded at Cactus and the floor manager started reset-
ting cameras and cast.
Since Amber and Kelli each had a camera on her, I could
watch their closeups in the booth. At Ma's announcement,
Amber's elegant face tightened up and she shot a glance
toward Kelli, whose panicked expression said she was terrified of having to read new answers without any chance
to rehearse them. Her look in Amber's direction seemed
like an appeal for help. Amber studied Kelli a moment,

then turned away, her image revealing nothing. I felt sorry
for Kelli's fear, but her spontaneous terror was the best
proof to Amber that Kelli'd had nothing to do with this.

The director said, "Roll down to raw stock." The on-line
monitor gibbered in fast-forward. "Ready on the floor. Roll
to record."

"We have speed," from a tape tech.

"Ten, nine, eight . . ."

Cactus Pomeroy picked up the count and the show got
under way again.

At first Amber and the redheaded woman divided most
of the spoils between them—when Kelli wasn't making
hash of those answers the players had failed to come up
with. But as the questions got tougher, the plump Chicana,
who'd replaced yesterday's low-scoring male player, began
to surge ahead.

"Literature: Whaddya call a spear used to butcher young
sheep?"

"A lampoon!"

"Right, Lupe, for three hundred *dollars*!!"

"Fashion: Whaddya call the sound you make when you
tickle a baby?"

"Gucci!" Amber almost got that easy shot, but Lupe beat
her to the buzzer.

"Television: Whaddya call what spiders do for a living?"

No guesses. Put on the spot by the players' failure, Kelli
gulped hard and said, "Network!" correctly, then grinned
like a felon reprieved.

"Books: Whaddya call the science of keeping babies clean
during meals?" No takers again, but Kelli had reached her
limit here, and her shot at *bibliography* was a dismal fiasco.

"Mark it for pickup," said the director.

"Plastic surgery: Whaddya call a passionate French kiss?"

"Liposuction!" Score another one for Lupe.

And so, as they say, it went—right down to the typical killer question that always ended the show:

"Cooking: Whaddya call where a picnic ends up when it's eaten by hungry insects?"

"In-greedy-ants!" But that was beyond Kelli too, and though she giggled and mugged as always, her unsparing camera revealed the anguish behind her manic performance.

As Smilin' Jack wrapped up the program, I studied Amber's face on the screen; but all she revealed was the tremulous smile of a good sport who finally had lost.

10

As soon as the director called, "Cut," I hustled up to the Chyron cave to plug a possible leak. Sure enough, I found the assistant Sondra just coming to a boil.

"You wanna get us fired? You got a death wish, or what?" She glared at Tolkis through her spectacles.

Tolkis grinned and winked at me as I said, "Sondra . . ."

Turning at the sound of my voice, "I swear, Stoney, I had nothing to do with it."

"I know."

"The Chyron did not go down. It printed 'fardelglup' because Tolkis keyed it in!"

"I told him to do that. Listen." I drew Sondra closer to Ron and lowered my voice. "Someone was feeding Amber the answers."

Her eyebrows shot above her spectacle rims. "Who? How?"

My prepared story: "We couldn't really prove it, so we had to get her off the show quietly." Her anger faded toward puzzlement. I put my hands on Ron's and Sondra's shoulders. "And you guys . . ." significant look at Sondra, ". . . were the only ones we could trust completely." Sondra liked the sound of that, and even Ron looked proud. "Now we have to trust you to forget the whole thing."

Sondra glowed at being one of we happy few. She nodded briskly.

I smiled. "Outstanding. And Ma Barker's really pleased."

Sondra resumed her seat, grinning, and Ron got up to follow me out of the booth. At the top of the stairs he caught my arm. "Think Kelli's home free?" I nodded. He puffed his breath out and Foghorn Leghorn brayed, "Mag—, ah say, mag*nif*icent!"

"As long as we keep it just between us."

He grinned, and Elmer Fudd whispered, "I'll be vewy, vewy quiet!"

"Kelli, stand by for pickups." The director's voice boomed from the studio speakers as the announcer left his hideout and crossed to center stage, where he'd keep the audience entertained enough to remain while Kelli repeated the answers she'd flubbed. Edited into the broadcast tape, these isolated shots would be indistinguishable from the rest of the program.

"What's *really* going on here?" I turned around to discover the well-dressed woman I'd seen in the audience: petite, late twenties, professional looking in a green power suit.

"I'm sorry. . . ?"

She aimed a pink nail at a studio monitor. "When computers go down, they don't say 'fardelglup,' and they *sure* don't say 'great horny toads' and 'ya lop-eared galoot.' "

Damn Ron and his Warner cartoons: he'd waxed just a bit too creative. Smiling to take the edge off, I said, "Who wants to know?"

"Katherine Halbreck." She offered a smile and a hand. ". . . Kat. I write for the Sunbelt Group."

Uh-oh. "Have you checked with P.R., Ms. Halbreck?"

"*Kat*. No, this is different. I'm writing a feature from the audience point of view."

I pointed politely to the bleachers. "Then you need to get back to your viewing point."

"But really, what's going on? I mean, readers want to know."

Ah yes, "enquiring minds." "So do I, Ms. Halbreck, and now I have to go find out." I waved to one of the pages who wrangled the audience, and she moved to join us. "Got us a stray dogie, Pilgrim."

With a smile and a shrug, Kat Halbreck allowed herself to be herded back into the stands.

I wandered away to join Sally in the Green Room. The Sunbelt Group. What did they publish? In today's world of conglomerates eating conglomerates, it was hard to remember—but I'd bet the enquiring Kat Halbreck didn't write for *The New Yorker*.

• • •

I found Sally in her usual Green Room chair. Arlo was off someplace, but since Amber Sung Li sat alone in the opposite corner, I kept my voice low. "Watchman, what of the night?"

Sally did one of her leopard stretches. "I could never be a private eye. This stakeout is driving me bats."

"Pretty quiet?"

Sally flicked a glance at Amber and muttered, "She walked in ten minutes ago—face like a rock—started toward Kelli's dressing room—noticed me—slowed up, like she was thinking—went and sat down—hasn't moved since."

"Got to get her out of here. People coming in I don't want her to see." I stood up and walked toward Amber, thinking at warp speed.

"Ms. Sung Li?" She nodded with wan politeness. "I'm Stoney Winston, the producer's assistant. I'm sorry it was close-but-no-cigar for you." The same brave smile she'd closed the show with. "But you did win twenty-five thousand dollars, and we need to make arrangements about your money." Her face remained opaque. "So let's go up to Ms. Barker's office."

Still no reaction, but she rose and followed me.

By the time I'd stashed Amber in Ma's office, explained that it would be a few minutes, and returned to the Green Room, the troops were assembled as planned: Sally, Kelli, Ma, and the agent Ernie Drenko, whom Ma had contacted that morning. We all piled into Kelli's dressing room, where

Drenko made for the sole arm chair as if it were only his right.

He established himself on his throne and tried to take charge of the meeting. "Okay, we need to run over some things."

"What things are those, Ern?" I kept my voice flat.

"The hell *I* know? *You* got me over here."

I smiled. "So we did—for a little demonstration." I scanned their faces: Ma Barker's phlegmatic scowl, Kelli's kooky puzzled look, Sally's calm alertness.

All right, show time. I stripped a sheet off the scratch pad on the makeup table, pulled a rubber band from the drawer, and held them up.

Drenko: "What is this, magic tricks?"

"All in good time, Ern. Kelli, why don't you get the straight coat hanger out of the closet?"

"What hanger?" But Kelli's best talent defeated her: every thought in her head marched across her face like a moving sign on a marquee. I waited. She shot a worried glance at Drenko, whose expression told her nothing, then looked at me again. "I . . ." I waited some more. Nobody moved.

Suddenly, Kelli wheeled around, flounced into the closet, and emerged holding the hanger. She held it out to me and tears welled in her eyes, spilled over her long lower lashes, and flowed down through the video makeup on her pretty child's face. I took the hanger from her.

Drenko jumped to his feet. "What *is* this?" He wrapped a thick arm around Kelli. "What is it, honey?"

I rolled the sheet around the hanger. "For the last three weeks, Kelli's fed answers to Amber Sung Li."

"Stoney . . ." Kelli's croaking cry sounded heartbroken. She started trembling.

"By writing them on scratch paper and pushing it into the women's room through a hole in her own bathroom wall." I snapped the rubber band in place and held up the rod. "With this."

Ernie's face said he couldn't think which gear to shift into. "To be frank about this . . ."

"So today, we switched questions without telling Kelli —and Amber went right down in flames."

Ma said, "In the nick of time too."

By now Kelli was sobbing aloud.

I tried to go easy on her. "I guess it wasn't Kelli's fault. Amber extorted those answers with slides her ex-boy-friend'd shot." I stared at the agent. "You know the pictures I mean."

"I told you . . ."

"Now Amber's off the show, but she's got to be furious at losing and she still has those pictures. So *you* have to tell us how much damage she could do with them."

When the agent still looked mulish, Ma Barker jumped in. "Here's the bottom line, Ernie: if those goddam slides could hurt us bad, then Kelli's out right *now.*"

"You wouldn't do that; she's half the show. Besides, we gotta contract." But doubt had crept into his tone.

Ma jumped on that: "What's your contract worth if our markets cancel and the show folds?"

She'd said the magic word, *fold.* Drenko stared into space a long moment, then put his big hands on Kelli's shoulders. Reluctantly, "Babe, I think I better tell 'em."

Kelli's face went cotton-white. "Ernie. . . !"

"Shhh." He patted her shoulder. "No show, no dough, kid; capeesh?" Her face said *no she didn't* and her trembling escalated into outright shaking.

Drenko dropped his arms, sighed, and turned to me. "Okay, you're right, Winston: it was sorta rank stuff."

"How sorta? Oral sex? Intercourse?"

His wave dismissed that. "Nah, not even *Raunch*'d print that shit."

I tried to ignore Kelli's heartbroken sobbing. "What, then?"

Drenko actually looked embarrassed. He glanced at Ma, sized up silent Sally, and puffed out his breath. Avoiding the women's eyes, he addressed himself to me. "We got this clown with a shlong like a . . ." He spread his hands like a man telling a fish story. "Well, *you* know. And Kelli, like . . ." quick glance at the women ". . . well," his voice dropped ten DB, ". . . played with it."

"Ernie, please; oh Ernie, *please!*" Kelli was heading right over the top. Ernie wrapped his arms around her and she huddled in them, moaning and shaking and soaking his tie.

But Ernie's news didn't faze Ma. "Anything else?"

Drenko mumbled, "Shdpnk."

"What?"

Belligerently, "I said she showed pink—okay, *lotsa* pink." Kelli shrieked like a widow at a wake and Ernie smoothed her hair. "So how's that grab ya?"

Ma looked relieved, though I couldn't see why. "And that was it?"

"Thawasall, thawasall!" Kelli howled into Drenko's shirt.

He muttered, "Isn't it enough?"

I said, "Why, Ernie?"

Impatiently, "That shoot was, like earlier. Kelli was nobody then, broke. She needed work—some kind of exposure."

By now, Ma looked almost cheerful. "Exposure she got."
Ma actually smiled. "I think we're okay."

But *I* didn't. "You're going to tell Amber to publish and
be damned?"

Her expression bordered on glee. "And I'm going to
goddam enjoy it!" Without warning, Ma wheeled around
and lumbered out of the dressing room.

I looked at Kelli, who by now was in gale force hysterics,
then at Sally, who nodded toward the door. I nodded back
and took off after Ma.

I caught her up in the corridor. "Ma, I don't think you
should . . ."

"Shut up, Cocky; I'll take it from here."

11

And take it she goddam did. Ma told Amber we knew
that she'd cheated and knew how she'd done it. When
Amber denied everything, Ma waggled the hanger and
paper at her and told her to think about this: she had
$25,000 in prize money coming; but since we could prove
that she'd cheated to win it, we could legally withhold the
money. So why not take this consolation prize and disappear
just quietly? The subject of pictures was not raised at all.

In the end, Amber agreed to the deal and left. Throughout the confrontation, she never raised her voice or showed
any emotion.

That bothered me. "How can you be sure Amber won't
peddle those slides someplace?"

"Because I'm betting she can't." Patiently, "Look: now
that I know what's in the pictures, I can tell you the photographer sold them *already*." For the first time since I'd
met her, Ma seemed positively jubilant.

"Ma, the garbage Drenko described is *exactly* what
Raunch publishes. They'd eat it up."

She nodded, grinning. "I'm sure they did." Ms. Attila
blew a smoke ring and looked at me with pity. "You're a
smart enough kid, Winston, but you can't see the goddam
obvious."

That stung. "*Raunch* buys pictures of Kelli—some good
taste, some bad taste. They're famous for bad taste, but
they publish only the *good* taste. And the reason is obvious?"

She spoke very slowly to dim, childish Winston: "Because the publisher owns this show." My jaw descended
to basement level. "And this show is four times as profitable
as his dreck magazine. So it's better for him to protect Kelli
and *Oh-Pun Sesame* than to trash her in *Raunch*. Is that
simple enough for you?"

But I was still digesting the fact that *Raunch* and our
empty but innocent game show were siblings.

Ma stared at her cigarette ash. "I know how Carlisle
works."

"Who?"

"Russell Carlisle, the publisher. Sure as hell, he bought

all the slides, suppressed the no-nos, and printed just enough of Kelli's skin to get our show—*his* show—publicity."

"Then what pictures did Amber use on Kelli?"

"Dupes, prints—who knows? Who cares?" Ma Barker actually chortled.

She was making a lot of assumptions here, so I pushed her a bit. "Can you check this out?"

"I'll call Russ tomorrow." The dragon blew smoke from scaly nostrils and her grin drained away. "Listen, be at the office by nine for that meeting."

"That . . . ? Oh, those letters. I'd forgotten."

She nodded grimly. "Don't say anything to Kelli, though—she doesn't know about them."

"But if they're a threat, shouldn't she . . ."

"I *told* you, Junior: she's one crumbly cookie. Didn't you see her in there?"

Yes, I'd seen her, falling to pieces like a six-year-old scared by a bogeyman under her bed. As I left the office, I cursed myself for failing to come up with a gentler way to pry the truth out of her.

To help conceal her connection with me, Sally'd come —and now gone—in her own car, leaving me to pilot my Beetle. I made my way toward the parking lot, trying to sort matters out. I should have suspected that *Raunch* and the show were linked when Ma told me she'd helped set up the sale of Kelli's pictures. Why else would she get involved in that? And why else would—what's his name? Russell Carlisle—print shots that were far too mild for his scabrous magazine? Publicity for his quiz show; publicity that made money for Ma and Carlisle—and possibly even for Drenko—while sweet, obedient Kelli, who had far more talent than brains to direct it, was terrified out of her minimal wits and splashed all over a rancid rag that rednecks perused on the toilet.

And I was Ma Barker's devoted assistant. Stoney Winston: the panderer's apprentice. I said out loud, *"Jesus!"*

"He's on his dinner break. Can *I* help?" The reporter I'd talked to stepped out of the shadow beside the artists' entrance door and fell into step beside me.

"Oh, Ms., uh . . ."

"Kat Halbreck." Brightly, "Hi. Can we talk a minute?"

Just what I needed. "Well . . ."

"You're Winston, right, the producer's assistant?"

I stopped walking. "Mm-hmh, how'd you know?"

She grinned. "Happens to be my business. Listen, what was all that today?" She put a small hand on my arm. "I mean, just between us."

In her business, there was no "just between us." "Which magazine do you write for?"

"Newspaper—well, several." She waved off the question as if it were trivial. "I move around the Sunbelt Group."

"Then whatever the question, no comment." I resumed my trek toward B. Bumble.

She slipped her hand around to take my upper arm. "So let's talk off the record."

I stopped at my car. "Fine, you go first. Why are you here and what are you looking for?"

She put on a candid smile. "Right now, I'm not sure. This morning, I was after background on Kelli Dengham —you know, color for a, well, sort of feature."

I didn't like the sound of that. "Sort of?"

She stared at me intently. "But today I find this contestant who's one game away from a million dollars. Then the computer gets amnesia, the questions get switched, and all of a sudden this crackerjack player can't answer a single one right." Her brown eyes had an odd intensity that hinted of contact lenses.

Neutrally, "Yes?"

"So I'm thinking maybe I'm onto an even better story." Her delivery slowed for added emphasis: "A nice, juicy story my editor would love."

"And maybe not."

My carefully empty answers changed her tone to irritation. "Look, you ever hear of damage control?"

"It has a familiar ring."

"You might want to try it." She shifted to sweet reason: "If there's some explanation, then tell me and I'll drop it. My editor doesn't print lies."

"Ben Franklin would be gratified."

That made her mad again. "But he *loves* to print innuendo. Can you see it?" Palms outward, she spread a banner headline in the air between us: "*IS MEGAHIT GAME SHOW CROOKED? Was Beautiful Contestant Cheated of $1,000,000? Show Officials Mum about Scandal.*"

My announcer voice: "Film at eleven." I opened Bumble's door and climbed in.

She pushed her small face through the open side window. "Okay, fella, but I'll tell you out front: I'm going to dig up the truth here, and I'm *very* good at my job."

"Horatio Alger would also be pleased." When she snapped erect angrily, I fired my engine. "Good night, Ms. Halbreck." I started backing out.

She yelled, "Kat!" over the Beetle's roar and stomped off into darkness.

I got home to find Sally at her computer, communing by modem with the business service she subscribed to.

"Hi, Sally. How's the Hetty Green of Laurel Canyon?"

"Market's closed Sunday; I'm doing research while the phone rates are cheap."

That gave me an idea. "Can you get corporate information, you know, like Standard and Poor stuff?"

"S and P? Sure."

"Bring up the Sunbelt Group, will you? I want to see what newspapers they own."

Sally clickety-clicked through an endless labyrinth of menus, submenus, commands, and options until the screen finally displayed the Sunbelt paper stable. "I never heard of most of them."

I peered over her shoulder, inhaling the dividend of her apple smell. "Hm: *The Anaheim Shopper, The Foothill Advertiser, The . . .* They all look like weekly throwaways. Scroll down for me." I followed the smell to its source and kissed bare shoulder, just inboard of her tank top strap. "Wait a minute: *The National Insider.* That's a supermarket tabloid, not a throwaway."

"Though it should be thrown away; it's the worst of the bunch. What's this for?"

I told her about Kat Halbreck. "She wouldn't name her

paper, but it has to be *The Insider*." I sampled Sally's neck. "The kind of dirt she's after doesn't run in *The Cucamonga Bugle*."

"That tickles. What *was* she after?"

"At first, Kelly's background; but now she suspects something about today's show." I kissed her neck again. "And that's bad news."

"Have you shaved within living memory?"

"Mm."

"Next time, stand closer to the razor." But Sally contradicted this by offering her mouth.

12

*I*n due course she offered more than that, beginning with Chateaubriand for supper and ending with other delicacies that were vastly more precious and far longer-lived. The resulting euphoria lasted all night and made even Monday morning seem cheerful.

I howled downhill in the mighty B. toward my nine o'clock meeting at production headquarters. Whatever the problem with Kelli's "mash notes," it had to be minor compared to what we'd just been through. As I swooped into the garage and flung my car at its very own space with my very own name on the wall above it, I felt I was in for a glorious day.

An hour later I wasn't so sure, as I sat in the darkened conference room, enduring a dog and pony show by one Herbert Parames, Ph.D.

He placed a new chart on the overhead projector. "Our database holds almost three hundred thousand crank letters to celebrities—not only letters to our own clients. We share with police and sheriff's departments—and of course, the FBI."

Of course. His pompous delivery was irritating.

"Some letters are serious enough to check out. They often include threatening gifts: human teeth, excrement— always a favorite—and dead animals or animal parts. Quite nasty."

Another transparency: "A few of these people actually seek encounters with celebrities, and they are often deranged and dangerous."

Ma sounded impatient, as usual: "We don't need a goddam sales pitch, Parames; you're already hired."

"I'm simply presenting the total picture." Somewhat huffily, Parames killed the projector.

I reached behind me and switched on the room lights. Even in flattering pinspots Parames was not prepossessing: a middle-aged man with thin hair and thick waist, wearing gold-rimmed bifocals. His short beard and checked shirt announced a professorial contempt for dress codes, but his jacket and tie said maybe not *utter* contempt.

But for all his pedantic manner, Parames ran one of the bigger celebrity protection services. It would pay to take him seriously. I said in a placating tone, "How would you judge the letters to Kelli?"

He handed me two Xerox copies. "What do *you* think of them?

So the prof. was putting his class in its place by springing a pop quiz. I sighed and read the first letter:

> *My Sexy Kelli*
> *The minute I saw you I knew you were the girl of my damp midnight fantasies. I would tell you this myself but I know they wont let me (though I am much closer to you than they think!) We will come together soon and I will slip into your slim body and fill you like you fill my head now my slippery one. I will find a way no matter what I have to do.*
> *Your Lover Who Will Come For You*
> *Hassan*

Parames said, "What does that tell you?" He sat back with a satisfied look and waited for me to prove my incompetence.

I studied the letter. "In no particular order: the writer's a male who's uneducated, or at least indifferent to punctuation. Or maybe foreign: Hassan is Middle Eastern and 'damp midnight fantasies' is too purple for an illiterate. He used a nine-pin-dot matrix printer—looks like Epson, but I'm no expert. He threatens an encounter and says he's closer than she thinks, so that could make him a serious contender." I handed back the letter.

Parames stared at me silently, then smiled as if he'd never doubted me. "The second letter's much in the same vein, though more, ah, erotically graphic. Now read the third one. It arrived four days ago."

You Slut Kelli!

You bared your body to everybody in that magazine. You have no right! Your mine!! I have been too easy on you but no more! I will soon reveal myself and I will make you strip your clothes off and lick my toes while I spank your round pink ass until it glows like fire. You must be humiliated to pay for mine and when you beg for mercy and swear you will not whore again I will forgive you and protect you forever from bad people who make you do these bad things.

Your Furious Master
Hassan

Ohboy. "Threatens kinky sex, physical harm." I frowned at the sheet. "Another thing: he says he will *reveal* himself again, as if he's already someplace near." Parames nodded. "Any postmarks?"

"90038."

"Hollywood. So he's not writing from Kalamazoo."

"No such luck."

Ma addressed an appeal to the ceiling: "Who needs this?"

Parames made a calming gesture. "Major stars often have fifty such letters on file at a time. It's regrettably all too common." But he sounded as regretful as a dentist deploring plaque.

I said, "Then what do you suggest we do?"

"You stick close to Kelli, because the writer may be connected with the show, and if we brought in my people, we might tip him off."

Ma added, "His people will keep an eye on Kelli, discreetly."

I nodded.

"So let's get started debriefing you."

"First, I need a word with Ms. Barker."

"Fine. I'll just take a break or something." He buttoned his jacket across his small paunch and walked stiffly out of the room.

"Ma, did you check with Russell Carlisle?"

Her doughy face brightened as she nodded. "I was right on the goddam money, Junior! Russell bought every last frame. And Kelli's shots with Freddie Footlong went right into the shredder."

I could only nod, though I wasn't half as sure as she was. Carlisle may have bought the original slides, but Amber, it seemed, had copies. Not for the first time I remembered the slide-duping rig in Arnesen's darkroom.

She waved a plump hand at the Xeroxed letters. "So if we can plug The Ayatollah here, I think we're home free."

"Ma, we have other troubles too." She assumed her kill-the-messenger look, so I filled her in quickly on Katherine Halbreck, girl reporter for *The National Insider*.

Ma tried to look on the bright side: "Maybe she's only trolling."

I shook my head. "Barbra Streisand or Dolly Parton might be worth a fishing expedition—but Kelli's not hot copy yet. They wouldn't bother snooping on general principles."

"In other words, they must know something about her."

I nodded. "Which is more than we do."

She twiddled a Marlboro nervously, then put it to the torch. "Goddammit!" She'd lit the filter. Ma stubbed it out and said, "Come up with something, laddie; earn your pay."

"Well, she's been trying to pump me. Maybe I could talk to her and try to pump her back."

A doubtful nod. "Can you do that without giving her anything?"

I shrugged. "What's there to give?"

But after stonewalling Kat Halbreck twice I couldn't plausibly approach her now. I'd have to wait for her to resurface. Meanwhile, my job was to see if I could spot a nutball correspondent on the program staff.

The printout from Personnel yielded nothing, but that wasn't surprising. In Hollywood, those few workers of the Muslim persuasion generally opted for zero-profile. I knew an Arabian sound tech who passed himself off as a Lebanese Christian.

In any case, a dingbat fan was not likely to be on the staff. Industry people see too many stars with their hair down (or off) to romanticize them. More probably he was a sad little man out there someplace in a one-room flat with only his hand for company. And "out there someplace" belonged to Parames, who was far better qualified and equipped to patrol it. I felt a distinct relief at telling him all I knew and turning things over to H. P. Security, Inc.

After briefing Parames I'd little to do except wander about or play with things on my office desk, and by quitting time I was twitching with boredom and bothered by fifteen things that weren't right. The problem was out of my hands now, but I couldn't put it out of my mind.

I had just turned off the office lights when the phone rang.

"Punny Place Productions, Stoney Winston."

"*Stoney?* Uh, this is Kat Halbreck."

"Yes, Ms. Halbreck." Wait a minute: don't turn her off. "I'm sorry, yes, *Kat.*"

Cheerfully, "I'll take that as progress." Then to business: "Listen: we talked about damage control?"

"Yes?" I kept it neutral but receptive.

"You might want to think about that again."

"I might?"

"Yessir. I checked out Amber Sung Li today."

I paused two beats before saying, "I see."

"Found out where she lived. Didn't talk to her, though."

"You didn't?" Okay, Kat, now tell me why not.

"No, she was busy being murdered."

"Being . . ."

"She'd been beaten to death."

This time my silence was not contrived. First Arnesen, now his ex live-in. Both beaten; both dead.

"Still there? Want to talk?"

"Uh . . ." But I couldn't make my head work.

"I'm not far away."

I rubbed at my eyes as if trying to knead the brain behind them. Finally, "Cafe Dijon—on Melrose?"

"I know it. Give me twenty minutes." Kat Halbreck hung up.

I stood by the desk in the unlit office, attempting to picture Amber Sung Li; but all I could see was generic product: young, beautiful, Chinese-American, dependably lively on camera. Off camera, though, she'd been silent and passive—a virtual blank. The killing of a human should be more affecting than the sight of a flattened possum, but the

off-screen Amber had barely existed, and I had the eerie
feeling that, like any other TV actor, she hadn't really been
murdered—just written out of the show.

As I walked, half numb, to the Beetle, I remembered
the third letter: *"You bared your body to everybody. . . .
I will protect you forever from bad people."*

13

West of La Brea, Melrose Avenue is a two-mile strip
mall of framing shops, tarot parlors, nosh joints, hair salons,
wine saloons, poster barns, punk boutiques, bistros, clubs,
bikini vendors—an endless pop bazaar of things ephemeral,
superfluous, and false. Tonight, as every night, the street
was jammed with rapt consumers lurching onward, stoned
on store displays and glitzy neon—or just stoned. I inched
the Beetle past a shop whose sign proclaimed CAMP MEL-
ROSE. They'd caught the tone exactly.

Cafe Dijon was Prop House Gallic: ice cream chairs and
tables under faux-Vermouth umbrellas, faux-Picasso
posters under beams of Ye Olde Styrofoame, faux Edith
Piaf on the faux-forties juke box. The seated couples, a
random sample of sexual permutations, were locked in the
deep discussions expected in French cafes: ". . . Midler
and Streisand? Oh, they've been saying that for *years!*"
"I kid you not, sweetie; Elaine May's already done a
draft . . ."

"Hello, Kat." She was sitting at a table by the wall, sipping from a tall glass and watching the action with a quiet smile.

"Hi." She gestured to the other chair. " 'Stoney,' did you say? Where'd that come from?"

I sat. "What would *you* do with Spencer Churchill Winston?"

"Oh." She giggled.

A waiter floated up, costumed in white shirt, black tie, linen apron, and Reeboks.

Kat wagged her glass. "I'm having a spritzer."

I nodded to the faux-garçon and paused until he'd left, then, "Tell me about Ms. Sung Li."

Kat smiled across her glass. "Tell *me* where we stand. I don't give freebies."

I was in no mood for games. "I stand at *Oh-Pun Sesame*; you stand at *The National Insider*."

She had the grace to look embarrassed. "I don't write the two-headed baby stuff."

Wearily, "You and I are reciprocal parasites: without your publicity we wouldn't get viewers; without interest in our show you wouldn't get readers."

She stared at me a beat, then nodded. "Simplistic but more or less true. Here's to professionalism."

"So you tell me about Amber Sung Li and I'll tell you about yesterday's show."

She pondered that while the waiter set down my drink, then said, "Sounds fair."

But she couldn't, or wouldn't, tell much. Kat had managed to dig up Amber's address; but when she got there she hit a wall of blue uniforms and yellow plastic tape. All

she got was the fact that sometime during the day the victim
had been battered to death and probably raped.

"Raped?" I thought of Hassan again.

"That's when the cop shut up." A rueful smile. "I made
the mistake of saying who I worked for."

We sipped our drinks awhile. Finally, Kat said, "Now
it's your turn."

"First, a question: is there *really* such a thing as 'off the
record'?"

Her lip muscles tensed as she leaned forward. "There is
with me."

I liked this small, intense, straightforward woman who
neither flirted nor played tough cookie. "Off the record
then, Amber Sung Li was cheating."

"How?" Her tone was more eager than surprised.

"Nobody really knows. But you were right: I did switch
questions—to get her off the show without confronting
her."

Kat looked pleased at her perceptiveness. "Why?"

I had my answer well prepared. "Because the fifteen
programs she'd taped are worth a million-five. Can you see
the producer scrapping them?"

She seemed to buy this, then looked suspicious. "What's
the connection with her murder?"

My innocent puppy look. "Coincidence, I think. These
things do happen."

"Maybe." But her tone added, *and maybe not*. She scru-
tinized me for a long moment, then drained her glass. "So
now where do we stand?"

"I can't ask you to sit on the story: *Sunday, she won a
fortune; by Monday she was dead.*"

That brought a smile. "Not a bad lead, is it?"

I nodded. "But if you bring in the cheating thing, we'll slam you with a libel suit."

A snort. "We've been there and we've always won."

"Not this time. Nobody knows the questions were switched except me, and I haven't breathed a word, now have I?"

"Aw come *on*. Somebody had to screw up the computer."

I had this answer ready too. "It's not a computer, exactly—just a system you type answers on to put them on the screen. The techies don't know what the answers mean; they simply get them from me and key them in."

Her expression said *what do you take me for?* "You're telling me you fed them fake answers without even consulting anyone?"

"I'm telling you the producer said, 'Who will rid me of this man? . . .' "

"*Man?*"

"Or words to that effect. And I took it from there. If nobody knows anything, they can't lie about it."

Kat stared at the red-checked table cloth, apparently sorting this out while I sipped my drink and left her to it. After a long pause, she looked at me with a new expression. "Why do you believe I'll keep this off the record?"

"Because we're coming from the same place. You're a scandal rag reporter; I'm a game show flunky. But we both have standards and we're both looking for more honest work."

That must have appealed to her. "All right, I'll drop the cheating angle."

I put ten dollars on the table. "And let's keep in touch on this."

She stood up with me. "Yeah, that reminds me: why the sudden cooperation?"

"Partly what you call damage control. Partly because my producer taught me the publicity value of scandal."

She only nodded, but her face betrayed a faint distaste.

As I rumbled homeward through the darkness, I reviewed my strategy. I'd hoped to steer Kat away from the contest and Kelli, while throwing her the bone of Amber's death. Why not? She'd write that story anyway, no matter what I said.

I chugged up Sally's driveway in a crushing depression. Amber was a bad guy, but nowhere near *that* bad—not bad enough to rape and murder. No crime deserved that hideous reprisal.

I found Sally rigid at the dining table, glaring across her half-empty plate. "Where were you?" When I told her she sneered. "Drinkies with a lady."

"Woman."

Wrong thing to say. She slapped her napkin down and rose. "You might have phoned, at least."

"Death upsets me."

"So you take it out on me." And Sally stalked out of the room.

I stood awhile, wondering what the hell was happening, then tracked her to the bedroom. She was lying on the bed, her face away from me.

"I'm sorry I was thoughtless." No response. "I should

have phoned." More pregnant silence. "Come finish supper."

"Don't want any."

"Then come keep me company."

"I don't feel good."

I let that hang, but when a freezing minute passed, I
sighed, repeated "Sorry," shuffled out. Then I wandered
lonely as a cloud toward the wine supply in the kitchen.
What had I done *this* time?

14

At breakfast I apologized again, pointing out that I'd
been only half an hour late, and asked her what was wrong.
But Sally shook her head, said sorry she'd overreacted, and
sent me out the door with a quick pro-forma peck that told
me things were definitely not well.

Sigh.

By ten A.M. I was in the courtyard of Amber's apartment
house, ringing the bell under the card that said HERMAN
COOGLE, MANAGER. Himself opened the door, dressed in
exactly the same T-shirt, rubber sandals, and underquali-
fied shorts.

"Morning, Herman, Stoney Winston. I was here a week
ago?"

"Yeah." His fatty face turned grave. "But I can't talk to

you. Murder witness, that's me, and the police said don't talk about it, not a word."

I feigned puzzlement, then, "Oh, you mean Ms. Sung Li! Well, you're absolutely right."

"My lips are sealed."

I nodded, trying not to smile. "Terrible about her, but that's not why I'm here."

"You're not?"

"No, you see, I told the producer about you . . ."

"You did?" in a tone that came out *little old me?*

". . . and she was very interested."

Coyly, "Well, I dunno. I'm still shooting for *Jeopardy.*"

"But you also had ideas for game shows."

I'd said the secret word. "Hey, sure!" With the heartiness of a used-car salesman, "Come right on in, Stoney." Herman whacked the screen door open. "See, I remembered your name right off. All part of my training." His fat index finger stabbed his temple. "Siddown. Want some coffee?" But even before I could answer he was off and running: "*Grab Bag!*"

"I'm sorry?"

"Name of the show. *Grab Bag.* Like they got this huge bag, okay? Full of *plastic eggs.* Great concept, right?"

"Plastic eggs."

"Like they sell panty hose in. Got the idea from Alice. She never throws them out, y'know. The eggs, I mean, not the panty hose. And . . ."

As he burbled on, I put my face through a very slow dissolve from friendly interest to a faint, distracted fearfulness.

". . . So the contestant opens up the egg, right? And guess what's in . . . Hey, whatsa matter? What are ya looking at?"

I shook my head. "It feels, I don't know, *eerie* here."

"It does?" He glanced around the frumpy room as if he'd smelled a chilling whiff of dread.

My who'd-have-thought-it tremolo: "Only a week ago we were standing in this very room, talking about Amber Sung Li."

"Yeah, just think." So Herman thought.

I maintained the Unsolved Mysteries tone: "Young, beautiful, on her way to wealth . . ."

"She had her whole life ahead of her." He almost whispered it.

"Little did we know that tragedy would strike her . . ." I broke off, brushing a hand before my eyes. "I'm sorry."

"Hey, does you credit." He shook his head again at the wonder of it all.

"To think a killer would just stroll across this court and walk right in on Amber."

That broke the spell. "No, they didn't."

"Hm?"

"I got my desk right here. I do my work here, my ree-search. Anybody goes through that patio, I see 'em."

Stir in a pinch of admiration: "You don't miss a thing."

"Observation, that's the secret."

"And no one went to Amber's apartment."

"Except this cute chick came for lunch—prolly her girlfriend."

"How do you know?"

"Observation. Look: she shows up at noon with a red-

and-white-striped chicken bucket, stays forty-five minutes, leaves without the bucket: lunch. Amber's smiling when she opens the door and she's smiling when the kid leaves: girlfriend."

"Amazing, my dear fellow!"

"Aaah . . . Yeah! *What does Watson say to Sherlock Holmes?*"

"Hm?"

"*Jeopardy!* They give the *answer* and you gotta come up with the *question*. I'm in training." The manager looked past me and his face abruptly changed. "But listen, I got a lotta work right now, so maybe some other time."

"What about the panty eggs?"

Herman shuffled to the door and held it open. "Yeah, right, but maybe not right now, right?"

I turned to find his monochrome wife standing in the doorway to the hall, arms folded, lips tight, drab eyes fixed on Herman. "Right. Well, thanks, Herman. Morning, Alice."

As I started down the walkway, Alice was reminding her husband of his promise to the law.

Out on the street, I walked to the corner and turned right toward the alley behind the apartment block, then strolled toward the open-fronted carport attached to the building.

The more expensive flats, like Amber's, backed directly on the carport. Their spaces were marked with apartment numbers on the wall that also labeled private entry doors. The door by Amber's number showed no signs of forcing.

Nonetheless, it was a way inside unmonitored by Herman Coogle, doing ree-search at his window.

• • •

Parames was at his most pedantic as he led me around his office complex, lecturing, expatiating, and spreading himself generally. To be fair, he had something to show off: an astounding database of people, pictures, letters, cases—all instantly accessible to report-writing software that could seine it with a microscopic net. Did you seek a left-handed crazy in Portland who believed Dustin Hoffman ran a PLO conspiracy? No problem. A warlock in Detroit who yearned to eat Michael Jackson's toenail parings? Easy. Parames held the world's most massive file of nut-balls, kooks, and psychopaths—a digital parts bin teeming with loose screws, all utterly different except in their shared perverse obsession with celebrities.

Parames' own office proclaimed the inner man: a fugue of rectangles in framing square rigidity. Stacks of sheets and folders checkered his square desk, all perfectly aligned and each stack equidistant from the others on a square glass desktop shield that was itself protected by a square green blotter pad.

We stood by his credenza as Parames counted coffee beans from three square cans. "Our files hold almost six thousand cases."

"I didn't realize it was this bad."

"It's worse. Not even *we* have everyone. Was that five beans or six?"

"Five, I think." I hadn't really noticed.

"Good. You don't want too much Turkish in the blend."

"What makes these crackpots do it?"

"A general increase in social pathology and a culture that offers ever-decreasing contact with reality. The only vivid world these people have is media, and its stars are their possessions, their pipelines to importance, their intimate friends." The explanation sounded canned and practiced.

Still, I recalled a conversation overheard in a low-rent coffee shop: . . . *and Oprah told me only yesterday . . .* "It's frightening."

He closed and realigned the cans, then dumped his mixture in a Braun grinder—a defiant cylinder in this right-angle world. "Oh, by the way, another letter came today." He nodded toward his desk. "Top right-hand stack."

While Parames fussed with his coffee machine, I read the letter:

> *My Servant And Lover Kelli*
> *I am more calm today. I wish I could tell you what Ive done but you wouldnt understand yet. Be ready to receive me. I cant wait and I know you cant either but if you are patient just a short time more I will reveal myself and end your pain forever.*
> *Your Determined Master*
> *Hassan*

I reviewed the letter. "He orders her to receive him . . . he'll end her pain forever. And there it is again: he will *reveal* himself, as if he were near—maybe on the show. When was this postmarked?"

"Saturday."

"The day *before* we exposed Amber's cheating. So whatever Hassan has 'done' that he can't tell in this letter, it wasn't killing Amber." I handed back the letter. "Still, it doesn't take a psychologist to spot trouble here."

"That's why we have to line our ducks up. My staff is working on Kelli's background." He aligned two mugs. Somehow, he'd managed to find square ones.

"Anything so far?"

"As you said, she doesn't seem to *have* a background. That's significant. Everybody has a background—a paper trail all the way to a birth certificate. We'll pick up the scent someplace."

"I keep suggesting this and people think I'm simple. Why don't we just ask Kelli?"

"My understanding. . ." He decanted coffee. "Well, Ms. Barker told me that Kelli's . . . equilibrium, you might call it, is fragile. She doesn't want it jeopardized."

I took the mug he offered.

Parames continued his lecture: "I've worked with many creative types. Some are stable citizens, but for every Jack Lemmon in the solid center there's a dozen John Belushis out riding the ragged edge. A by-product of talent, I suppose. That's how they can do what they do and the rest of us can't."

Ah yes.

"Meanwhile, your job is vital. As Ms. Barker's assistant, you have the run of the operation. Normally, as I said, I'd put my own people in place, but if Hassan is already with the show somehow, he might spot them."

"Wouldn't that deter him?"

"The opposite." He sipped. "Nine times out of ten, these people never act as long as they don't feel threatened. But if they do, they lose their cool, as it were."

I tapped the letter. "You still think Hassan killed Amber?"

"We don't yet know."

"Speaking of which, did you contact the police?"

A complacent nod. "I have good connections with them."
He paced over to his desk and plucked his notes from grid
coordinates three-dash-four. "Let's see: skull crushed by
just two skillful blows—probably a sap—extensive bruising
of inner thighs," his dandruffy voice turned even drier,
"pudendal, vaginal areas . . ."

That confirmed the rape and ruled out the girlfriend.
"Any pubic hair or semen traces?"

Primly, "Negative. Probable time of death, late afternoon."

"Prints? Evidence of robbery? Drugs in the system?
Stomach contents?"

"Yes: ah, fried chicken, soft drink, nothing else."

"What do you think, Herb?"

He restored the page of notes to its designated spot.
"The rape business bothers me. Rapists often beat their
victims . . ."

"But not with a cosh."

"Hm?"

"A sap." After all these years, I rarely used an Anglicism.

"Exactly, Stoney."

"Would Hassan do that?"

"Impotence is often associated . . ." He broke off and
there was something odd about the way he shifted topics:
"By the way, we have a two P.M. appointment, you and I,
with Russell Carlisle."

"Owns *Raunch*."

"And *Oh-Pun Sesame*. He wants to know how we're protecting his property." Parames piloted his mug to a desktop

landing two inches from the west edge, two inches from the south.

15

We rolled out to Westwood in Parames' Volvo, a car as close to square as cars now get, this side of Jeeps.

Carlisle's headquarters was in a glass and concrete highrise: five floors of offices thrust aloft by five above-ground parking levels—a typical ratio in these parts. The directory in the onyx lobby disclosed that Carlisle's publications filled the building: *Raunch*, of course, and a journal of arty erotica called *Priapus*—but other magazines as well.

A security guard phoned upstairs to confirm our appointment, then led us around a corner to an unobtrusive elevator, activated its door with a key-switch, and waved us in. I pushed the top button, marked PENTHOUSE.

When the door reopened, the penthouse receptionist smiled and buzzed the latch on one of three carved doors. We walked into an office as vast and stuffy as a bankers' club lounge, except for one tinted glass wall framing a raised terrace outside and a background of UCLA buildings that marched up the hills to the west. We hiked across a parking lot of Oriental rugs deployed on the hardwood floor, our footsteps going *mmp-mmp-mmp, klok, klok, mmp-mmp*, toward the desk where Russell Carlisle sat facing backward as he stared at a forty-inch video screen on which a game show was in progress. He was balding on top.

"One minute, guys." He waved us into chairs without turning around and scribbled on a legal pad.

The sign above the game show set said HOPSCOTCH. A player tossed a marker like a yellow hockey puck, then hopped one-legged toward the square on which it landed. As she reached it, the square flashed on and off and the host boomed, "Classic TV series, for three hundred points!" The contestant smiled triumphantly.

"Damn!" Carlisle swung around, slapped the note pad down, punched buttons on a tape deck hidden in the desk front. *"Damn!"* The deck whirred and he brought the ejected tape into view and slammed it on the note pad. "My concept." He banged on the cassette. "The sonofabitch stole my concept!" He was a well-set-up man of fifty-plus with a rugged face under a pompadour like Ronald Reagan's.

I said, "What sonofabitch is that?"

"Savick, that's who, Manny-fucking-Savick, and I'm going to sue his ass." He rose, extending a hand that emerged from a custom-tailored oxford-cloth shirt. "Russ Carlisle."

We introduced ourselves, and as we returned to our leather club chairs Parames asked, "Can you prove he stole it?"

"Don't have to." He held up the tape. "This, gentlemen, is the pilot Manny's pitching to ABC." Carlisle's voice had the hearty ring of a veteran salesman. "Don't ask how I know or where I got it from. When I tie this show up in court, the network'll pitch it back at him so fast it'll knock that asshole right out of his lifts." As he said this, Carlisle's expression changed from fury to vindictive glee.

Parames' tone showed only cautious interest. "What'll you gain by that?"

"Justice, brother . . ." Carlisle kissed the tape dramatically ". . . simple justice." He put down the tape, composed himself, and folded his big hands. "But that's a different story. Let's talk about Kelli Dengham."

Before we could begin, a young woman entered through an inner door, bounced up to Carlisle's desk, and handed him a file folder.

"Thanks, Clipper."

She flashed a cheerful smile, turned toward us, smiled again, and bounced off the way she'd come.

As a post-macho male, I sweat to suppress the ancient instinct to size up women sexually, but Clipper shorted my control circuits and I gawped like an adolescent. Her lines were all distended into curves, her planes inflated to convexities, her tan, pneumatic flesh buffed shiny as the office floor. In her white linen shorts and halter she was a sexual icon—a tribal fetish from a *Raunch* cartoon. As she opened the door, she tossed her tumbling auburn curls and wagged her tumid rump. She was barefoot.

Carlisle grinned at our bemusement.

During the next ten minutes we told what we knew about Kelli, and while Parames did the talking, I watched Carlisle's reactions: alert, responsive, and overtly friendly. But it was the practiced, dangerous bonhomie of a cutthroat marketing manager who smiled and murdered whilst he smiled.

Parames summed up in his usual lecturing way: "This

Hassan person has vowed to protect Kelli from people who 'do bad things' to her. We know he thought her spread in *Raunch* was one of those bad things. We don't know whether he knew that Ms. Sung Li was blackmailing Kelli—but that might constitute another bad thing. Whatever the case, both Sung Li and Arnesen were murdered."

"And the cops don't know who or why. They know about Hassan?"

Parames shook his head. "The letters alone wouldn't interest them—most entertainers get such things. And we thought it imprudent to mention Kelli's link with Arnesen."

I tried a little fishing: "Or Arnesen's with *Raunch*."

Carlisle just shrugged. "His photo credit's in the magazine if anybody looks. But he shot lots of different pussy."

That reminded me. "Ma Barker says you bought all of Kelli's pictures. Could you describe the ones you didn't print?"

Carlisle deployed his toothy grin. "Just say I wish I could have printed them; they were perfect for my magazine. Too bad they were lousy for my TV show."

"So you shredded them."

"Ever try and shred a strip of film? No, I burned them —they flamed up like crazy. Almost set my wastebasket on fire."

I pressed it: "But Ms. Sung Li used the shots on Kelli long after you'd bought them. That means there were dupes."

Carlisle waved this off. "Or maybe Amber saw Arnesen's originals and *described* them to Kelli—you know, just pretended she had them."

"Maybe." But that didn't satisfy me.

At that point Clipper strolled into view along the terrace

outside with Walkman earphones on her head, sunglasses
on her button nose, and lotion in one slender, pink-nailed
hand. She lazed up to a rattan chaise, divested herself of
the Walkman and lotion, stripped off her halter and shorts,
scratched with her thumbs where her white bikini panties
seemed to chafe her undulant stomach, reinstalled the
Walkman, uncapped the lotion, anointed breasts as big and
hard as melons, though more complexly contoured.

Parames' dry voice: "Is this show for somebody's benefit?" He was staring through the glass with open interest.

"No, she does that all the time." Carlisle chuckled with
rueful fondness. "In here Clipper can see my office wall is
glass, but out *there* all she sees is mirror. She thinks she's
alone because she's so shit-for-brains dumb she can't connect the outside with the inside."

I asked, "Is she your secretary?"

Another chuckle. "She can barely read and write. No,
she drives my car, runs my errands, decorates the place."
He gazed benignly out the window at the now recumbent
girl. "Some people rent a Renoir or whatever to brighten
up their office." He gestured at the image behind the glass.
"I'd rather hang a Clipper on my wall."

That figured. If *Playboy* decorated with transparencies
of centerfolds, the mastermind of *Raunch* would outdo
them in piggery by flaunting the originals.

Carlisle recaptured our attention. "Here's what I want:
you focus on the show. I'll bet this creep Hassan's around
there someplace."

Parames said cautiously, "I think we should explore Kelli's background too . . ."

"Forget it if she hasn't got any background! Who cares

what she's covering up. That's like a constitutional right or
something." Carlisle leaned forward and pointed a mean-
ingful finger at us. "I want her protected, not investigated.
Anything happens to that lady . . ." He stared at us with
a sudden, cold intensity that finished the sentence for him:
. . . *it's your ass!*

Parames drove us back to his office in a mood of mild
abstraction. "Interesting display Miss Clipper gave us."

"She's certainly voluptuous."

Parames smiled and nodded. "The best volup that cash
can buy. I spotted gluteal augmentation, nose reduction,
lip enhancement—probably cheekbones too—and breast
enlargement. As you may have noted."

"I recall that vaguely, yes." Either Parames had the eyes
of a red-tailed hawk or the concentration born of unsus-
pected prurience.

"Quite well done too, except for the scar lines around
the areolas."

"The . . . ?"

"With the bigger implants they often have to move the
nipples. Otherwise the silicone beneath them would dis-
place them north or south or someplace."

"You seem something of an expert."

He smiled again. "One of our corporate sidelines is en-
suring that when celebrities disappear for a spot of physical
revision their absence goes unnoticed by the public. Over
time I've learned a lot about cosmetic surgery."

"And there seems a lot to learn."

"You'd be amazed. I've seen whole personalities built of
silicone."

And yet, to what effect? After the initial impact Clipper's body was oddly offputting—an artifact like a plastic doll that overinflation had only made even *less* human, a blow-up sex toy for sad, seedy loners like Hassan.

Hassan. Protect Kelli from Hassan and forget about her blank background. Carlisle didn't care what she was covering up. Funny, though: we hadn't told him Kelli had no background. It seemed he already knew that.

As for Amber, Parames and I'd politely called her "Ms. Sung Li," so how did Carlisle know her first name? Smilin' Jack had used it during tapings, but these shows had not been broadcast yet and Carlisle never came near the production at any time. Had Ma Barker told him? Check that out.

Another thing: Carlisle described the way he'd burned the slides, but modern film doesn't flame. It only bubbles, curls, and blackens. I'd bet he hadn't burned those slides, he'd kept them.

Why?

16

I spent the balance of the day digging, sluicing, picking tiny information nuggets out of veins already overworked —or in Ma Barker's case, varicose.

"What do you know about Manny Savick?"

"Biggest goddam game show developer around—bigger

than Merv Griffin." Ma blew a Marlboro ring, then shot a small ring through it.

I watched the rings drift toward her office ceiling.

"And a sweetheart of a man. I produced two shows for him." Poof, poof, poof. "Damn. Time was, I could blow a three-ring pretzel. Manny's a gentleman, one hundred proof. Why?"

"Carlisle says this gentleman stole a concept from him."

Ma chortled and coughed. "You don't know this business, Bucky. A show like *Password, Dating Game, Let's Make a Deal*—ten years later eight people claim exclusive credit for the concept and each calls the other seven liars." Another spastic cackle. "That's why they all hate each other."

Casually, "Carlisle does seem to hate Savick."

"Yeah, they started out as partners, then split up." Ma's doughy face looked strangely mellow. "Carlisle diversified into publishing and stuff, but Manny focused on what he did best. Now he's three times richer than Carlisle and Russell hates him."

Still very offhand: "But Carlisle's feeling no pain financially."

"Who knows?" Puff, poof, wheeze. "Last few years he conglomerated any goddam thing that moved. Now I wonder if the interest's catching up with him."

"You think he has financial troubles?"

Ma suddenly noticed that she was being pumped. She glared at me. "Who wants to know?"

"Oh, just idle curiosity."

"Idle, I don't like at four o'clock. You got nothing to do?"

I rose. "I'll go see Dr. Herbert P. He was going to check the cops again." Before she could answer, I was off toward

the room where Parames camped out when he worked in
our production offices.

But Parames hadn't learned much more. The time of
death had been narrowed to just before five P.M. When a
neighbor'd heard screams and thumping noises, she'd come
in through the unlocked front door, discovered Amber, and
phoned 911. Death due to massive head trauma. No evidence of robbery.

"And no rape either, I suspect." Parames tapped his note
pages into perfect alignment and set them on the table.
"The bruises on, uh, the areas we discussed looked more
like blows than forceable entry. Why would someone sim-
ulate rape?"

I gave the answer that we both suspected: "To divert
attention from a set of stolen duplicate slides."

Parames nodded. "Who would want them enough to kill
for them?"

"The hypothetical Hassan, perhaps, to protect 'his' Kelli
from 'bad people.' "

Doodl-loodl-loodl-loo. My electronic phone had a ring
like a sonar echo.

"Punny Place Productions, Stoney Winston."

"Yo, Stonewall!"

"Yo. Uh . . . Katcall. Is that the countersign?"

"How are you, Stoney?" Kat Halbreck's voice was warm.

"Functional. What's up?"

"I thought I'd tell you I filed the Sung Li article. Are
you ready? Two hundred words on page thirty-six."

Buried in the bust creme ads. Outstanding.

"Editor said since Amber's shows weren't out yet, no one would know who she was."

"Makes sense."

"But he put me back on the Kelli article."

Uh-oh. "You said . . ."

"No, not the cheating bit, the backgrounder."

"Ah." But that was worse.

"Thing is, she hasn't *got* a background."

Stalling while I thought, "There is a handout bio . . ."

"And it stops dead a year ago." I didn't answer. "So what's the story?"

"I don't know anything about Kelli's background." Which was all too true. "Why'd your editor put you on her in the first place? She hasn't got that big a public yet."

"What I said too. He told me it came from upstairs."

"Where upstairs?"

"Not *where* but *which floor*? The paper's in the Sunbelt Group, which is connected to de back bone, which is connected to de neck bone—all the way up to some press lord in Fleet Street or something."

"In short, you don't know where."

"Yeah. So you have nothing on Kelli's background?"

My most reasonable tone: "No, or Jack Kilparrow's or anybody else's. It's not my department on the staff here."

"Who would know?"

A pause, and then an idea hit me. "Try her agent, Ernie Drenko—on Robertson."

"Much grass, Stonewall."

"*De nada.*"

She rang off. If she wanted a real stone wall, let her go bang her head on Ernie Drenko.

• • •

At dinner I told Sally what I'd learned that day. My description of Carlisle and his surgically inflated handmaiden was greeted with proper contempt; but otherwise, Sally seemed abstracted. Her responses trickled down to monosyllables and then to nods and grunts; and the more I tried to keep discussion lively, the more artificial I sounded. Supper finally guttered out in littered plates and silence.

Since Sally'd cooked tonight, I did the dishes, to Mozart on the kitchen radio, then wandered off to find her. Living room, TV room, bedroom were empty, so I walked out to the wide front deck. She was leaning on the railing and looking at the distant lights, her linen skirt lapping at her shins in the breeze, her discarded shoes beside her on the redwood planks. I propped my elbows on the railing at a distance nicely calculated: close enough to tell her I was with her, far enough to say that I would not intrude 'til asked.

I spent a long, patient time counting lights and smelling eucalyptus, then Sally moved close enough to pick up the wine glass I'd set on the railing. She sipped and put it back, but didn't move away again.

That, if I knew Sally, was my signal. "You want to tell me what's the matter?"

"Nothing, really."

"You've been edgy for days."

"Just out of sorts." She looked at the view again and shook her head very slowly, perhaps six times. "I guess I don't know where I am. I walked out of the jungle when I quit selling mainframes. Where did I go?" She addressed the question to the darkness.

"Here."

"Where's here?" She took a deep breath of chill January air. "Tell me more about Carlisle."

Quietly, "No, tell me about the jungle."

She sighed. "It was brutal but clear." She stared out as if it lay beyond the deck. "This animal is what you eat; that animal will eat you if it can. This is where the swinging vines go; that's how you swing on them. Me Tarzan, you Jane." Her big peasant toes had a prehensile grip on the deck edge. "Let's talk about Carlisle."

"Finish the jungle."

"I did." I let that drift away into the night. At length she sighed. "Now I'm—I don't know—out on the savannah: no trees, no landmarks, endless grass."

"You're thirty-three, financially secure, and at loose ends."

Half chuckle, half snort. "Too true."

"What you need is structure."

Sharply, "Oh, profound, Winston!" She softened it with a smile. "Back to Carlisle."

No way, lady. "So let's get married."

I expected Sally's usual exasperated look, but her face showed only quiet curiosity. "For the hundredth time, why make it permanent?"

"Because I permanently love you."

She looked at me for a long moment, then turned to address tree shadows. "I never fell in love with you."

"I know." Hard to keep a level tone there.

Pause. "Then I woke up one day and thought, *I guess I sort of love him, more or less.*"

"These searing passions happen."

"All right, *I just plain love him.*" Still looking at the night, she put an arm around my waist. "How'd you do that to me?"

"Snuck up on you." I matched her arm with mine.

"Nobody sneaks up on me."

"That's what Custer said."

She chewed on that awhile, then, "Why would marriage give me structure we don't already have?"

"It would say, this isn't simply happening to me; this is what I *choose.*"

She shook her head. "It's just a different jungle."

"No predators in this one."

This time her snort was humorless. "There were the last time." Sally'd wed at twenty-two, divorced at twenty-four, and spent the next nine years in wary independence. "And in this second jungle it would be me Jane, *you* Tarzan."

I turned us face to face, put my hands on her hips, and looked her in the eye. "Do you believe that, Sally?"

She studied me carefully, then smiled. "No, I guess I really don't."

"So. You want to catch the nine o'clock vine?"

"I'll think about it." She backed away, then turned and started for the house. "Weather report said it's going to rain."

But my own forecast showed promise of clearing.

17

*N*othing more happened during the rest of the week, and we taped five weekend shows as always. Hassan remained anonymous, though he did check in on Wednesday with another masturbation fantasy that couched his impending union with Kelli in the florid prose you'd expect of Omar the tentmaker.

I read the opening paragraph and grinned. *"I will whisper hello my honey as I suck the honey nectar from your navel.* That's choice."

Parames pursed his lips. "I wish I could find it funny, but I can't." He looked anxious and irritated.

By now I'd got used to his pompous manner and I found the man sharp, original, and likable enough to care about. "You look tired, Herb."

He removed his bifocals and held them up for inspection as if they were smearing his view of the truth. Speaking to his glasses: "Some showbiz clients—many, I should say— are simply not nice people." He reinstalled his specs. "But Kelli *is.*" Then, as if to change the subject, he pointed at the letter. "Read the rest."

"Let's see, um . . . *kiss your mothering breasts . . . drink the milk of paradise* . . . well, he knows his Coleridge."

"Hm?"

"He's quoting poetry. Is that significant?"

Snappish, "Will you just read it?"

I skimmed until my eye caught *You will degrade yourself in worshiping my great manhood like you did in those pictures.* Those pictures! "Herb, what Ma calls the Freddie Footlong shots were never published."

"Precisely. Hassan has seen the other shots."

"Which Amber used to blackmail Kelli and which maybe got her killed." I thought a moment. "Killed by Hassan?"

Parames' middle-aged face looked gray. "I'm almost sure of it."

I considered this, then said grimly, "I think it's time to check out Kelli's background."

Parames shook his head. "I concur, but Carlisle is my bottom-line client here and he says no."

"We wouldn't have to tell him."

"Carlisle says *no!*"

I couldn't judge Parames too harshly. His business depended on obedience to the whims of often capricious clients. But I was indifferent to Carlisle's opinion of me, and the threat to Kelli Dengham was now manifest. A nut who'd killed two people could easily kill a third.

In vowing to pollinate Kelli Dengham's belly button, our crackpot poet was just warming up. His next emission came the following Tuesday:

> *I will put jelly on your nipples and butter in your slender thighs and I will eat the fruits of Kelli and you will lead me from this sin and darkness. Your expiation will cleanse me as I dirty you.*

And he detailed his plans for this by reference to some of Kelli's more gynecological poses—more confirmation that he had those pictures.

Thursday's effusion returned to sado-masochism:

> *I bought a suit for you today all shiny leather with three holes in it and you know where and a face hood with no holes at all and a red rubber ball to strap in your pink mouth. Will you cry behind that ball? Will you weep at your humiliation when I tighten your buckles or will it turn you crazy with longing for me? I am crazy for you.*

Crazy, period, and as dangerous as plastic explosives in a 747.

In the letter I collected at the office on Sunday, before completing another weekend of tapings, Hassan's erratic prose had finally fractured into cubist shards of passion, hate, and incoherent rage:

> *Soon oh so so soon I will be in you nobody can stop me its fair its fair! Youre in me now in my head all the time and I didn't ask for that you made me soon I will feel you feel how it feels you devil oh how can you make it so black for me I cant see what Im doing bad things and I must break your curse or you will make the black come if I end you you will break my heart and kill me but no one will have you we will together where we cant be bad*
> *no more bad no more*
> *waitwaitwait for hassan.*

That tore it! No more, all right, no more waitwaitwait for Hassan! After one look at this murderous rant, I charged off to the TV channel offices in search of Attila the Ma.

I found her behind the program director's scabby desk, cloaked in her usual Marlboro smog. Parames stood near one windowless wall, studying the ancient awards on it as if checking their alignment. I handed the letter to Ma, and when she'd read it, took the sheet to Herb.

He scanned it and gave it back. "He's reached new levels of pathology, no question about that."

I waved the letter at him. "The question is, what do we *do* about this?"

A shrug. "More of what we're doing, only better."

"Zero plus zero is zero."

Ma's dragon mouth shot smoke. "Look who's talking, Junior. You've snooped around here for two goddam weeks—on my payroll, remember—and what have you found?"

"I can't do a thing with my hands tied."

"Like what?"

"Like talking to Kelli."

"Hell no!" She smashed the cigarette butt on the ashtray.

"Does she even know about these letters?" Ma shook her head. "Has she no right to know she's in danger?"

Ma's jaw locked in barracuda mode. "Look, Bucko: you saw her go to pieces that night in her dressing room. But you *didn't* see the whole goddam week it took me to glue her back together enough to tape the next weekend. Miss Flake is just *that* far from flipping out—and if she's freaking bonkers, I haven't got a show!"

"But you'd still have a show if she were hurt or dead?"

Parames cleared his throat. "I'll put more people on checking out the staff."

"Including Kelli?"

He shook his head. "You know what Carlisle said."

"Why did he say it?" Then to Ma: "What does he know about Kelli's background?" Ma and Parames looked at each other, then at me. No answer. "Then at least protect her. Get someone to stay with her."

Ma tapped her gray head with one pudgy finger. "Use your goddam brains, Winston. To do that, we'd have to tell her why."

"Have someone watch her house."

Parames shook his head ruefully. "Park a man in a car down the street? In that rural canyon, how long would he last before the neighbors called their security patrol?"

Boiling with frustration, I paced a little circle on the shabby carpet. "Let's add it up. We can't tell the police because the letters by themselves aren't enough to act on. We can't get help from Kelli—or even tell her about the letters. We can't dig up her oh-so-mysterious past because Carlisle says no—for reasons unexplained. And we can't even protect her at home from a psychopath who may well have committed two murders!"

Parames sighed. "Succinctly put."

"We can't do *shit*," Ma said.

Parames nodded. "Even more succinct."

"You want succinct? Kelli Dengham may be killed, murdered—you know, like *dead*? And I can't even *start* to find the killer!"

I stormed out of the office, shaking with worry and frustration.

• • •

A few minutes later I was knocking on the door of Kelli's dressing room.

" 'Tsopen!"

She stood half in, half out of a green-sequined paint job like a tropical snake in mid-molt. The top of the dress hung on her slender hips from a point just below the provocative pout of Hassan's beloved navel. She grinned at me, seemingly unconcerned about the effect of her pearly flesh or the breast tops pushed into small, lush mounds above her punishing black lace bra. She cocked a hip in her goofy Mae West burlesque and said in her little-girl croak, "Zip me, big boy." She struggled into the rest of her gown and presented her undulant back.

I zipped her, then we stood there as if neither quite knew what came next. Finally I said, "Kelli, I've wanted to tell you I'm sorry I upset you that night—you know, in here?"

A small voice: "Yeah. It's okay."

"That business wasn't your fault at all. You got trapped into it."

"Because I'm not all that swift." Before I could reply, she turned to face me. "I'm not real good at . . ." She tapped her temple as Ma had just done and chuckled almost sadly. The big soft eyes above the smile turned sadder.

"Maybe you're smarter than you think. Look at your ad-libs and your business on camera. Where do they come from?" Her eyes crinkled as she shrugged. "All talent comes from smarts, Kelli. It just comes out a more original way."

She pondered that a moment, then her smile said *that was sweet of you.*

"But I did want to apologize."

She shook her yellow curls. "Don't hafta; I could tell. Y'know, I got another talent: reading people, kinda like my cats."

"Cheddar, Jack, Velveeta, Zola."

She nodded. "They, like, checked you out, Stoney. You passed."

My turn to smile. "You communicate with your familiars?" Her look said she couldn't process that, so I added, "Thank them for me."

Kelli moved in, snaked her arms around my chest, and pulled me into the hug of an affectionate friend. "You're a real nice man, Stoney. Don't ever let that go." She kissed my cheek and unwound herself. "And thanks for worrying. It's okay."

I nodded, smiled, and left her—smelling the jumble of scents at her ear: hair spray and pancake base and, underneath, a slightly sweet but uninsistent musk.

By the time I'd driven home from the taping, helped Sally with the supper, and washed the dishes, I knew what I would do.

"Do you have any forms design software?" I was on my back, propped up by couch pillows so I could see the TV screen between my big flat feet.

"For my 486?" Sally lay on top of me with the back of her head on my solar plexus. "No. Will PageMaker do?" She zapped the end credits of *Masterpiece Theater*.

"Does it make lines and boxes?"

"Easy. Why?"

"I need to fake an insurance report form." I tried to

kiss her hair but my big chin banged my chest. "You're
heavy."

"Poor baby." She revolved and lay facedown. "That better?"

"Better for smelling your hair, but you're embossing my
chest with my own shirt button."

"There's an obvious cure for that."

"Not with your weight on top of me."

"Well ex-cuuuse me!" Sally raised herself on her elbows
and started to work on my shirt buttons.

18

After breakfast the next morning Sally fired up her computer and desktop publishing software and set to work on
my form.

I set to work on my form as well: washing it, shaving it,
dressing it up in sharp-creased pants and a chaste white
shirt and a tie that proclaimed me a model of probity. I
even swapped my sneakers for a pair of leather bunion
builders and trimmed the straggles of hair at my ears. Then
downstairs to my desk in Mildew Manor for a government-
issue clipboard and back up to where Sally was lifting the
last of ten sheets from a tray on her PostScript printer.

She handed me the stack. Each sheet was headed SOUTH-
LAND INSURANCE SUPPORT GROUP, INC. in 30-point Hel-

vetica Bold, with *Auto Insurance Field Report* below it and then rows of headings, boxes, type, and lines. Sally'd got into the spirit so well that the bottom right corner said *form 3632 REV. 01/22/91.*

"It's gorgeous, Sally, thank you. And I love the mint-green paper."

"Makes it look official. You sure you don't want to take my Supra? It'll be more at home than your Beetle in Conejo Canyon."

"But out of character." I snapped the sheets into the clipboard and stowed the lot in my briefcase. "I'm not supposed to live there. I'm a poor but honest leg man for a great American company." I kissed her and then patted her computer. "Stand down from forms design; resume amassing obscene wealth. Bye."

But first a stop at Punny Place Productions.

"You rang, madam?"

Ma Barker sat at her office conference table. "Yeah, I want to go over these . . ." She broke off, staring at my funereal tie. "You got goddam jury duty?"

"I deliver religious pamphlets door to door."

She snorted smoke. "You look it. Siddown."

Despite her contempt for my gag writing, Ma knew I was a fast editor, so she kept me for two hours polishing show questions. I filled the printout margins with notes and she filled the ashtray with Marlboro corpses. It was eleven o'clock before I got away and pointed the Beetle toward Conejo Canyon.

Plan A was to pose as an insurance sleuth checking Kelli

Dengham's application for an auto policy. When I'd once
toiled briefly at this work some years ago, I'd found that a
deferential smile and an official-looking form routinely
prompted folks to answer invasive questions about neighbors. Neighbors like Kelli Dengham.

I knew my way this time, so I zigged and zagged deci-
sively and soon fetched up at her steep, narrow street.
Kelli's downhill neighbor had no cars in the driveway and
nobody answered my ring, but her uphill neighbor was
outdoors, puttering in the wide, shallow yard.

The gardener was a hulking woman with a face well up
in years but a still-straight body hung on bones scaled for
a soccer forward. She was troweling the gravel that paved
the yard around an anthology of cacti that would shame the
local arboretum. An ugly little specimen with evil spines
lurked in a plastic nursery pot beside her.

"Morning, ma'am, my name is . . ."

"This a petition?" She was squinting at my clipboard.

"No."

She stared sourly from under the Stetson that was her
unlikely gardening hat. "Whales, redwoods, voting districts
. . ." she got one big, sandaled foot beneath her and struggled upright ". . . unborn babies, hand guns, faggots,
homeless bums?" She stalked toward me, glaring.

"None of . . ."

"You smoke?"

"Well, no . . ."

"You smell. Who smokes?"

"My boss does, heavily."

A grim confirming nod. "You keep your distance."

"Sorry." I stepped back two paces, impaled my calf on a vicious spine, hopped forward.

"Thirdhand smoke! They don't tell you that. Secondhand, yes, but thirdhand, they don't tell you." She pronounced this with the finality of those people for whom there's always an evil cabal christened *they*.

"Ah."

"Any fool knows it's dangerous to breathe around a bunch of vicious smokers. But what about afterward, when *you* breathe on your wife and babies?" Her tone said *and you will, you swine, you will!* "That poison comes reeking off your clothes and hair and skin and out your mouth and turns their lungs to charcoal."

"I hadn't thought . . ."

"Of course you hadn't thought." She thrust a grubby finger toward the clipboard as if pointing it out in a lineup. "But that's what your petition *should* be against: thirdhand smoke!"

"It's not a petition."

This time her tone said *gotcha!* "Why did you mislead me?"

"I haven't even *led* you, yet."

Suspiciously, "Then what are you doing on my gravel?"

I showed her my impressive form with Kelli's name and address penciled in and said I was checking an application for car insurance.

She peered at the form as if its top said KGB in giant letters. "What right have you to snoop for personal information on my neighbors?"

I needed what she might tell me, but my politeness

started cracking with the strain. "I don't care about their taste in music, clothing, veggies, sex—or what they do with any of them. I just have to verify who drives which cars for what purposes." Her suspicious look dampened, so I added, "It affects her insurance rates."

Wrong move: her expression said *aha!* "Affects them *upward*, I'll just bet. I don't support the big insurance companies."

A malignant subset of *they*, but I played to it: "Confidentially, I don't either." Improvising, "But I *do* support the wife and babies you described. Please?"

Grudgingly, "All right, let's see: who drives what. She drives the little red Miata thing. Housekeeper comes and goes in her own car—a clunker like those Beaners always drive. He drives some kind of Ford."

Hello! But keep it bland: "He? We don't list a second driver in the household. Would this be her husband?" Her glare dialed up again. "Well, does he live there?"

"Yes, but that's getting personal. Stick to driving."

"He drives some kind of Ford, you said. What kind?"

"Small, white, cutie-pie license. Says ACME. I don't get the joke." (Surprise, surprise.) "Just a way to show off." She glowered at my Beetle behind me. "Like your plate there. Why's it read B BUMBLE?"

"SCHWARZENEGGER wouldn't fit."

That pushed her over. Clamping her jaw, she jammed hard fists on her hips, bunching the denim of her blue tent smock, and stomped backward. "When you showed up I didn't like you, and now I don't like you even better." A second stomp, but this one squashed the spiny little horror at her feet. She glowered down at damp white pulp and shards of plastic pot, then looked at me with fury. "Get off my gravel!"

My pleasure, Gertie.

I spiraled out of Conejo Canyon, picked up Sunset Boulevard, and rumbled east toward Hollywood through yet another winter day as hard and bright as forty zircons.

He drives a small white Ford and lives with Kelli in her chalk-blue cottage. The news that Kelli had a live-in boyfriend was unremarkable—in fact, it would be odd if a woman of her age and sensuality had no love life. But why did no one know about him except for Madam Cactus with her thirdhand smoke and her contempt for funny license plates?

I cut south on La Brea toward Melrose. Vanity plates like ACME. Hmh, ACME: summit, pinnacle, peak . . . all-purpose company name . . . mail-order vendor to Wile E. Coyote . . .

Warner cartoons!

No, it couldn't be *Ron Tolkis*. Nerdy Ron, the Chyron king, with his horn-rim spectacles and narrow little shoulders and generic facial features you forgot in twenty seconds? Ron was stunning Kelli Dengham's lover? Aw, come on!

Then a memory floated to the surface: after we had played the trick that'd finessed Amber off the show, Ron had asked me if Kelli was home free. But I hadn't told him that Amber's cheating had anything to do with Kelli. How else could he have known unless she'd told him so herself?

So where would Tolkis be on Monday? When I reached my office I called his union hall and told them I needed to check with Ron about our taping schedule. They said he was working a show at CBS and should be off by five.

Assuming Tolkis was my man, how could I pry him open? If he lived in Kelli's house, he shared her life—perhaps her past life too. He might know someone with a hinge pin missing: a former friend, a would-be lover—someone capable of writing notes that shredded devotion and dominance, love and pain, into a jumbled schizoid salad.

That was it: just let Ronald read those letters. If he cared about Kelli, he'd cooperate. I put the Xerox copies in my briefcase, then took off for Larry Edmund's Cinema Bookstore on Hollywood Boulevard. I already knew a fair amount about cartoons, but I had some time before Tolkis got off work—time for a spot of research to learn some more.

19

*C*BS Television City is a handsome complex of fifties-modern buildings with an artists' gate on Fairfax where I explained a bogus mission of mercy to the guard.

"Ron Tolkis called me; he's working *Up Your Ante*. His battery's dead." I held up the clips of the jumper cables I'd pulled from my trunk and stowed on the seat beside me.

The guard checked his production staff roster, then nodded cheerfully. "No problem." He waved me in.

I drove slowly up one line of cars and down the next,

hunting a small white ACME Ford and boggling at the lim-
itless variety of southern California wheels. Three rows,
four rows, five . . .

What ho! A white Ford Escort in the newer porpoise
profile with ACME on its shiny stern. As if that weren't
enough, the plate holder around it was embossed BEEP
BEEP. Unlikely as it seemed, luscious Kelli's boyfriend had
to be Ronald N-for-Nebbish Tolkis. As I hid the Beetle in
an unobtrusive slot and ambled toward an entrance, I reflected that ol' Ronald was a model for us all. If he could
land a beauty, then *anybody* could.

At the check-in desk I explained my mission, pinned on
a visitor's badge, and followed directions toward *Up Your
Ante*. CBS was a far cry from the dusty barn where we
taped our shows: high, clean corridors; endless carpentry,
paint, and prop shops; and taping stages built to the same
scale as the parking lot outside. This is the big time, Winston, so look all you want but don't touch.

On the set the crews were wrapping for the day, and I
spotted Tolkis just emerging from his Chyron cave.

I sneakered up behind him. "Donald McRonald!"

Tolkis snapped around, recognized me, did his Daffy
Duck voice: "Don't even withper that duckth name in my
prethenth, Buthter!" In his normal tenor bleat, " 'Cha
doing here, Stoney?"

"Came to look you up. How's it going?"

Suspiciously, "Look me up?"

"Mm-hmh, can I lay a beer on you?"

The suspicion deepened. "A beer can only mean I'm
fired."

"Oh, everyone's delighted with you. I wanted to get you lubed enough to give me free advice: cartoon books."

Puzzled, "Like The Far Side?"

"No, animated, as in Looney Tunes." Ron's mealy face cleared instantly. I gave my tone a rueful shading, "Larry Edmund's has what looks like fifty different books. I think I need expert advice."

Expert advice was the password that unlocked Ron's encrypted ego. His thin face shone like a ten-watt sun. "The guru is open for business."

"I did buy *Chuck Amuck*," I started toward the exit and Ron came with me, "but I wondered if I should get Mel Blanc's memoir too."

"Well . . ." Ron launched into diatribe 43B, and by the time we'd reached the street, crossed Fairfax, and found a *gemütlich* saloon, he was so blind to everything but animation that he wouldn't have noticed if I'd put him on a plane to Walla Walla.

Through the first glass of Anchor Steam beer we traded favorite lines (". . . Actually, it'th a buck-and-a-quarter quarterthtaff . . ." ". . . Could you direct me to deh Coachella Valley and deh carrot festival—dere-in?")

By the second beer Ron was telling tales about collectors: "So once a year we all go to his house and lock the door and pull down all the shades and screen his 35mm print of *Coal Black and De Sebben Dwarfs*."

By sud number three—or four?—we'd agreed that the *ne plus ultra* was *What's Opera, Doc?* Ron spread a sappy smile on his face, pressed a palm to his sparrow chest, and Elmer Fudd burst into Wagnerian song:

We-tuuuuuurn, my wuv,
I have a wonging inside me.

I picked up Bugs Bunny's Brunhilda:

Re-TOINNNNNN, my love,
I wont yew ol-way-hays beside me!

We traded two more lines and then belted the climax
together in thirds:

ELMER: Won't you we-turn, my wuv, to me!
BUGS: Won't you re-toin, my love, to me!

We lolled on our bar stools, helpless with bibulous mirth
while a nearby table of stagehands applauded and one
yelled, "Which is the fat lady?"

Still giggling, Ron looked at me with the affection re-
served for the anointed. "Brunhilda Bugs." Another giggle.
"Ever notice how often Bugs gets into drag?"

"Now that you mention it . . ."

"Y'know, I did my master's on that at UCLA: 'Gender
Identity in Warner Brothers Cartoons.' "

"Scholarship marches on."

And so did time, so I sidled into my real agenda by
looking at my watch. "Lot of traffic between here and Conejo Canyon?"

He shrugged. "Takes me half an hour." Then the impli-
cation hit him. "How . . . ?"

My own shrug said no big deal. "Open secret." I smiled
at Ron. "What a lucky guy you are—lovely lady like Kelli."

But Tolkis had retreated to his closed, suspicious look. "Hope the secret's not *too* open."

Offhandedly, "Why? I'd be proud if I were you."

He couldn't resist the compliment. "I am. She's so crazy-funny."

"But why do you have to keep Kelli secret?"

With a disgusted grimace, "It's her . . . well, it's her agent."

"Ernie Drenko."

"Yeah. He says . . ." Ron broke off and thought a moment. "He says I'm not good for P.R. He wants her seen with actors, stars—you know." He sipped his beer and sighed. "I guess I got to admit his point. Imagine our picture in *People*: 'Glamorous star attends premiere with unidentified geek.' "

Ron was not without self-knowledge and I liked him for that. "Maybe Kelli values a man who's not a phony—and who loves her for her own sake."

His face turned as sappy as Elmer Fudd's again. "She's so generous. You know she got me my job on the show."

Which cleared up that coincidence. I said cautiously, "You knew her before the show?"

"We go back a way—but that's a long story."

It's the story I'm after, Ronald. Aloud: "How'd you meet?"

But Ron just shrugged and waved it off.

Time to bring up Hassan's letters. I said, "Underneath her fun, Kelli seems like a delicate personality."

He nodded seriously. "She's very vulnerable."

"That worries me."

Ron stopped a handful of bar nuts en route to his mouth. "Worries you, why?"

"Because some psycho's writing her threatening letters."

"*What?*"

I got the copies out and showed him. As Tolkis read through them, his expression shaded from worry through anger to outright fear.

He dropped the letters on the bar and scraped his hand on a napkin as if he'd fingered excrement. "My God, I didn't know there were people like that." He thought a moment, then his face changed again as he looked at me and his reedy voice was quiet. "You don't just carry those things around, you brought them to show me. In fact, you looked me up to show them to me."

I owed him that much honesty. "I did indeed." I explained that the writer might be someone Kelli knew, but we couldn't smoke him out and we couldn't tell Kelli about the letters for fear of upsetting her.

Ron nodded. "Yeah, her head's winched up awful tight."

So when I'd learned she lived with Ron I'd come to him for help. "You said you two go back a way?"

Ron noticed the beer nuts in his hand still hanging in midair, and delivered them to his mouth. He chewed and swallowed, sipped his beer, and thought. Finally, "We met when she came here three years ago. The old story: crack the big time in glamour city. Nothing happened for a year, so she took off for San Francisco."

"Not much show biz there."

"Well, Kelli's not too big on logic." Tolkis smiled fondly. "Took her a year to figure that out, so she came back and, well, we got together."

"Can you think of *anyone* who could be obsessed with her?" Tolkis screwed up his thin bland face in thought, then shook his head again. "Did she ever do drugs—or maybe hang around with . . ."

"No way!"

"Did she work at fill-in jobs?"

"No, soon after she got back she hooked up with Drenko." His face turned proud. "Fact is, *Oh-Pun Sesame* was the first interview he sent her on."

This was going nowhere, so I tried a different tack. "Ron, I find it hard to believe you've loved Kelli and lived with her a year—been friends for, what, three years?" He nodded at his beer glass. "And you don't know a thing about her life."

Ron misted the glass with a long, moist sigh. "Kelli doesn't really *have* a . . . It's real hard to explain. I guess she lives for her career, or something."

Or something. I thought again of Daffy Duck, who didn't eat or sleep or use the bathroom—didn't even breathe, except inside the four tight walls of his cartoon cosmos.

I studied Ron Tolkis, who felt most at ease in life with folks like Elmer, Bugs, and Porky, and I realized that he and Kelli were not such an odd pairing after all. Theirs was a match made in Toon Town.

I rumbled up the drive around six and wandered into the house, which appeared to be empty.

"Sally?"

"Ihdah kicha!" From the sound of her voice, Sally was upended in a fifty-five-gallon drum stashed at the back of a closet. I strolled into the kitchen to find two breathtaking Amazon legs emerging from the under-sink cabinet. The

legs and attached bare feet were tangled in a tasteful still
life of detergent boxes, used Brillo pads, and jumbled paper
sacks.

"S'matter?"

"Sprayer hose." Though still muffled, Sally's speech was
now comprehensible. "Damn things only last a year." More
clanks and mumbled imprecations. "Damn! Slipjoint
pliers?" A large, capable hand emerged and waggled
vaguely, palm up. It was filthy. I filled it with pliers. "Uh,
uh, UH!" Sally grunted with each twist, then dropped the
pliers and extruded the hand again. "Basin wrench!"

I slapped it on her palm, feeling like a surgical nurse.

She bonked and grunted some more, then shimmied
out of the cabinet on her rump like a caterpillar belly
dancing. "There!" Sally said in sweaty triumph. Her hair
was a cornsilk rat's nest and her shirt had said goodbye
to her greasy white shorts. She looked gorgeous, and I
felt a rush of delight as I recalled my saloon philosophiz-
ing. Unlike Kelli Dengham, Sally could never be mistaken
for a Toon—despite her topographical kinship with Jessica
Rabbit.

20

As conscientious L.A. citizens, Sally and I save water
by showering *à deux*—a reliable way to get into a lather–

and at eight-thirty Tuesday morning we were well into reciprocal scrubbing and things when the phone rang.

I stepped out of Sally's Olympic-size shower and puddled over to the wall phone by the toilet. "Stoney Winston."

"Winston, get your goddam buns down to the office."

"At present, Ma, my buns are dripping soap all over the bathroom floor."

"Then wipe your ass. You must know how to do *that* at least."

"You're not your cheerful self today. What's up?"

"The balloon is what. The goddam show's been sold."

"To whom?"

"Now he's a goddam grammarian. Just get your buns down here. And Winston? I want a shirt and tie, slacks, and real shoes too—not those goddam sneakers!"

CLICK!

I slopped back into the shower, where Sally cocked a soapy eyebrow at me.

"Ma Barker, and she must be really steamed. Four goddams in thirty seconds has to be a record."

"I'm getting steamed myself. Here, have a nozzle." In fact the shower offered four heads to choose from, but Sally turned quickly under stereo sprays and then stepped out into the bathroom, taking the neighborhood scenery with her.

It was eleven before Ma summoned me to her throne room. Her big sunny office was smog free this morning, and I noticed that her usually groaning ashtray glistened with virgin virtue. That may have explained the nervous way she fiddled with papers on her desk.

Not to mention her sunshine temper: "Whadja do, Winston, stop for lunch on the way?"

"No . . ."

"Meet your new boss." She wagged a plump hand at the tall man sitting opposite. "This is Manny Savick."

Manny Savick? Carlisle's nemesis? What was going on here? "Stoney Winston, Mr. Savick." He smiled and shook the hand I offered.

Parames completed the group. "I've filled Manny in on the situation and explained my services." I wondered if he'd brought his show-and-tell today. "We feel . . ."

"Thanks, Herb. Let's you and I huddle on that later." Savick smiled to take the dismissal out of it, but Parames got the message and his answering smile was meager as he turned and left the room.

I sat back and studied my new employer. Swarthy skin, hatchet nose even bigger and sharper than mine, and watchful eyes set deep in pouches so dark they might have been lined with mascara. His curly gray hair lay thick on his head and his rumbling bass voice carried New York harmonics. He could have been sixty-five or sixty—or even fifty if he'd lived hard enough. Except for his camel's hair jacket and flannel slacks, he looked like a Warner Brothers gangster, vintage 1940.

But Savick didn't act like one. The fragrance of big money wafted off him like a fine cologne, tastefully understated but unmistakable.

As the meeting wrapped up, he turned to me and said, "Stick around a minute, Stoney."

I looked at Ma Barker. One pudgy hand hovered near her desk drawer and a look of pure anguish crossed her face. Suddenly she stood up, yanked the drawer open, and snatched a pack of Marlboros. "Well, I got a ton of work to get through." She hustled out the door as fast as her old legs could go, torching a Marlboro with a dope fiend's panicked intensity.

Manny sat back and shot me a measured smile. "What do you know about me, Stoney?"

"Not much. You've been a major game show producer for years, you're seen as a decent man in a business where that's distinctive, and you don't like people who smoke." When Savick cocked a shaggy eyebrow, I added, "Ma Barker's ashtray was empty this morning and she was only too eager to leave her office."

Savick's laughter was an unexpected bellow. "You call her *Ma* Barker?" He chuckled some more—a rumble at down around 100 Hertz. "That and your ashtray bit confirm what Marcia said about you: you're an independent bastard and you have a funny mind."

"Don't start that again." He cocked his head but I shifted the ground: "Tell you what *I'd* like to know: why you bought *Oh-Pun Sesame.*"

"Why do you ask?"

"I met with Carlisle at his office. When Parames and I walked in, he was watching a tape of one of your pilots."

"Which?"

"*Hopscotch.*"

Savick gaped. "Now where did Russ get hold of that? Go on."

"Said he was suing you over it."

"Good old Russ." Savick's idling-diesel laugh again.

"He seemed to have a grudge against you—a real hate thing. Went out of his way to tell us about it."

Savick's face showed nothing as he thought about this, then, "But what's your point?"

"If he hates you so much, why would he sell you a show that will literally print money for you?"

After a long pause, "I'll ask *you* one: why did he just happen to be watching my pilot when he called you into his office?"

Come to think of it, the coincidence was implausible. "For our benefit? To cover the fact that he'd sold the show?"

He nodded. "When was this?"

"Uh, two weeks ago today—Tuesday."

"That was about ten days after he offered me *Oh-Pun Sesame*, very, very quietly."

It didn't want to compute. "But Parames and I aren't important. Why the charade to mislead us?"

A shrug. "Carlisle's a funny kind of man."

"If I may ask, why *would* he sell his hottest property—to you or anyone else?"

"Cash flow. The way he's been eating up companies, his revenues don't half cover his interest payments. So he hit me for a loan. When I refused he said he was desperate—would do anything. He got all emotional; practically did Al Jolson down on one knee; finally asked what I'd pay him for *Sesame*." Savick shook his gray curls. "Surprised the eyebrows off me. But I gave him a quote and we haggled and finally shook hands."

I mulled this over a bit, then, "Corporations aren't much in my line, but isn't eighteen business days a *very* short time to complete a sale this size?"

Savick grinned widely, showing teeth that looked only ten years old—and, for all I knew, were. "That's how I got his price down: promised I'd get us through the paperwork to meet his interest deadline." His smile drifted away. "Now let's talk about Kelli Dengham. Parames filled me in, as he said, but I want to hear it from you."

So I told him. Savick inspected his manicured nails. "Blackmail and two murders, an Arab fanatic, *The National Insider*—anywhere from one to three problems, depending on how they're connected."

"Four, if you count Kelli's soft-core slides."

"The worst Carlisle can do is print them." When I shot him a look, he smiled sadly. "I don't like that junk, Stoney, but I'm a realist: publicity's the fuel our business runs on."

So there we were again, even Manny Savick: any public embarrassment was worth its cost in publicity. I couldn't help sighing for poor, simple Kelli. "You knew Carlisle said not to investigate Kelli's background."

"That's changed. I told Parames to dig up the bodies—use every resource he's got."

Welcome news. "And how about me?"

"Do whatever you feel like." Savick's face was friendly but serious. "You know, Marcia wasn't kidding about your original mind. She has a great respect for you."

I snorted. "Beneath her bluff and crusty surface."

He shook his head. "I've known Marcia for years. She's a good egg." Savick stood up to end the interview.

I walked back to my office, delighted that Savick had unlocked the lid on Kelli's past. Somewhere in that past was a psychopath who'd killed two people and might kill

Kelli next. I knew I had to find him fast—but where to begin looking? Damn! The frustration was making *me* crazy.

21

I was sitting in my office, still trying to figure out where to get a lead on Hassan, when the phone rang.

"Stonewall!"

"Hello, Kat." Warily, "What's happening?" I liked Kat Halbreck, but her phone calls meant some kind of trouble from *The National Insider*.

"New goodies on Kelli Dengham."

"Aha." Pray it's not some dirt in Kelli's past.

"Get this letter that came in: *I have written and written to my love slave but her captors will not let her reply so Im sending them to you the voice of truth so you can print them and sweet sexy Kelli can read them and her goons on the Open Sarsparilla show cannot keep them from her.*"

This was worse than background dirt. "Let me guess: it has no punctuation and it's signed 'Hassan.' "

"Thought it might ring a bell." Her voice was chirpy as a schoolgirl's. "So what's the story?"

I tried to get more out of her. "Did he send any other letters?"

"Hoo-hoo! And what we got here is one very disturbed Arab."

"Tell me about it."

"No, you tell *me*."

"I'd rather not—for Kelli's sake."

"Stoney, I've already written the article. It comes out in this week's issue. Friday." When I just sat there trying to think what to do, she added, "Stoney?"

"Uh. . . . Where are you?"

"The office, here in Glendale."

"Maybe I'd better come see you. I'd like to check out the letters too."

Cheerfully, "I'll be here."

"Half an hour?"

Kat repeated, "I'll be here," gave me the address, and rang off.

I roared out the Hollywood Freeway, snaked along the shortcut past the Forest Lawn and Mount Zion cemeteries, picked up the 134, and aimed the B. eastward at the copse of new high-rises that marked the metropolis of Glendale.

I got off at Brand Boulevard and rolled south between ranks of post-modern office blocks whose designers had not yet recovered from the discovery of colored granite. Glendale had given Brand its municipal all: a divider full of greenery, shopping mall lighting, and wide pedestrian walkways paved in decorative blocks.

But somehow it didn't quite work. Caught between Burbank and Pasadena, the city seemed to be masking the banality of one with the pomposity of the other.

Or maybe it was just my mood. Why take it out on harmless, necessary Glendale?

The *Insider* preempted the fifth floor of one of the granite eyesores, and I spent ten minutes in the lobby, watching the San Gabriel mountains bask in the hard light beyond the picture windows. Then Kat emerged to collect me, looking trim and professional as usual, and led me back into the antiseptic factory that built *The National Insider*.

Modular "office" dividers stretched away in a grid no less forbidding because they were faced with burlap in cheerful colors. All I could see as we walked past doorless entrances were wall-hung desks and the backs of staffers hunched above them. The only sounds were the bleats of ringing phones, the mutter of sound-damped voices, and the chuckle of workstation keyboards.

I remembered the open, ramshackle newsrooms of Hollywood films and sighed at the death of another romantic illusion. "So it's all computerized now."

"Sure: writers' workstations, copy desk, graphics, layout and production—all the way to plate making."

"Is this on a network with file servers and good stuff?"

"No way!" She smiled at this primitive notion. "We feed a humungous mainframe someplace—I dunno where it is."

"Somehow the romance is gone."

"But you can't argue with efficiency. Here we are."

She popped through an opening with a plastic sign beside it: KAT HALBRECK, STAFF WRITER.

Like so many workers imprisoned in uniform six-by-six cubicles, Kat had worked overtime to make her cell her own: Garfield and Kathy and Far Side comics pinned to the walls, parents and lover(?) in frames on the metal desk, a plant in one corner so riotous that it must have been bred for fluorescent light.

Most of the desk was paved with a workstation linked to

a laptop computer by a gray umbilical. "I suppose you can modem your copy."

She patted the laptop. "I plug in a phone line wherever I am and just dial up Big Bertha. Would you believe it? The phone number spells I.N.S.I.D.E.R." She held her nose in comic embarrassment.

"Cute."

Kat waggled the laptop's modular phone cable. "But what a time-saver for research. I can access libraries, tap our own database . . ."

"Forgive me, but I wouldn't think the *Insider* was big for research."

"Maybe not, but it's all there. Every publication in the group dumps into that database."

"Another blow struck for knowledge."

Suddenly, Kat seemed to realize that I'd been having her on. Her face set. "Stoney, I know what you think of this paper, but so far it's what I've got."

She was absolutely right. "Point taken—and the setup *is* impressive." Time to shift the topic: "Have you got the Hassan letters handy?"

The manila file she gave me contained the letter she'd read on the phone and, sure enough, all the other effusions we'd got at the production offices. They were duplicate printouts, not copies, and all from the same dot matrix printer.

I handed them back. "Would you mind if I glanced at your article?"

"Preemptive damage control?"

I shook my head. "I'd just like to know what's going to hit us."

She punched it up on the workstation screen. It was what I'd expected: a sensational summary of the letters, with some of the juiciest quotes that were not flatly unprintable.

I couldn't say the piece was unfair, except for the head-line, which I read aloud: " *'Kelli Terrified by Secret Arab Threats'*? It sounds like a Saddam Hussein."

Kat's shrug looked a trifle defensive. "Just a grabber."

"And not accurate. Kelli isn't terrified by these letters; she doesn't know they exist."

"You're putting me on!"

I shook my head. "She's so unstable that her people keep stuff like this away from her."

Skeptically, "What are they, afraid she'll freak on them?"

I nodded. "And I am too." We stared at each other a moment, then I began, "I don't suppose there's any chance . . ."

"No, there isn't." Kat's expression turned defensive. "Look, Winston, grow up. These folks are celebrities: they earn a hundred times what we do, they're treated like oil sheiks, and papers like this one feed their giant egos by telling them that every time they take a leak it's news!"

"But Kelli doesn't understand that."

"Aw, poor baby! I'll tell you this, my friend: old Arafat here's just part of it." She slapped the manila folder with her fingers. "We got a murder, a game show cheating cover-up, and a dark, mysterious past—and it all connects with Kelli Dengham."

I held up my hands, palms out as if to fend her off. "The article runs. Message received."

She shook her head furiously. "Transmission not yet fin-ished. You better believe the article runs, but that's just the start." Kat lowered her voice but not her intensity. "I feel just as much contempt for this paper as you do, Winston, though I'm not as obvious about it as you are. I had to start here, but I'm not going to stay here long. And the only way I can get a better job is by proving what I can do as a journalist."

"An *investigative* journalist."

"You got it: Kelli Dengham."

I chewed on that, then gave it one last shot: "You keep saying that my job with Kelli is damage control. That tells me you know that what you're doing to her is damage."

"Maybe." But she didn't look as tough as she sounded.

"You can really hurt her, personally, you know."

Primly, "No more than necessary."

I started for the opening to her mauve-padded cell. " 'Necessary' is the very last word I'd apply to anything connected with this paper." I turned left past KAT HAL-BRECK, STAFF WRITER, and made my way out of the rat maze.

An hour later I stood hunched over the printing easel in my darkroom, slurping chablis number three and staring at the image of Kelli Dengham, which was still dressed in just a silver bracelet and draped with shy abandon on a prop chaise longue. I could almost see a magazine binding staple in her navel.

Hassan's beloved navel, and on Friday Kelli would read all about it in *The National Insider*.

I took another slurp. Two slurps.

Damn!

"Supper time!" Sally was outside my front door.

Three slurps. *DAMN!!*

"Stoney?" Her voice was closer, and in a moment she stuck her head through the open darkroom doorway. "Oh. Printing, or . . . ?" She broke off at the look on my face. "What's the matter?"

Still looking at Kelli's image, "Terminal stupidity."

She stood beside me and looked down too. "Just a big snarl. You'll find the end of the string."

I indicated the picture. "I can't even find the beginning." I snapped off the enlarger irritably. "I keep thinking about Kelli and about a man who could kill her any time." I sighed and shook my head. "I dunno."

Sally said, "It'll come to you," but that was just a soothing noise.

I grunted. "On top of that, I just pulled a beauty, even for me."

Sally's nod and smile said, *okay, unload it.*

I summarized what'd happened in Kat's office. "So by the time I was through, I'd dumped on her job, sneered at her automated office, read her a lecture on professional ethics, and left with a snappy insult, gathering my toga about me."

Sally's tone was measured. "That seems to cover it."

I stomped out into my dreary living room. "And if Kat Halbreck had any qualms before about digging dirt on Kelli, I made sure she doesn't have any now."

"You never know." Sally followed me. "Sometimes things'll sink in later—when she isn't angry."

I doubted that. "Why am I so insensitive to people?"

A smile and shrug together. "Oh, that comes and goes."

"Well, I'd like it to go, and just anytime soon." That came out sounding pettish, which it was.

Sally looked at me with big blue eyes. "You want me to lie to you?"

I couldn't help smiling. "Well . . . yeah, a little, maybe."

"Okay, you never tune out other people, you never live in your nice, square chessboard head instead of the real mess outside . . ."

"I feel better already."

". . . and you never sit around whimpering, 'Why me?' " Her tone carried just a hint of sharpness.

I sighed. "My love, you're a positive tonic." But somehow, Sally made me feel better.

Wonder Woman strode over to the door. "Supper's waiting: beans and wienies."

I chuckled. "Just right for my low-rent mood."

"Well, it's Polish sausage, really, but I didn't want to upstage you." Sally turned and walked out.

I followed her, then stood at the bottom of the stairs beside the house, watching her powerful figure climb them briskly and disappear around the corner.

God knew why, but I *did* feel better.

22

When I reached the office the next morning, I learned that Savick had called a strategy session for after lunch. That meant I had little to do until then, so I hung about the place, killing time. I couldn't get excited over secretaries typing, and when I wandered past the writers' meeting room, I heard a burst of raucous laughter that only reminded me of my demotion from that warm and raffish fellowship. I ended up at a room in the back, where I found Arlo Bracken, black-clad and spiky as always, holding a fluffy pink strapless dress in front of her as she peered in a full-length mirror.

"Yo, Arlo. Changing your style?"

She sneered at her frilly image. "Sure, Winston, I'm going nelly. Whaddya want?"

"Distraction. What's with the pink number?"

"Kelli's in this morning—trying wardrobe. I'm her clothes rack." She contradicted this by slapping the dress on an actual rack beside her.

"You do wardrobe too?"

"Except Saturday and Sunday. Weekdays, I'm half the production staff and you're the other half—though I never did figure what the hell you do."

"Keep Ma's temper sweet."

"Then you don't earn your money."

At that point the door behind her burst open and Kelli stood there in a green sequined number that fit her like the skin on a bratwurst, except that bratwurst didn't have Kelli's subtle contours. When she saw me her blue button eyes goggled in comic surprise, then narrowed to torchy slits. She propped her hands on her hips like Mae West again, snapped a leg forward so it played peekaboo with the high slit in her dress, and ankled forward as if on a runway.

She started "A Pretty Girl Is Like a Melody": "Dah da da *daaahh!*"

When she got to the end of the first phrase, I contributed brushes on a cymbal: "tsh-ta-*tsshh*, tsh-ta-*tsshh*." Kelli giggled at this, dah-dahed the second line in her little-girl croak, and we carried on through the rest of the verse, while Arlo regarded us children with patient amusement. Kelli switched to Marilyn Monroe moves, fanning the fingers of both hands on her sternum so that her sharply bent wrists became two extra breasts. As the verse ended, she shimmied up to me, held my left hand up in dancing position, and segued into "Hernando's Hideaway."

Something in Kelli sparkled irresistibly, and I found myself playing Valentino to her Vilma Banky or whoever. We tangoed all over the room while Kelli squeaked out the words and I did castanet sounds with my tongue. Arlo rolled her eyes and muttered, "Oh, Jesus!" But she was grinning.

We came to a big dip-and-glide finish in front of the open hall door, where we found Manny Savick watching with a smile not unlike Arlo's.

"Ready for that meeting, Stoney?"

"Uh, right away." To Kelli, "Thanks for the dance, miss."

And Kelli responded by kissing me on the mouth. Not a peck this time, but a 240-volt smooch. Then she giggled, grinned, and turned me loose.

Manny kept his own counsel but his pouchy eyes remained amused.

And now we were all in the conference room, drawing battle plans. Parames, in fact, was really *drawing*: covering a sheet of graph paper with the lines and boxes of a project flow chart.

Ma Barker fiddled and twitched at one end of the table, deprived of her Marlboro fix by Savick, who presided at the other end with the calm control bred of long practice.

He said in his gentle rumble, "By Friday, Kelli's going to find out about this crazy Arab . . ."

"That's the day after tomorrow," Parames added helpfully.

"So it is." The very slight dryness in his tone suggested that Savick too had noticed Herb's pedantic little ways. "And secondly, some reporter wants to make her reputation by destroying Kelli's." Savick turned to Parames. "Let's review your part."

Parames put his pencil on a flow chart box. "Her boyfriend said she spent a year in San Francisco, trying to break into show business. I have people on that now." His pencil moved to the right. "Kelli Dengham is her legal name, but probably not her birth name."

Savick nodded. "So she changed it. Are you checking court records?"

Parames sighed. "In L.A., Orange, and San Francisco

counties. The trouble is, she could have changed it someplace else—any place at all." His pencil moved back to the
San Francisco box. "We may do better up north."

Savick turned to me. "Stoney?"

"I've sounded like a stuck record for weeks: we could
save a lot of work if we simply talked to Kelli."

Parames shook his head doubtfully and Ma mimicked his
gesture. "Still too goddam risky."

But Savick gazed at me in silence for a moment, then
said, "I think you may be right." Herb and Ma both made
noises as if to begin speaking, but he patted the air with a
calming hand. "I'm not blaming anybody—we all have to
play it day by day—but I think we let this mess develop
because we were more afraid of Kelli's instability than we
were of potential scandal."

Despite Savick's diplomatic "we," both Ma and Herb
caught his message, and they acquired the wary look of
corporate team players trying to guess the boss' new opinion
so they could endorse it before he told them what it was.

Savick continued, "Stoney, you seem to have a rapport
with Kelli." He smiled just slightly. "Why don't you talk
to her?"

Predictably, Herb and Ma chimed in: good idea, I guess
you're right, go for it, etc.

So I was delegated. As the meeting broke up, I wondered
if Manny Savick knew more about me than I did. After the
subtle finesse with which I'd managed Kat Halbreck, I
couldn't see myself as a genius at diplomacy.

When I got back to the room where Kelli'd been trying
on costumes, I found Arlo departed but Kelli still standing

in front of the mirror, assessing first the pink dress, then the green one. She seemed calm enough, but Kelli could blow up to hurricane strength in nothing flat and my news was just the thing to set her off. I took a deep breath and tiptoed into it.

I started gently by saying that media stars often had nutballs bothering them, and, well, one of these kooks was writing her letters.

Kelli looked puzzled.

And the letters were, you know, sort of *intimate*.

I was poised to batten down the hatches, but Kelli only nodded.

"Not just wanting to go to bed, but, um, tie you up and, well, things." Get ready to duck.

Nothing.

What was going on here? Had we all misjudged her? "I mean, he's not just crazy about you, he's crazy, period."

Kelli looked into space a moment, then said, "Aw, the poor lonely guy," as if she was pleased nonetheless by his ardor. "Y'think I should, like, write him or something?"

"Ahh . . . no. It would just escalate." She knitted her brow at that, so I added, "Make it worse."

"And this newspaper's going to print it?"

"I'm afraid so, Kelli, on Friday."

Again her stare of comic concentration, then she smiled. "Well, it'll be real good publicity."

Hmh: Kelli was the same as all the others. Get their name in print and spell it right and they were tickled. But I couldn't really blame her. It was part of how she earned her living. A stripper could as well refuse to take her clothes off.

But I'd made an amazingly good beginning, so I eased cautiously into the matter of her background. "Kelli Dengham's your professional name, isn't it?" She nodded absently. "What's your real name?"

Something crossed her face as swiftly as the shadow of a flying bird. "Why?"

Super-casual: "Oh, just curious." I grinned. "I use 'Stoney' because my father named me Spencer Churchill."

Kelli looked faintly puzzled. "Nothing wrong with Spencer."

"What was *your* name, Fannie Mae McCrockpot?"

"No."

My joshing tone: "Come on: I confessed my silly name. What was yours?"

"Just different. I don't talk about it." She looked at me searchingly, as if she could feel something afoot but couldn't figure what it was.

"Sorry."

A small, abstracted voice: "S'all right."

And the conversation turned up its toes and died.

But Kelli seemed uneasy still. She held the pink dress up for about the fifteenth time, hung it on the rack, picked up the green dress, put it back, fiddled with the hangers. She didn't look at me.

Gazing at the curve of her neck below her tight blond curls I was struck by her fragility and doubly reluctant to threaten her.

But Kelli Dengham's well-being was not the only issue. She was the catalyst of an otherwise mundane show that wouldn't last six weeks without her. If Kat Halbreck shot

her down, she'd blow away the program too. Push had
finally come to shove.

I took Kelli's two small hands and made her look at me.
Gently, "I'm asking for a reason, Kelli. The *Insider*'s not
through with you. They're digging up your past as well.
They're far enough to know you haven't got a past—at least,
none that anyone can find, and so they smell a scandal.
You understand?"

Her nod was almost imperceptible and her blue Toon
eyes got bigger than I'd ever seen them.

I went on in the same gentle tone, "If you have something
you don't want talked about, we can help you."

"How?" It was a whisper.

"Keep it quiet if we can, and if we can't do that, then
soften it, show it in a better light." I smiled. "That's what
our P.R. folks are for: damage control."

She stared into my eyes for a long time, her two hands
still in mine. Her pretty face looked sad but not distraught.
Then she said, still whispering, "I told you before, you're
a real nice man." Another pause. "How come. . . ? How
come everybody isn't nice?"

"Just the way life is, I guess." My cliché words were
unimportant. I hoped that my affection and concern showed
in my voice.

She repeated, "The way life is," in a tone I couldn't read,
then gently pulled her hands away and smiled. "Thanks,
Stoney, but I'm not damaged."

In the eye blink it took me to connect her words with
"damage control," Kelli turned abruptly and left the room.

Well, she hadn't opened up, but then, she hadn't hyperventilated either. That troubled me. Her reaction to Hassan was hardly true to form, and her almost zombie calm was so unfathomable that I couldn't even guess what she was feeling.

Or, more important, what she might do now.

My office was at the other end of the floor, and as I plodded toward it my uneasiness built with every step until the feeling was approaching dread. So it didn't help to discover Kat Halbreck, chic and professional looking as always, camped on my only visitor's chair.

"Hi, Stonewall."

"Hello, Kat; what's up?"

She smiled. "Couple things. First, I'm sorry about the last time."

I sat in my desk chair. "Me too. My high and mighty attitude was out of line."

She shook her head. "Not by much. I think I got mad because I secretly agreed with you."

"Whatever. I'm glad we're friends again."

Her smile brightened three notches. "And we're not on opposite sides anymore. That's what I came to tell you."

"Good." The more cheerful Kat became, the more I always wondered what she wanted.

But this time she surprised me. "Yup, I got promoted!"

"Hey!"

"Not just promoted, *moved*. Ladies and gentlemen, please welcome the associate editor of the *La Crescenta Beacon*."

"Hey!" Why did Kat always make me repeat myself?

"It's a weekly in the Sunbelt Group: paid circulation, news, columns, editorials—a real paper!"

"Tomorrow, the world. Congratulations."

By now she was grinning all over her pert face. "And the best thing about a little weekly is I won't be stuck at a desk. I'll be on the street too." Her joy was infectious and I smiled back. "So." She broke off, looking almost shy, then, "I figured my news is a peace offering. The *La Crescenta Beacon* doesn't cover celebrities."

"I guess not." In other words, Kat's archeology on Kelli's past was over.

Hallelujah. But I didn't want to show undue relief. "Thanks. It was nice of you to tell me."

Kat stood up. "That's it, I guess. Just one more thing." She gave me a serious look. "You said we were in the same boat, remember? Well, I just got a better boat." Her eyes behind their contact lenses were penetrating. "You will too, Stoney. You're more than worth it." We looked at each other a moment more, then she shook my hand firmly, turned, and walked briskly out my door.

My sense of relief lasted until I was rumbling home in Bumble. Driving the familiar route on semiautomatic pilot, I allowed my mind to wander. Why had Kat Halbreck been promoted? Why associate editor, an unlikely jump for a lowly staff reporter? Why to a suburban weekly where the dubious techniques perfected at a scandal sheet would not be needed? And most of all, *why now?* It seemed as if someone had called off the hound that was baying along Kelli Dengham's scent.

But who was someone?

I roared up the driveway, killed the Bumble's thunder, and went in search of Sally. I found her standing on the bathroom scale.

"Here, hold my towel."

"Best offer I've had all day."

She stood in her perfectly splendid skin, peering down at the scale dial. "Am I getting fat?" She pressed her stomach with two palms.

Sally's always "getting fat" but never does, so I was used to this trifling neurosis. My sincerest tone: "Not a single ounce."

"Hmh." And with that cryptic grunt she stepped off the scale. "Can I have my towel back?"

"Must you?"

She grabbed the towel. "If you have to leer and slobber, go read *Raunch* or something."

I echoed her grunt. "Women have been paying me compliments all afternoon. You're a bracing return to reality."

"What women?"

I ignored that. "But you gave me an idea. Remember when you looked up the Sunbelt Group for me?"

"Mm." She walked into the bedroom and I followed.

"Could you track them up the corporate tree—find out who they're connected with?"

"Sure." She stepped into bikini panties with that bend and lift that always looks like dancing. "Why?"

"Something tells me I know who owns it."

Something told me right. In due course Sally's computer screen showed three groups of publications: one of weekly newspapers that included the *Insider*, one of trade journals, and last of all the Eros Group: *Priapus*, *Think Pink!* and *Raunch*.

Kat's ultimate boss was not "some Fleet Street press lord." He was Russ Carlisle.

Sally looked up from her screen and said suspiciously, "What women?"

"Hmh? Oh. Kelli Dengham said I was a nice man."

"She did? Mmmm." Sally's dismissive little hum implied that Kelli was not worth keeping an eye on.

Or maybe *I* wasn't. Or maybe none of the above. Where women were concerned I was like a passionate music lover who was nonetheless part tone-deaf. No matter how glorious the melodies I heard, the complex harmonics that I knew escaped me drove me crackers.

23

*D*uring the night my industrious subconscious sorted out what I knew about Carlisle, and by morning I decided that the next step was to sort out the man himself.

A secretary answered the phone at *Raunch*, took my name, went through the usual who-are-you-with? routine, and parked me on hold with the usual pancake syrup music for comfort.

When Russ Carlisle picked up the phone his memory proved oddly spotty: "What pictures you talking about?"

"The slides of Kelli Dengham."

"I told you . . ."

I kept my tone ominously flat. "Fact is, there's quite a lot to discuss—about you and Kelli both."

A long silence, then, "Be at the office at ten. I'll give you five minutes."

"My cup runneth over."

CLICK.

I was at the lobby desk at five to ten. The guard phoned upstairs and then directed me to the fourth floor, where I opened the only door in the tiny vestibule and stepped into the creative heart of *Raunch*.

This studio would have turned poor Arnesen pale green: eighty feet square at least, and fitted with every strobe, reflector, scrim, and seamless backing a photographer could dream of. I threaded among the props and floor stands toward a shooting session in progress near the opposite wall.

A lanky photographer with hair done up in dreadlocks bent over an eight-by-ten Sinar view camera on a massive tripod while two assistants fiddled with the modeling lights, tripped the wireless slave strobes, and peered at digital flash meters. Russ Carlisle stood by in flannel slacks and penny loafers, directing the action on a beach set complete with sand, umbrella, and a twelve-by-thirty-foot transparency background of palms, more sand, and ocean.

The focus of attention was on Carlisle's assistant, Clipper, nonchalant as always in her birthday suit, while the makeup on her violent breasts was amended by a gray-haired granny with a cigarette in her mouth. An equally naked male model stud lounged nearby, flaunting the elastic fixtures for which he had clearly been hired.

"Come on, let's shoot it." At Carlisle's impatient tone, the makeup granny backed away, the photographer bent to his ground glass, the beefcake struck a standing pose, and Clipper knelt before him in overflowing profile.

Clipper chirped, "How much ya want?"

" 'Bout half."

Matter-of-factly, "Okay." She grasped the stud's equipment as clinically as a nurse and caressed him to half staff, then pouted her red lips in a fleshy O and froze. Enough lightning for a minor storm went off.

"Keep it." The photographer slipped the dark slide into the film holder, pulled the holder, reversed it, pushed the holder in, removed the second dark slide, changed the F-stop. ZZZZZAAAAAPPPP! The strobes went off again.

Carlisle directed the poses and checked the compositions as if he enjoyed his work. If he'd seen me, he gave no indication of it.

After an interminable time he said, "Take a break," and everyone relaxed. Clipper stood and stretched absently.

The Beefcake grinned at her dirigible breasts. "Hey, do them things honk?" He grabbed her breasts like bulb horns and squeezed them—hard.

And then a strange thing happened. Without visible warning or windup, Clipper had gone from zero to sixty and Beefy found himself on the wrong end of a kick to the groin, a slam in the solar plexus, and a blinding feat of leverage that somehow dumped him facedown in the property sand with his beautiful buns in the air.

"Only on business, Jack." Clipper's tone was relaxed and her empty doll face looked as cheerful as ever. She wasn't even breathing hard.

Carlisle said, "Ten minutes, guys. Come on, Winston."

One floor down, he led me through another maze of the same modular cells filled with the same prisoners hunched over the same keyboards and terminals. I said, "Looks like the *Insider* office."

"They're all part of the same system." Carlisle's tone was indifferent.

We walked another fifty feet in silence, then I said, "I didn't know you shot your own stuff here in the office."

"When I take a personal interest." He came to an actual full-height wall and opened a door in it. "Here."

This office was smaller and more businesslike than Carlisle's palazzo in the penthouse: desk, work tables, backlit racks for slides. He pointed me at a conference table and I sat down while he plucked something off his desk and joined me. "Okay, like I said, five minutes." The object from his desk was an antique hourglass. He flipped it over on the conference table. "Whaddaya mean about Kelli pictures I didn't destroy?"

I sat back. "Let's start at the beginning."

Coldly, "I said five minutes."

I ignored the trickling sand. "When Dr. Parames and I spoke to you two weeks ago, you said forget it if Kelli hasn't got any background. Who cares what she's covering up?"

"So?"

"So you knew her history was blank before we told you. Then you told us to stay out of her past, as if you knew something about that too."

Colder: "Your sand is still running."

I matched his tone: "So is everybody's. Also, you referred

to Ms. Sung Li as 'Amber,' but we didn't tell you her first name. You already knew that as well."

He looked at the sand piling up in the bottom chamber. "I'd call it three minutes, tops. Better cut to the climax."

"Yes, the big fire scene. You went out of your way to describe how you burned Kelli's other slides. You said the flaming film nearly set fire to your wastebasket."

Indifferently, "So what?"

I'd prepared for Carlisle's stonewalling with a theatrical gesture of my own. Instead of answering I pulled from my pocket a strip of film collected in my darkroom and lit it with a plastic lighter. I held the film until it smoked and bubbled down to blackened bacon, then dropped it on the hardwood table.

It had the right effect. "Shit!" His face livid, Carlisle jumped up, swept the ashes off his table, and stomped them into crumbs. "Shit! The hell you doing?"

"Proving that film doesn't flame up the way you described it."

"Meaning?"

I stared at him. "You didn't burn Kelli's outtakes. Why did you say you had?"

Carlisle sat down slowly and leaned back. "Where do you get off, playing district attorney?" He looked at the hourglass and faked surprise. "Wup! But don't answer that. Time's up."

"But whose time is it?" I suddenly slapped the glass off the table so hard that it bounced off a light box six feet away and shattered on the floor.

Carlisle jumped up again, his face furious. "Okay, that's it. Out!"

I relaxed in my chair. "Before you call your rubber Amazon to bounce me, chew on this: a certain Kat Halbreck of *The National Insider* did two stories on the show—one of them some dirt on Kelli Dengham. She was all hot to dig some more manure when, lo and behold, she got transferred to another paper."

Carlisle looked at me, his thick face frozen.

"And lo and behold again, you own both the *Insider* and the paper she was sent to."

For the first time he looked uncertain. "Just looking out for *Oh-Pun Sesame*."

"Why bother? You didn't own the show anymore—and you seem to hate the man who bought it far too much to do him any favors."

Silence again, as if Carlisle couldn't answer that.

I leaned in and gave him my fishiest stare. "So here's the bottom line: I think you're somewhere in the past that Kelli buried and I think you want that body undisturbed. But you got a big, big problem."

I waited, but Carlisle was still turned to stone.

"Some crack-brained fan may be in Kelli's past as well, and he's a threat to Kelli. To find him, Manny Savick told Parames to use every resource he's got, and that's a lot of resources. He'll dig up Kelli's past and you with it."

He still didn't answer, but a hint of uncertainty shaded his face.

I shifted to sweet reason: "Look, we're not interested in your affairs. We only want to protect Kelli. So if you tell us where you fit in, we may not need to dig into that ourselves. And you may just give us what we need to flush a man who's killed two people."

Another lengthy silence, but this time it felt as if Carlisle
was deciding what to do. Then he said, half musingly,
"You're just protecting Kelli."

"That's all."

He nodded. "I am too." Carlisle sat down again.

"Why?"

He rubbed his forehead with a palm and sighed. "Okay."
He nodded his head several times as if he'd made a decision.
"Okay." Tiredly, "About three years back she shows up
here at the magazine. Complete yokel, cow shit between
her toes, right? She's broke, she wants a photo spread, she
needs the money, blah blah blah. So I shot a test. Didn't
work out. She's cute all right, but, like . . ." he searched
for words ". . . too delicate."

"*Raunch* wants them more like Clipper."

"Right, you're right. But something about her craziness,
her personality, I dunno—I took her on myself—I mean,
if you follow."

"I think so."

"So here's the corny part: I . . ." He looked away and
started over. "That is, she gets herself knocked up." He
shook his head, incredulous. "How fucking stupid can you
get?" Carlisle pulled the anger back out of his voice. "I say
okay okay I'll buy an abortion—it's no big thing. But what
does she do? She goes bananas, then she *disappears*, for
Chrissake! Months later—I mean we're talking *months!*"
He hit the table with a fist. "She calls from outta town."

"San Francisco?"

A puzzled look, then, "Yeah, I think it was."

"Then what happened?"

He spread his arms and looked affronted. "Nothing! More

months go by. Next I know, she's back in town and reading for the show." I raised an eyebrow. "Barker told me. I called Kelli but she wouldn't see me—wouldn't even talk. All she said was, please leave her alone."

Neutrally, "So you did."

He looked defensive. "Well, I saw she got the job, didn't I? Barker woman didn't like her at first."

"And *that's* why you wanted her past history buried?"

He nodded.

This didn't compute at all. "What, exactly, did you want to cover up?"

Carlisle's expression modulated to a faintly shifty look, as if he were trying to think up a good one; then it collapsed, as if he'd failed. "Well, I guess I dunno; I guess . . ." the man actually cleared his throat ". . . to be honest, twats like Kelli don't kick me out. I kick *them.*"

Ah: the bull gored by one of his own cows. That figured. "And the film?"

Carlisle looked even more embarrassed. "You know the funny thing? I shredded it just like Barker said."

"Then why . . . ?"

He sighed and said impatiently, "When I told you I burned it, I was showing off. You know, giving it more drama." He waved vaguely at the city beyond his window. "Kelli and that jerk with the twelve-inch . . . well, they're ten feet down in the city dump someplace, in tiny pieces."

He looked so mortified by this confession that I moved on: "Amber?"

A shrug. "I knew her name because Arnesen brought in a spread on her too. I didn't even get the connection 'til you told me. But how many Sung Lis would Arnesen know?"

Remembering the nude shot of Amber on Arnesen's wall, I nodded. "Okay, then how about Hassan?"

"There you got me." I raised an eyebrow. "Look, I didn't know Kelli all that well." The defensiveness was back. "She was just a bimbo, right? They come and go. Who asks?"

"You never knew a Hassan, never heard of *anyone* who had a thing for Kelli?"

Another shrug. "Oh, there must of been—sexy little piece like Kelli—but she never told *me*."

I poked around in everything he'd said but couldn't find anything more to pursue, so I stood up. "Okay."

Carlisle stood too and started for the door. "I gotta get back to Clipper."

Why hurry? Unlike her partner, Clipper wouldn't deflate.

24

I drove out of Carlisle's office garage into a blast of white sunlight that made his strobes look puny. Another bleak baking day in a solid run of fifty. By summer, southern Californians would be spitting on their grass to water it.

As I rumbled east on Wilshire, Carlisle's story started raveling at the edges. He went through a big rannygazoo

to protect Kelli's past merely because it included a rejection
of himself. Uh-huh, and he lied about the film just to make
a more dramatic story.

Sure.

My subconscious had been overachieving as I drove, and
without thinking I'd pointed Badass Bumble toward Beverly Hills and Ernie Drenko's agency on Robertson. I
parked my rolling garbage can and sat a moment, hauling
to the surface my reasons for coming, then went off to visit
Drenko in his Sharper Image office.

Young Golden Delicious the receptionist was as campy
as ever. I sat on the hard-edged couch pretending to read
The Hollywood Reporter while he twittered about like a
budgie in a cage.

It was half an hour before the inner door opened and
Drenko ushered out the actor who played Daddy Warm-
andwise on a sitcom so banal that I couldn't recall its name.
The two of them strolled to the outer door in a blizzard of
showbiz bonhomie and Drenko played the doorman to his
client.

Then he turned to me. "Hello, Winston. How's the fire
fighter?"

"Still hosing down the embers. Got a minute?"

Drenko nodded. "Just about that long. Come on." He
contrasted my status with the actor's by walking into his
office and letting me trail behind.

Today's toy of choice was a putting green: a shallow can
with a sunflower ring of plastic petals curved up like beg-
ging hands and hinged to tilt a rolling ball into the cup.
Beside it a waist-high stand held up a digital readout box
with numerals an inch high. Drenko picked up a putter,

addressed a ball with the droll Zen calm of the passionate
golfer, and knocked the ball into the cup. The box tinkled
a digital fanfare and the readout blinked blood red.

Drenko consulted the box with the gravity of a doctor
reading a CAT scan. He shook his head. "Two inches short."

"Of what?" He could hardly miss this cup, which must
have been eight inches wide.

"The pin. See, the chip in that thing computes how hard
the ball hits the sensor and tells you how close you'da come
to a real pin."

"The wonders of technology."

"Done wonders for my game, I'll tell you that much."

"I'm hoping you'll tell more than that."

"Like I said, I'm all up front. What about?"

"Kelli Dengham's past. You know more about it than you
admit."

"I already explained . . ."

Time to belt him with my trusty two-by-four: "Look, Ern,
there's a few things we haven't told *you*. Two people connected with Kelli are dead—murdered by a psychotic who
writes dirty letters to Kelli. He's repeatedly threatened to
'reveal' himself to her and make her his love slave."

The two-by-four got his attention. Drenko stood up
straight and let the putter slip to the carpet. "You serious?"

I showed him just *how* serious, laying out everything we
knew about Arnesen and Amber and maniacal Hassan.

Drenko shook his big head. "A goddam A-rab. Wouldn't
you know!"

"His origin's not important. But what connection could
he have with Kelli?"

"Zero zippo zilch!" He retrieved the putter and snapped

it under his arm like a swagger stick. "That Kelli kid's a
dip all right, but she wouldn't hang out with a goddam A-
rab." To him the ethnic label was a single word: *goddam-
a-rab*.

I tried another route: "I just talked to Russ Carlisle."

Drenko pushed another ball into position. "That spread
on Kelli give us good exposure." He fiddled with his grip
on the putter and addressed the ball.

"You knew he got her pregnant."

WHACK! The golf ball soared into an orbit intercepted
by the TV screen in the video chapel behind Drenko's desk,
and the great glass tube exploded into sparkling shrapnel
that rained on Drenko's carpet and tinkled on his desk top.
He gawked at the disaster stupidly, as if the news and the
accident together had shorted his circuits as well as the
set's.

Finally he turned to me. "Carlisle said *that*?"

I repeated what the publisher had told me while Drenko
stood blankly, holding his forgotten putter. As I talked, he
turned and walked slowly around to his desk chair, oblivious
of the glass shards he was grinding into his carpet.

He dropped the putter and sank into his chair. "Jee-zus!"

Was *everyone* having me on today? "Ernesto, you're a
Hollywood agent in the 1990s." He gave a little comic nod
as if he'd only just thought of this. "So why are you stunned
by the news that a client got pregnant?"

He looked at me. "Frankly . . ." He tried again: "To be
honest about it, I'm not stunned, no, no way. It's . . ."

And then Drenko's business face dissolved into an
expression of such honest tenderness that I couldn't doubt
it. "Poor li'l kid—like a stray kitten or something. I dunno

what to do about her." He stared at the glass shards on his
desk as if he'd forgotten me, while I recalled his protec-
tiveness that night in Kelli's dressing room.

I tried a soothing tone. "Start by telling me what you
know about her."

His eyes lifted, locked, and focused in three discrete
steps. He said very quietly, "I wish I could, but . . ." His
shrug and upraised palms added *but I really don't know
anything.*

"You don't know, Carlisle doesn't know, Ron Tolkis
doesn't know. Nobody don't know nuthin'—except Kelli,
and Kelli won't say." I stood up to leave. "Oh: and one
other person." Drenko lifted shaggy eyebrows. "Hassan
knows, Ernie." I crossed to the door. "Think about it."

A corny exit, but the expression on Drenko's heavy face
suggested that I'd reached him.

By eleven P.M. Sally and I were sitting tensely in her
living room, thumbing vapid magazines, half listening to
music, dispatching one too many jugs of wine—in other
words, avoiding going to bed. Each was alternately talking
while the other tried to read, and at the moment I was
downloading my frustrations with Kelli and Hassan and all
the good people who refused to talk about them.

"So I've been running about like a chicken for nearly a
month—when I'm not hiding in my office goofing off. Ma
Barker keeps asking what I do for my pay." No response,
so I added, "I *was* writing gags, but . . ."

"Yeah." Sally turned a page.

I poured four inches of wine, gulped half of it, and sighed.
"Maybe I'll look for another job."

Her eyes stayed on her magazine. "What kind?"

"The usual: production manager, editor—anything."

Sally looked at me. "Where will that get you?"

"You never know."

"Yes you do." She closed the magazine. "Nowhere."

"You have to start someplace." I didn't like the defensive tone that leaked into my voice.

Sally's voice had an edge of its own: "You've been 'starting someplace' for ten long years."

"It's the industry."

Her turn for another gulp of wine, then, "No, it's *you*. You take a job, leave the job, take another job—same damn job!" She threw the magazine on the coffee table.

"Not always . . ."

"Because, underneath, you don't *really want* a career." I stared at Sally and her face pulled tight as she spoke. "You just like to make mudpies—and movies are the best mudpies around."

What was going on here? "That may be *partly* true, but . . ."

Her face and voice wound tighter still. "So you wake up and you're thirty-five and you're still a gofer without a bean in the bank or a prayer of doing better."

This unpleasant truth turned my voice dry: "Stoney Winston, boy failure."

Sally jumped to her feet. "But that's just it: *you're not a boy!*"

I goggled up at her. "Hey, where did this all come from?"

"Down deep, you just don't care."

"Now *wait* a minute!" I stood up too.

Sally's look raked me stem to stern. "Look at the way you dress. When you *look* like a gofer, people get the message."

I glanced down at my jeans and five-dollar golf shirt. "Everybody's casual."

"There's a difference between casual and crummy." Sally grabbed her wine glass from the table. "Between running shoes and ten-buck sneakers, for God's sake!"

I was starting to get angry. "What do sneakers have . . . ?"

She gestured toward my head, slopping wine in the process. "And where do you get your hair cut, at a power mower shop?"

Angrier: "I like my hair."

"Exactly! And look at your place downstairs: a sty, a *dump!*" Her volume rose ten DB: "Don't you see what your living habits say about you?" She swung away impatiently, and when she swung back she added another ten DB: "How the hell could you've lived down there at all?"

I didn't need this tonight, lady. I said tightly, "It was *quiet.*"

"Your cold bastard sarcasm!" By now she was half yelling. "It was quiet, sure; and you had yourself all to yourself." She was stomping toward me and now she shoved her face at mine. *"Which is what you really want!"*

That did it. I said, "Okay," in a dead-neutral tone and started toward the door.

Sally shouted at my back, "That's it: walk out. Don't deal with it; walk away from it!"

I paused at the door but controlled the impulse to turn and deliver a phony exit line. In the same dead tone, "G'night, Sally."

"You get out; tomorrow you get out! This is *my* place!"

My God, I'd never heard Sally scream that way before. "You mean that?" I turned to look at her.

My God again: Sally was shaking with fury and tears were pouring down her cheeks in quarts. She waved wildly at the glass doors. "You want me to throw all your shit out the window? I will."

"Sally . . ." I took a step toward her.

She backed away. "I will tomorrow." I tried another step. "I will *tonight* if you don't go away!"

I went away. Through the dark kitchen, where I snatched up another three-liter jug, out to the near-freezing winter night, down the long flight of concrete steps—whoops! watch it; must be a broken step—and into my unheated flat.

I stood there in the clammy darkness, weaving only slightly, and listened to the bangs and thumps that filtered through my ceiling from above. Don't want to think about what that might mean. Gotta be a glass in here someplace.

There was: a jelly tumbler half paved with volunteer plant life. I sluiced some of it out at the bathroom sink, then said the hell with it.

The alcohol will sterilize it anyway.

25

*I*n the dawn's early light I felt seedier than a pumpkin's guts, and the face in my smudgy mirror looked like a carved jack-o'-lantern a month after Halloween. I washed the wreck of that face three times, tongue-squished toothpaste through my teeth because my brush was still upstairs, and trembled into yesterday's clothes.

Today's clothes and tomorrow's and tomorrow's festooned the upper deck rails and the shrubs beyond them as I tottered toward my ratty Bumble. The ground was littered with my books, tapes, CDs, and even the few pots and pans I'd moved upstairs. They were soaking in the drizzle that had finally snapped the string of sunny days and I thought of taking them indoors and then thought *let 'em rot.*

To hell with everything.

At the office, Arlo Bracken found some Alka-Seltzer, microwaved a foam cup of patent ramen soup, and sent me to to my office with a motherly solicitude.

And so I just hid out. For two leaden hours I stared at my desk blotter and thought wearily about Sally and then Kelli and then Sally and then Kelli as if they were two books I couldn't choose between because I couldn't concentrate on either. Then I thought about a killer who remained as elusive as he'd been two weeks ago. By eleven

A.M. I was half comatose from hangover, depression, and something very like grief.

Then Parames bustled in with his usual fussy energy and laid a Xerox copy on my desk. "Another letter from Hassan."

I said anxiously, "Any worse than usual?"

Parames sniffed. "The same."

"Then I'll read it later."

The phone went off like a fire bell at close range. "Aaaaahh! Pick that up, will you, Herb?" He nodded. "And do me a favor: *whisper.*"

"Winston's office, Herbert Parames." The bellow on the other end was Ma's, so loud that I could hear it like rock noise escaping from a teenager's headphones. She yelled at Herb for thirty seconds while his face tightened and his thin mouth tensed in a sour curve.

He put the phone down. "Kelli's disappeared."

"Ohgod."

"Ms. Barker got a call from Ernie Drenko. She's a bit concerned."

And the hydrogen bomb was a bit disruptive. But before Parames could repeat her message, my door banged open and Attila herself galloped in.

"She's gone, the stupid goddam bitch left town!" Ma stabbed a pudgy finger in my face as if I were to blame. "I do not need this shit. I don't care if she's Vanna White and Meryl Streep and Mother goddam Teresa rolled in one! I got five shows to tape this weekend and no Kelli goddam Dengham to tape them!" She swung on Herb. "You got a cigarette?"

Parames looked surprised. "I don't smoke; you know that."

Back to me: "Am I the only leper left?"

"I . . ."

"Forget it. Okay, Winston, for once you earn your money."

"What did Drenko say, Ma?"

"You deaf? She's gone; took off."

Patiently, "Where did she go?"

"She went to Pismo fucking Beach! Would I be this upset if I knew?"

"Drenko didn't tell you?"

"He was too upset himself, and no wonder: if his client blows five shows like this, she's *out*—and so's his precious thousand bucks a week. *You* don't have a cigarette?"

I shook my head.

"Goddammit!" She waved an arm around as if dispersing smoke. "All right all right. Herb, get out. I wanna talk to Winston."

Parames stared at her a moment, his face under rigid control, then left without a word.

Ma trained her guns on me again. "Now hear this, Jocko: I'm switching schedules so we tape two shows tomorrow, three on Sunday. You have exactly twenty hours to get that bimbo back."

"How do you expect . . . ?"

"I don't *care* how. You get her back, or else!"

I was mad enough to shout, "Or else what?" but it got smothered in the door slam as Barker thundered out.

Trembling with frustration and generic adrenaline, I

looked down to find that I'd crumpled the Xeroxed letter in my fist.

Hassan's epistle. Which arrived just after Kelli disappeared. I smoothed the paper on the desk and read it. His usual rant, as Herb had said, and I found myself skimming toward the bottom of the page:

> . . . *your jailers are looking for me now but they will not find me Kelli darling and if they do I will chop them in tiny pieces and flush them down the toilet!*
> *Your angry master*
> *Hassan*

Oh, whoopee: Hassan will chop me up and flush . . .

I froze. Hassan will chop? *Hassan chop?*

Oh, no! I yanked open my desk file, pulled the other letters, and skimmed them all.

It had been right in front of me: In one letter, "Hello my honey." "Open Sarsparilla" in another. And now, "Hassan chop." All quotes from Warner cartoons. Unlikely as it seemed, Kelli's psycho pen pal was none other than her boyfriend Ronald Tolkis.

But why on earth would he do such a thing?

A machine answered Kelli's phone, and Ron's union hall said they didn't think he was working today, so I slogged out to Conejo Canyon in the persistent drizzle and banged on Kelli's door at about noon.

After three full minutes while the heavens gleefully pissed on me, Tolkis cracked the door. "Stoney! What are you doing way out here?"

"I came to talk about cartoons, Ron." When he didn't widen the opening, I pointed a finger up at the clouds. "May I come in?"

An odd pause, then, "Gee, Stoney, I dunno right now . . ."

"Specifically, about *one* cartoon: *Ali Baba Bunny*."

"I don't get it." But his bland potato face said *yes he did*.

"You know the one: where Bugs and Daffy tunnel into Ali Baba's treasure cave—the cave guarded by *Hassan*, who's too dumb to remember 'open Sesame,' so he says 'open Sarsparilla'? The fat Arab with the huge scimitar?" I dropped into a gravely basso voice, one of Mel Blanc's hundreds: *"Hassan chop!"*

"Yeah, I remember. Yeah." He swung the door and motioned me in.

I said, "Sort of thought you might," to his back as Ron walked past the foyer's teensy-weensie wallpaper flowers and into the living room, a rustic stage set with oak beams and maple chairs and sofas swathed in patterned chintz.

He stopped before the photogenic blaze in the used brick fireplace, turned, and leaned an arm on it. "So what about it?" His lord of the manor pose was compromised by the fact that he had to stretch his elbow past his ear to reach the high mantelpiece.

I pulled the copied sheets out of my pocket. "You're Hassan. You wrote these."

"Gimme a break!"

I walked over and wagged the letters in his face. "Friend Tolkis, I'm in no mood to play. My head is killing me, my lady threw me out, and my boss gave me twenty-four hours to find Kelli Dengham."

"To find . . .?"

"She's gone and you know it, but we'll get to that later. Let's focus on these letters."

Stubbornly, "I don't know a thing about them."

"Then we'll focus on Kelli instead. As of now, she's fired from the show." Not true, but for all I knew, she might be.

"Why?" He looked genuinely surprised.

"And so are you, in case you care."

"But *why*?"

"You two are becoming expensive. Canceling the taping because Kelli's disappeared will cost us maybe fifty K. Hiring a security firm because you wrote crackpot letters to her has already cost us twenty more. You may work again—eventually—but Kelli's through. She's not a star, not yet, not big enough for people to put up with that behavior."

As I said this, Ron's look evolved from defiance to worried amazement. He repeated, "Through?"

My most reasonable tone: "So why don't you see if you can save a little something? At least clear up the Hassan business so Parames can pick up his flow charts and go home and stop billing us seven K a week."

Tolkis pulled his elbow down and stared into the fire, absently rubbing his miniscule biceps. Finally his shoulders slumped—though in his case they hadn't far to go. "Okay. You're right about the letters."

"Why?"

A sigh. "To help her career."

That made no sense whatever. "Elucidate."

He swung around. "For the status! You know any big star doesn't have crazies?"

"I don't know any big star, period."

"Look, I got it all figured out: how hot you are in this town depends on how hot people think you are."

"Old news, Ron."

"Sure, but *why* do people think you're hot?" He asked this with the patience required with a very slow child.

"You're about to tell me."

Ron started pacing the room. "Four ways to measure hot: talk shows, fan mail, tabloid coverage—and crazies."

"Crazies."

"No doubt about it." His weak eyes beamed conviction through his horn rims. "Look what a crazy did for Michael J. Fox. Made him a superstar."

I'd thought talent had played at least a tiny part, but I kept quiet.

Ronald resumed his lecture, holding up one-two-three-four fingers in case I lost track: "So I thought about the four measures. Talk shows I couldn't help with. Fan clubs: too much work. But a crazy I could do. So I did. Then I figured out how to use the crazy gag to get tabloid coverage too."

"The National Insider."

"You see: it was working!" His reedy voice was actually triumphant.

I didn't know what to say. Ron's picture of reality was as warped as a record on a hot radiator, but I sensed that the more I attacked that picture the more stubbornly he'd defend it. So I said only, "Okay, but that gag is over." A reluctant nod. "Look, Ron, regardless of your motives here, you cost a lot of money, made a lot of people very nervous, and created a lot of ill will toward Kelli."

I had him really worried now. "How bad?"

"Very bad, *potentially*. So far no one knows but me."

Ron said, "Yeah?" in a tone that added *what's the price?*

"And no one has to know if you do two things. First, tell me where Kelli is."

He set his face. "She made me promise not to."

"You want to break your promise or her contract? If I don't produce her for tomorrow's shows, Kelli's history."

Tolkis peered at me through his glasses for about a month, while I held my breath and matched his stare. The fire crackled, the rain hissed on the cute colonial window panes, and one of the Siamese cats gargled and spat in another room.

Finally he puffed his cheeks and blew. Then, "San Francisco; Ancient Mariner Hotel."

I released my own breath less audibly. "You should like that; you're a Coleridge fan." When Tolkis wrinkled his forehead, I quoted Hassan's own quote, "I will *drink the milk of paradise.*"

Amazingly, he grinned. "Kind of a neat touch, I thought. Those letters were fun to do." Then he remembered. "You said *two* things."

I nodded. "Got something to write with?"

Looking puzzled, he went to a breakfront desk, rummaged, and produced a pen and pad.

"Take this down. *My former darling:*—um—*How deceived I was in believing you were my destiny when it has been revealed unto me that you are not worthy of my pas-*

sion. *Now I know my soulmate is another and I banish you from my life and thoughts forever as I give my love to her.*"

Ron looked up. "Who's her?"

"Hm?"

"You gotta name somebody—makes it more realistic."

I nodded. "All right . . . *as I give my love to . . . to . . .*"

"*Roseanne Barr!*" said Ron, and he cackled with glee.

The stupid twit still thought it was a game. I nodded wearily. "All right. Finish with *Your life will be so empty now for you will never ever hear from me again. Hassan.* Print it out and send it today." He nodded and I started for the door. "Ancient Mariner Hotel?"

"Somewhere near Fisherman's Wharf, I think."

"All right, and if you value her career, don't call and tell her you told me." Another nod, though glum this time.

I stopped at the living room door. "I'm curious. Why did you put in those giveaway quotes from cartoons?"

He grinned. "Without any risk the game's no fun."

To Ron Tolkis that made perfect sense. Too weary and depressed to comment, I turned and left the house.

As I rolled away down the hill, I wondered how Ron/ Hassan had known about Freddy Footlong. Then I thought, why shouldn't he, with Kelli right there to tell him? What a pair of bozos.

Well, look on the bright side. If Hassan was a fiction, he couldn't have murdered Arnesen and Amber.

But *somebody*'d killed them! Somebody who was now an even bigger unknown than Hassan.

I *had* to locate Kelli, not to keep my job but perhaps to keep her alive.

26

When I returned to Laurel Canyon I found Sally's Supra gone. My clothes and things were missing too, probably thrown out by now. I descended through the stubborn drizzle to my cave, willing the energy to focus on my other problem, Kelli.

Inside my moldy flat I found the Ancient Mariner's address and number in the Triple-A tour guide—about all that club is good for nowadays—phoned them and asked for Ms. Dengham's room.

"I'm sorry; she doesn't answer." As if I couldn't figure that out after ten rings. "Any message?"

"I'll just try later." So she was there, or at least registered.

A shave and a shower, then into my closet. I wear a business shirt and suit so seldom that they were still downstairs—instead of in a trash bin or pitched into the canyon. I'd be okay if I could keep my underwear and socks from decaying into slime before I could buy replacements.

Then off through the rain to Burbank Airport and a plane for San Francisco.

Because the Burbank burghers are dismayed by aircraft racket, takeoffs from their airport are short and none too sweet. The ancient 727 stood on its tail engine and pole-vaulted toward cruising altitude while my stomach wired congratulations that I'd irrigated it with beer in an airport lounge. In fact I was feeling better, at least physically.

Mentally was another story. Everything about a plane ride fosters introspection. The travelers build an artificial privacy otherwise impossible in the sardine-can cabin, the droning engines flood the plane with isolating white noise, and the lurchings of the fragile craft at thirty thousand feet invite rejection of reality in general. As soon as we were off the ground, I squirmed into the least painful posture the sadistic seat allowed and drifted into meditation.

I was doing what I could about the problem of Kelli, but the problem of Sally was intractible. Lately she'd been veering from crabby to affectionate and back for reasons I just couldn't fathom. And giving her the benefit of every doubt, her explosion last night had been grotesquely out of proportion to my offense.

And what the hell *was* my offense? I cared nothing for my appearance. All right, granted. My apartment was a sty. Well, she didn't have to live there, and I was far tidier upstairs.

My career was going nowhere.

I sighed. It was only too true. After ten hustling, bustling years I was still living from hand to mouth, struggling with constant uncertainty, producing no real work of my own. I still loved film making—the silky precision of a Panaflex camera, the ballet of a crew with a Chapman crane, the cosy routine of a cutting room. . . . Maybe that was it: I loved the process too much to focus enough on the product. Or maybe I just lacked the fire in the belly, the ambition, ego, and, yes, talent to succeed.

Perhaps that was the reason for Sally's anger: she'd admitted that she loved me and agreed to think of marriage, but when she looked at my life and my career she saw a man of thirty-five who was not together, not grown up. If you marry Peter Pan you're transformed into a Wendy, and Sally was having none of that. No foster motherhood for her. Yes, that must be it: she'd decided to refuse me, and her rage had come from the realization that she'd been suckered into loving a man her good sense forced her to reject.

God, how I hated plane travel!

The Ancient Mariner Hotel was uphill from Fisherman's Wharf—but in San Francisco, what isn't? Its tan stucco cube housed a typical tourist barracks that escaped being a motel only technically: it boasted four stories and an elevator. The lobby was as personal as an airline lounge, with personnel to match—in this case a plump woman in a blue uniform who stared at her computer screen for several minutes before condescending to notice me.

Finally, "Yes?"

I had my story buffed and polished: my job on the show was to keep a leash on our flaky star, Kelli Dengham, but she'd eluded me for a weekend toot in San Francisco—you know how these stars are with drugs and all.

The clerk did indeed.

We'd saved her from one overdose already, but she was at it again, and it wouldn't be convenient for the hotel if Kelli checked out of this life before she checked out of the Ancient Mariner, now would it?

The clerk's attitude spun 180 on the spot and she accompanied me to Kelli's room, key card in hand. The room was empty, but a number scribbled on a pad by the phone offered hope.

In the lobby I made for the public phone and called the number.

"Doctors' offices."

Damn! That meant one receptionist for maybe eight physicians, and I didn't have a name. "Hi; listen, I'm on my way in and I misplaced your street address."

"Which doctor were you . . . ?"

"I'm already late; can I just get the address?" She gave it to me. "Right, of course! And the suite number?"

"Five-sixteen." Pause. "And what was your name, please?"

"Wilfred Bramble. Thanks." I hung up.

So I had neither a doctor's name nor the slightest clue about why Kelli had that number. I'd have to launch a fishing expedition that would make a tuna fleet look puny.

But what other lead did I have?

27

*D*riving San Francisco is a nightmare. The streets are paved with traffic, house numbers are capricious, and parking is a cold, sadistic joke. If you don't know where you're going—and I didn't—you can roll fat, dumb, and happy over a gentle rise and suddenly confront a stomach-churn-

ing drop—a road so steep you don't drive it, you rappel
down it. By now the February darkness had closed in as
well, so it took almost an hour to locate the address and
twenty minutes more to find even the illegal parking spot
in which I finally stashed my rented car.

The office building was a gloomy pile with a beaux arts
facade half bandaged in scaffolding. Even this long after
the '89 earthquake the city was still recovering. When I'd
blundered around it in my search for this address, I'd seen
holes where buildings once had stood and even empty
blocks. Walking toward the entrance, I heard a crash
around the corner like the sound of masonry dropped from
above. It seemed they went right on working after dark.

The lobby too was full of scaffolding, and so was the fifth-
floor hall to which the elevator lifted me with evident re-
sentment. The door of 516 said HAROLD HILDEBRANDT,
M.D., but offered no hints like "Practice Limited to Proc-
tology." I went inside with no idea of what to say.

As it turned out, I had a very different problem. The
waiting room was empty, as it might well be at six o'clock;
but then a nurse leapt into the hallway visible beyond,
sprinted to an open doorway, thrust her head in. "Denise,
call 911; she's trapped!" Then back down the hall at full
gallop and out the way she'd come.

I moved around the receptionist's booth, slipped through
the door where the nurse had gone, and followed voices
toward the rear. Down another hall, turn left, and . . .

The fire door at the end was ajar, and the opening was
swarming with people in lab coats. Somebody yelled,
"Don't move; just stay there!" I pushed my way through
onto a rusty metal landing and looked around.

There, on a two-foot cornice ledge, stood Kelli Dengham, twelve feet away and eighty feet above the street, her back plastered to the wall, fingers scrambling at the sooty stone, face locked in a rictus of fright.

"Hey, who're you?"

"A friend. I'll try to talk her down." I said this to the balding man beside me. He had *doctor* written all over his smooth round face.

His look said *oh, sure; everyone's a hero.* "Get the hell off this fire escape. It won't hold everybody."

"Then *you* get off." I grabbed a nurse's arm. "You too."

The nurse obeyed, but the pudgy doctor bristled. "You can't . . ."

"Yes I can. What'd you do to drive her out there?"

He goggled. "*Drive* her . . . ?"

"I hope you have good malpractice coverage."

The words of doom. The doctor blanched and backed into the hallway.

Quick survey: the cornice swept around from the front of the building, then ended between this fire escape and the point where Kelli stood. Logical: the decorative stone-work wouldn't extend much into the alley. And at least that alley had no pedestrians to stop and gape. So Kelli must have climbed through some other window.

I called, "Just hang on, kiddo," moved inside, and faced the doctor. "Where'd she go out?"

"Examining room window, but it's no good . . ."

"Show me!"

"I'm trying to tell you . . ."

I grabbed him, revolved him, and shoved. "Fast!"

He shook his head, but turned right and we trotted to a

room with an examining table, a chair, and a gaping window glazed with frosted glass. I raced over to it and looked out.

The ledge stretched toward the corner of the building, but halfway there a six-foot run was missing. I said, "How did she . . . ?"

Almost yelling, "That's what I'm *trying* to tell you!" He got control of himself, stared at me, and patted the air with his palms as if calming another crazy. "I go out for a minute, come back in, the window's open. I go look out. She's on the ledge, okay? I say come on back in, she shakes her head and sort of slides away along the wall. She takes four, five steps and right behind her a big hunk of ledge gives way, kaboom!"

That was the crash I'd heard below. So Kelli had no route back.

The doctor said, still soothingly, "Best thing to do is wait for the fire equipment."

But would Kelli wait with us? From the terror on her face, I wasn't sure. My brain was revving in neutral, but I couldn't shove it into gear.

The plump doctor made conversation, as if still gentling a nut case. "The whole building suffered earthquake damage. That's why we're doing these repairs."

Repairs! I raced to the reception room and out into the hall. Right: the scaffolding I'd seen there was floored with two-by-twelve planks—each about eight feet long. I unclipped one from the pipe supports, dragged it off the scaffold, and lugged it back to the suite, destroying a waiting room lamp, crashing through the inner door, bashing the walls at the endless right angles, wrestling it into the room, and finally shoving one end through the open window.

Now the tricky part. If I pushed the plank straight out, I couldn't control its weight and I'd lose it into the scaffolding two floors below. So I turned it edge up and fed it out diagonally, keeping it braced against the side edges of the window frame. Just before the left end cleared the frame, I turned to the doctor, who was gaping at this process. "Hold this end; keep your weight on it!"

"I . . ."

"Hold it!"

Obediently, he caught the left end in two hands and bore down as I eased another two feet through the window. At the last minute I grabbed the plank with one hand, placed as far out as possible, pushed the last few inches through, and hauled the heavy wood toward the building as it fell away. It bounced on the cornice top, skittered toward the edge, then miraculously stopped. I took a very deep breath and climbed out the window.

To push the plank across the cornice gap I'd have to crouch and nudge it forward. I sank to my knees in slippery pigeon dung and started shoving, inch by inch, looking at nothing but the plank and the dirty stone it rested on, while a cold breeze tugged me and traffic sounds floated up from the street.

And then, the same nasty physics problem: to bridge the six-foot gap I'd have to push the plank past its four-foot center of gravity and risk pitching it off the ledge. Nothing to do but try. I eased it out until the plank just teetered and then hunched over, wiping my necktie end through pigeon filth. One, two, *shove*! The plank end smacked the other edge of the gap, but I wiggled and bounced it until it rocked up onto the ledge beyond. It wasn't until I'd finished centering the plank that I noticed I was kneeling on my right knee and my left leg was dangling in the air. I started shaking.

No time for that! I stood and forced myself to focus on the problem. I couldn't knee-walk a board twelve inches wide, so I'd have to cross it standing up. Another shaky breath, then, just touching the wall for balance, I tightroped to the other side, eased up to the corner, and peeked around the edge.

Kelli's pretty face was still a mask of crazy panic. She shuffled her feet, wagged her arms vaguely in the air, and leaned out to stare at the alley far below.

I knew I had to reach her, soothe her, hold her still until the fire people got here. But at the best of times I'm no psychologist, and the strain of standing on a two-foot ledge five floors above hard concrete had deprived me of what little wits I had.

So I eased around the corner, stopped, and said in a silly baby voice, "I taught I taw a puddytat!" Kelli turned her head, and her eyes blinked at the sight of me. Edging forward, I kept up the Tweetybird chirp, "I did, I *did*, I taw a puddytat! Oooh, it a biiiig puddytat too!" Another cautious step. "You gonna fwy, puddy-tat? Ooooh, puddytats tant fwy; birdies fwy, not puddy-tats!" I flapped my arms and pranced along the ledge, insanely, in the circumstances. Kelli's eyes focused on me. "Oooh, you a *pwitty* puddytat!" Two feet away now. Kelli's eyes lit up and she smiled. "Give Tweetybird a gweat big hug!"

Got her! Kelli looped her arms around my neck and slumped against me, trembling.

I held her 'til the rescue squad arrived and brought us down.

And then I got a taste of what celebrity commands. Was Kelli jugged for breach of public peace? No way. Remanded to the bin for observation in a snug canvas wrapper? Perish the thought. The police, the fire people, the doctor and his staff all took it for granted that TV stars were exempt from inconvenient social processes. Regrettable incident . . . naturally upsetting . . . no real harm done . . . in your good hands now, Mr. Winston . . . have a nice day folks goodbye. I'd thought I'd really have to hustle to get Kelli out intact, but the worst mess I had to clean up was the bird lime on my pants.

Pleading patient confidentiality, Dr. Hildebrandt refused to tell me why Kelli was distraught, but the card I collected in his waiting room was eloquent. The doctor was a board-certified specialist in obstetrics, gynecology, and gynecological surgery. I was ready to bet on another baby, and Kelli's response to her last one was enough to explain today's hysteria.

So I collected the parking ticket from under my windshield wiper, drove Kelli back to the Ancient Mariner, filled half her tank with bourbon from the bottle in her kit, and ordered dinner in her room.

While we waited for it, Kelli disappeared into the shower and I phoned for reservations on a nine A.M. plane to Burbank.

I also called Ma Barker. "Got her, Ma."

"GODDAMMIT!" But her tone said *outstanding!* "Where'd you find her?"

"San Francisco, I'll explain tomorrow." I dropped my voice. "Can't talk; I'm with her now."

"You stay there, Bucky. Don't leave the goddam room. Use handcuffs if you have to."

"I'll have her at the taping by eleven."

"You hear me, Winston? Don't let that dingbat out of sight. I don't care if you have to watch her take a leak!"

"I get the picture, Ma. Good night."

Finesse personified, that's Ma. But come to think of it, Kelli *was* out of sight in the bathroom. No: one small, high window and no ledge outside this time. And through the hotel's cardboard wall I could hear her splashing in the shower and singing Paul Simon's "Fifty Different Ways to Leave Your Lover."

Kelli seemed to be recovering.

I thought next of telephoning Sally, who had no idea of where I was or why I'd be away all night. But then I put the phone down. In her present frame of mind Sally might say, "Why tell me? I'm not your keeper," and hang up.

Kelli's concert filtered through the wall. Who needed fifty different ways to leave your lover if your lover did it for you?

28

*B*y eleven P.M. the leavings of dinner were out in the hall, the chablis I'd ordered sat on the coffee table, and

Kelli lounged beside me on the couch in big pajamas and a fuzzy pink robe. We were far gone in domesticity. Kelli picked up the remote and channel-surfed awhile, then zapped the TV set and stretched.

"Well," she said in a bright, chirpy tone, "it's been a real long day."

I started laughing then; I couldn't help it.

"What's so funny?" When I carried on cackling, Kelli pouted. "You know, that bugs me. I always, like, say stuff and people laugh, but I dunno why I'm funny."

There was just no way to tell her, so I said, "I'm not laughing at you, Kelli."

"What, then?"

"Nothing, everything, I don't know." Time to change the subject. "We have to leave early tomorrow, so we'd better get organized for bed."

She pondered this problem seriously, then, "I'll take the couch. I owe you."

"No." Even for Kelli's length, the couch was under-qualified.

"Well, *you* can't sleep on this tiny thing." Kelli looked at me over her fourth bourbon and her piquant face turned thoughtful. "We could share the bed." Something wicked flickered in her eyes.

The mildest word for the situation was "fraught." I smiled and shook my head.

She pouted. "Just for sleeping, then. You don't *hafta* jump on my bones."

I let that twist slowly in the wind.

She sipped her drink. "They're kinda nice bones, you know."

"And what's hung on them is equally amazing."

Kelli giggled. "You'd be surprised. I mean I'm not as skinny as I look." Another giggle.

"You don't look remotely skinny." My enthusiasm was unforced.

But Kelli was flaky at the calmest of times, and today she'd been distraught about her pregnancy and unglued by half an hour on a fifth-floor ledge. Though she seemed becalmed in bourbon and my uninsistent company, she was still in a state where I could take advantage of her.

Before I could bask in this noble renunciation, Kelli snuggled against me and leaned her face toward mine. The face assumed a comic look of bogus candor, as if she were doing Nixon. "You can tell the truth, Stoney. Am I ugly? Am I really gross?" She crossed her eyes and stuck her pink tongue out.

She had to be the funniest woman I'd ever known. I met her goofy stare and tried to keep my own face straight; but as the seconds passed I slowly lost the contest, and my face shattered in a grin that mirrored hers. I said, "Yeah, you're yucky," in a tone of honest fondness.

She wrinkled her button nose. "Good!"

Then Kelli trapped my ears beneath her palms, pulled my head toward her, and kissed me. We leaned back against the couch while her fingers tickled my ear lobes and her tongue explored my mouth and a small, resilient breast nuzzled my ribs. The electricity was palpable, and so was her other breast under the robe when I covered it with my cupped hand. As the kiss went on for miles and miles, I smelled shampoo and hotel soap and Kelli's own subversive musk. I relaxed and held her closer, recalling another Paul Simon line: *There were times I was so lonely I took some comfort there. . . .*

That broke it. What was I doing, getting revenge on Sally? Kelli Dengham was as tasty as a strawberry cone, and I wouldn't mind taking a lick or two or three. But not to spite another person or revalidate my own attractiveness—and certainly not tonight, after Kelli's emotions had been shredded to confetti all day.

But as the wicked witch remarked, these things must be done *deh*-licately. I patted Kelli's sweet rump gently and gently pulled my mouth away. "You are one sexy lady, lady."

"Wait, there's more!"

"Pretty dove, I'd love to put you in that bed and see how long it took to break it." Her comic nods said, *Yeh! Yeh!* She made as if to get up.

I held her there and did my own Nixon, scowling and flapping my cheeks, "But it would be *wrong*."

She giggled at the impression, which is one of my better ones, then frowned. "How come?"

I sighed and pretended to think hard. Finally, "I didn't want to mention it—maybe upset you and all—but Marcia Barker's sort of mad at you."

Her eyes widened and she repeated, "How come?"

Reluctantly, "Well, you *did* run out on things and she had to reschedule the taping and, well, you know."

"I never thought of that."

"So tomorrow, you have to give the performance of your life to make it up to her." Kelli nodded absently as she tried to process this. "You've had an awful day today and it's pushing midnight. You'll be shot tomorrow if we stay up all night having fun."

The nods went on and on, like the bobbing of a spring-necked novelty bird, as Kelli's gears reluctantly meshed and turned. Then she looked at me with simple sweetness. "You're just so nice, Stoney; you think of *me*." She scrambled up briskly, shucked her fuzzy robe, and climbed between the sheets.

I sat and sipped chablis awhile. Yeah, big-hearted Winston. I thought of Kelli, all right, the better to control her; and she was as easy to manipulate as any other child.

Which many folks around her had discovered, to everybody's benefit but hers. Sighing, I got up, took off my shoes and socks, off-loaded the junk in my pockets, stripped out my belt, and lay down on top of the bed blanket with the spread to cover me.

I killed the light and lay there a moment, and then small fingers crabbed across the covers and took my own.

"G'night, Stoney," Kelli said.

When my wristwatch alarm tinkled at six, I discovered that sometime in the night Kelli had joined me on top of the blanket and now was asleep on her stomach with her head turned toward me and her pink mouth open like a child's. I eased off the bed and looked down at her. Her delectable rump in its cotton pajamas was cocked in the air and the curls on her forehead were damp. I decided to let her dream on awhile.

Feeling as dragged out as if I'd had no sleep whatever, I showered, shaved with soap and Kelli's plastic razor, unwrapped the socks and shorts bought yesterday, and climbed into my one good suit—well, good until the pigeons trashed it. And how'd I get guano on my *tie*? Only then did I wake Kelli up.

I should have done it sooner. She seemed to have the type of brain that fell to pieces in the night and reassembled, bit by bit, each morning. She woke up as dim as a snail and just as slow, yawned, scratched, stared at nothing, sat up, lay down, rolled over, stood up, sat down, stared again.

This did not bode well. "Kelli, we've got a plane to catch."

"Don' rush me." She addressed this to her knees.

I considered the logistics of modesty in this single room. "Better take your clothes into the bathroom."

"Mm." She lay down yet again.

I looked at my watch. "C'mon, kid."

Making a noise like one of her cats, Kelli struggled off the bed, zombied toward her suitcase, rummaged vaguely, then gave up and lugged the whole thing into the bathroom with her. Since time was so short, I phoned for breakfast from Room Service, to a background of intimate bathroom noises. One hundred thirty-five smackers a night for walls as soundproof as kettledrum skins. San Francisco sure does pamper the tourists.

First breakfast appeared and then Kelli, still half asleep, but at least fully dressed in a mauve cotton shirt, white jeans, ankle-length socks, and deck shoes. I smiled encouragingly. "I think we're making progress."

I spoke too soon. Kelli chose each bite of breakfast on a case-by-case basis and by the time she'd finally finished we were perilously late. But the closer we came to leaving, the more she displayed a maddening reluctance to actually haul off and *go*.

I looked at my watch again. "You ready?"

"Yeah." She wandered to the mirror, checked her face, considered, applied a lipstick touchup, dropped the lipstick in her purse, shut the purse.

Shifting from foot to foot, "All set?"

"Mm-hmh." She strolled into the bathroom, gazed around, strolled out.

I went to the door and opened it. "Let's go."

"I'm coming." She ambled to the window and sized up the weather outside.

Digital seconds marched relentlessly. "We'll miss our plane."

"Okay." She turned and started toward me. And then reversed direction.

This was driving me bats. "*Please*, Kelli."

"Be right there."

Stopping at the night table, she pulled four tissues from a dispenser, considered them at length, pulled out four more, thought about them for a week or two, then folded the tissues carefully and put them in her purse.

Sharply, "Kelli, *now!*"

"Okay, okay; don't be a grouch." She steamed toward the doorway at All Ahead Slow while I noted the time again. We would barely make our plane.

Kelli stepped into the hall and I sighed, "Right!" and picked up her bag.

She stopped. "I better go to the bathroom."

This was too much. "There isn't time!"

"Just be a minute."

Emphatically, "No way! We're fifteen minutes late."

"I think I gotta, Stoney." She looked about to cry.

Dear God! I said grimly, "You have thirty seconds."

Uncertainly, "Thanks."

My fiercest tone, "Exactly thirty seconds; then I'm coming in to get you."

She actually looked frightened. "I'll be super fast, I *promise.*" Kelli sprinted toward the bathroom.

I stood there by the door, counting backward from thirty: twenty-nine, twenty-eight, twenty-seven, twenty-six.

More bathroom noises. Nineteen, eighteen, seventeen, sixteen . . .

By God, I'd make good my threat! Seething with impatience, I started toward the bathroom.

But as I neared the partly open door, I caught Kelli's reflection in the bathroom mirror, profile toward me, not yet finished.

She was standing up.

It hit me: sweet forgiving Jesus, that unmistakable noise! The hydraulic sound effects emerging from the bathroom could only be produced by dependent *male* equipment.

As if in confirmation, Kelli stowed and zipped herself and then let down the toilet seat like the gentleman she was.

I stood outside the door as stunned as if a plank had fallen on my head. That's what those pictures showed, no doubt about it: *Kelli Dengham was a man!*

Kelli tripped out the door, fluffing her curls. She saw my stricken look. "S'matter, Stoney?"

I shook my head.

"You seen a ghost, or what?"

I shook my head again.

She said, as if trying to please a grownup, "I went as fast as I could."

And in fly-front jeans and without panty hose it was quicker to go standing up—if you were technically a male.

I fought to pull myself together. "Kelli . . ." Just in time I remembered that I had to get her home to Hollywood, emotionally prepared to tape two shows. How would she react if I told her that I'd guessed her central secret? So I ratcheted my chin back up in place, pasted a smile above it, and picked up the bag with a shaky hand.

"We can still make it," I said.

29

We did make the plane, by a margin a molecule wide, and the Keystone comedy pace I set to meet the deadline effectively prevented me from thinking about Kelli. But once we were aloft I surrendered to the engines' droning mantra and settled into rumination.

Was Kelli Dengham he, she, both, neither, *what*? Okay, call her *she*, or else the pronouns alone'll drive me bonkers. Besides, her sexual attractiveness supports it.

And I was attracted. Half out of her dress that day. Dancing with me in the fitting room. Her fingers on my face last night, sweet tongue in my mouth, soft breast in my hand—a hand just inches north of Jockey Gulch.

I can't believe this: I've been loving up a *man*!

What's so wrong with that, Winston? I mean, outside your prune-mouthed heritage.

My beliefs say nothing's wrong with it; my feelings aren't so sure.

Try this, then: does Kelli look, sound, taste, smell, feel like a woman? Does she behave like a woman?

To all questions, *yes*.

Then there you are.

Yes, but she's still a man!

Well, nobody's perfect.

Sure, but in *Some Like It Hot* Jack Lemmon was funny because his Hasty Pudding drag act was so clearly unconvincing. His voice, his skin, his very shape and walk said it's a *gag*, folks. But the vision sitting next to me was as feminine as Eve, from her delicate complexion to her brave vibrations each way free.

I snuck a glance at Kelli in the window seat peering out the window as avidly as if this were her first plane ride.

You're right: Kelli's female in every way but incidental plumbing.

Plumbing. The good Doctor Hildebrandt's a gynecological surgeon. Of course there wasn't any pregnancy. Perhaps she fled to San Francisco to complete her switchover. But why flee, and why right now, when she's been content with mere cosmetics for at least a year?

Nothing "mere" about those cosmetics. Breast implants and hormones, certainly; but look at her cheeks, her legs, her curvy hips. Remember what Parames said of Clipper: *"I've seen whole personalities built of silicone."*

Next to me, Kelli'd kicked her shoes off, and her small, high-arched feet were as delicate as the rest of her.

Start with Kelli's fine bones and short, slender build and you could sculpt a Cranach Venus on that armature, a body that would fool everyone. And everyone would *stay* fooled if she kept her knickers up, except with trusty Ronald Tolkis.

Did *he* know she was male? He must, he had to. Did he like her that way? Was he as wacko as "Hassan"?

Hassan: Ron could help her sell the trick by writing psycho letters, mash notes from a sex-crazed fan gone crackers over Kelli's *female* charms—charms unveiled seductively in *Raunch*.

That's why the published pictures were so tame. In full frontal nudity Kelli had to clamp her legs together with the telltale structures pulled back out of sight. Oh, pain! Don't even want to think about those shots.

Then think about how they were taken. In studio model work, professionals with motorized Nikons and powerful strobes shoot miles of film, knowing that one frame of each pose may be just slightly better. They'll begin as the model starts into the pose and continue until she moves on.

And in recording Kelli's transitions, the late Warren Arnesen captured her secret. And Arnesen had been killed by someone who remained an infuriating blank.

Kelli was digging through the seat pocket and happily checking out its contents.

Carlisle insisted that those shots were shredded and the secret buried in a landfill; but why invent a *fake* secret?

Why fictitious Freddie Footlong when the offending organ
was on the other model?

Or did Carlisle invent it? It was agent Ernie Drenko
who'd first explained, *"We got this clown with a shlong like
a . . ."* He said he'd been at the shooting session too, so
Drenko knew the truth.

Hell, Drenko must have organized the whole thing!
Where did a ditsy, penniless starlet find the megabucks for
surgery like Kelli's? Who had the shrewd idea of "exposing"
her femaleness in *Raunch*? Who conjured up "Hassan" to
sell her as a sex object?

As soon as Kelli was safe in the embrace of Mother Barker, I'd have to have a heart-to-heart with Drenko.

We made it to the studio by eleven, as promised, and
Arlo Bracken hustled Kelli off to dress. I found Ma with
Manny Savick, who had come to watch the first shows to
be taped under his ownership. I explained that Kelli'd run
away because she was upset about the Hassan piece in the
Insider, but I didn't tell them that their star was a pre-
operative transsexual. Let them get through today's tapings
before I dropped that anvil on them.

I called Drenko's office, waited for the voice of G. Delicious to finish cooing at me from the phone machine, then
left my message: "Stoney Winston, Ernie, noon on Saturday. I have a single word for you: *transvestite.*" I gave
my number and hung up.

Then I sagged into my office chair, exhausted. Worst
time I've spent in years. Just thirty-six hours since Sally
. . . Hmh: better call her.

The phone rang twenty times before I gave up.

I slumped there for an hour, too emptied out to move or even think; and then the phone rang.

"I picked up your message, Winston. What's it s'pose to mean?"

"Ern, I just brought Kelli back from San Francisco."

A very lengthy pause and then a sigh. "What I was afraid." Another long gap and then, "I'm home today." He gave me his address.

Drenko met me at the door of his Toluca Lake palazzo, dressed for the golf course that lay next door. "C'mon in here." He led me through a front hall done in Early Tasteless and into a living room big enough for squash games.

"You wanna drink?" He started toward the tufted leather wet bar. "Something to nosh? Siddown."

If I sat down I'd never get up again. "No, let's get right to it, Ernie."

He dropped ice cubes in a highball glass and poured. "I'm all up front."

I'd heard that once too often. "You're as close to the front as a Pentagon general—oh, never mind." No point in getting Drenko's back up. I used every ounce of will I had to focus on my job. "Okay. Kelli Dengham is a male, at least technically—a transvestite."

He raised a correcting finger. "Preop transsexual."

"A distinction without a difference where the show's concerned." Drenko shrugged. I walked over to the front side of the bar and looked at him. "You knew about Kelli. You set up that shoot for *Raunch* in order to sell her as a woman. Show Kelli *all up front* as you would put it, though some of her front wasn't *out* front in the pictures. A clever idea, in fact. But the outtakes showed the truth, and Amber Sung Li got hold of them."

"Bitch." He gulped his bourbon.

A dead bitch, though. "So when we asked about the pictures you invented Freddie Footlong."

Another shrug. "What was I supposed to do?"

"Was Hassan your idea too?"

He nodded as if this were no big deal. "I told Tolkis to use an A-rab name."

So he naturally thought of a *cartoon* Arab.

Drenko added with satisfaction, "Only people left to play the bad guys."

A lot of Muslim-Americans were suffering unjustly from that attitude, especially, post-Hussein. But back to business: "Something that happened Thursday made Kelli flip out enough to run to San Francisco. It wasn't the article about Hassan."

Drenko waved his empty glass. "She knew Ron was writing that shit."

"So what was it, Ernie, what happened?"

"*You* did. Well, in a way, like." Drenko rebuilt his drink. "You come to see me on Thursday, you talk about Hassan, that scandal sheet, some cockamamie murders—and what-all."

"What did that do?"

"Wait a second. Then you tell me Carlisle got Kelli *knocked up.*"

Of course. I nodded. "And one thing they can't do is a uterus transplant."

"At's it. I'm thinking, what *is* this? Why did Carlisle say that?" Ernie drained half his second bourbon. "So when you leave I call him up. I say, Russell, did you say this? He says yeah; then he laughs. I say, Russ, you're a reasonable person so give me a reasonable explanation. He says you were getting too close to Kelli so he tried to throw you off."

"Why should he care?"

"What I asked myself too, I mean he didn't own the show now. So we talk some more and he's yocking it up, you know, acting like it's all some kinda gag." Ernie cut to the chase: "After I hang up, I'm thinking it's starting to fall apart. Kelli can't keep it up much longer. Time to go for damage control. So I get her in my office and I talk to her like a father." Drenko dramatized the scene, with me as Kelli's stand-in. "I say, Kelli darling, the closet door is opening. You want them to find you hiding inside or you want to come out yourself—make a big entrance, get some *good* publicity?"

"Publicity."

But Drenko missed the disgust in my tone. Enthusiastically, "*People* woulda ate it up. But no, the kid can't see it. In fact she gets hysterical, rushes out. Next thing, Tolkis calls and tells me she disappeared."

"To see a gynecologist?"

"Can you believe that? She got this idea—well, Kelli's not too swift, you noticed—that if she like finishes the job she'll really *be* a woman and all this will blow away somehow."

"Do gynecologists even *do* that kind of surgery?"

"She musta thought so." Drenko lifted two thick arms toward heaven. "What can I tell you?"

I reran his explanation in my head, then, "Tell me *why*, Ern."

"Why what?" He drained the whiskey.

"Why you took the trouble. Kelli's very talented, but you didn't need her. You have lots of clients."

Drenko took a long time building his third drink and then wandered to the grandiose French doors that faced the golf course. He stood and watched a golf cart gliding by and his silhouetted shoulders slowly sagged. "I said I talked to her like a father." He sighed and turned around. "Well, I *am* her father."

With the bright sun behind him I couldn't see his face, but Drenko's tone lost its usual emphatic push. "Kelly— he spelled it with a *y* then, okay?—was . . . that way since, well, I don't know." He turned again and raised his voice to the sunshine, "Jeez, it isn't like I raised the kid in dresses, or . . ." The force leaked away and he turned back. "Anyway, when he told me what he wanted, I thought what are you gonna do? I mean your kid's your kid."

Drenko sighed again and returned to me at the bar. "So I thought, well, let him go off to San Francisco and be a drag queen. At least be happy."

"Why up north? There's plenty of gay culture here."

"Just to . . . make the change, you know? So the next thing I hear . . ." Drenko's voice began to tremble. "The next time I hear, he—*she* wants to go into show business! So I think what the hell: let her play around 'til she gets tired of it." Drenko made a hybrid noise, a sort of weepy chuckle. "Only the first thing I send her out on is *Oh-Pun Sesame*! Turns out my kid has talent—a career!" He sounded genuinely proud. "Can you beat it?"

No, I couldn't.

Drenko fought to control his face and started losing. He said very quietly, "I had to help her."

I looked at him silently. Every time I pegged somebody as a jerk, he fooled me. "I understand, Ernie. Thanks for telling me."

Drenko shook his big head. "Too late to make a difference." The face was going fast.

"Oh, I don't know . . ."

He slashed his arm down in a *shut up* gesture, stomped to the coffee table before the Italian leather sofa, and returned with a magazine.

A new issue of *Raunch*. "Check out the last page," Drenko quavered, and tears fought free and rolled down his cheeks into his beard.

The page was a teaser for the next issue, a preview of coming erections. There in the center was Kelli, and this time she was all up front.

Oh God oh God.

Wait a minute: not quite *all* of Kelli. She was seated facing forward with her pink knees wide apart—as if Arnesen had snapped her relaxing between poses—and her masculine appendages were obvious. But the picture was cropped to exclude her head. If I hadn't recognized the chaise longue and the bracelet on her wrist, I couldn't have been certain it was Kelli.

The caption underneath explained: "Which Hollywood celebrity has more between *her* legs than pussy? FIND OUT NEXT MONTH IN *RAUNCH*!"

That bastard! "Is this the only shot?"

Drenko wiped his eyes. "So far."

"So far, so *good*. Maybe we can stop it."

"What clout you got?" Drenko shook his head. "You don't know Carlisle." He started leaking again.

"I do know Manny Savick, though, and he has clout to burn."

"I wouldn't give you odds," Drenko said.

30

I chugged wearily through Cahuenga Pass toward Hollywood, thinking of Drenko in his big, coarse house, a house that all too clearly said he lived alone there. I tried to imagine raising a son who wanted to be a daughter, but I hadn't many referents for fatherhood. My own dad's picture was turned to the wall when my mother stomped off to America dragging me with her, and my own potential parenthood with Sally some day had just recently crashed and burned.

Be realistic, Winston: at age thirty-five, when the hell is "some day"?

On the way to the studio I detoured past the Cahuenga newsstand and picked up a copy of *Raunch* to show Manny Savick what he'd have to deal with. Crazy George was on station this afternoon, steaming up and down the sidewalk in cerulean panty hose and green skirt. His wig today was orange.

"Yo, George. Pretty stockings."

"The color of heaven itself, Stoney. Praise God!"

"From whom all blessings flow, George."

"Yes! Jesus in my corner, silver in my purse, and love, love, *love* in my heart. I am truly blessed!" And Hollywood's seven-foot Lily of the Field teetered off on his four-inch spikes.

Now *there* was a happy drag queen. George was a lesson for all of us: happiness doesn't require much; you only have to be nuts.

By the time I got to the studio, production had wrapped for the day and everyone seemed to have left. The dressing rooms, control rooms, and offices were empty and the set stood abandoned in the withering glare of the high studio work lamps. I wandered among the cameras and cables toward the plastic safe at center stage, noticing how cheap it all looked in the pitiless light. In closeup the bundles of cash in the transparent safe betrayed themselves. The printing on the bills read LOTSA LETTUCE and the president depicted was Bugs Bunny. Perfect, just perfect.

I heard a door and footsteps, and then Manny Savick strolled around the corner of a flat. "Hello, Stoney. Where you been all afternoon?"

I told him in full and at length.

I showed him the magazine picture too. Savick glowered at it, then stared at nothing for a long, quiet moment. Finally he nodded just slightly, as if satisfied with some conclusion he'd come to, and looked at me. "All right, let's talk about this."

Savick leaned across the bogus cash vault. "It isn't tough to figure, Stoney. Carlisle set me up."

"How so?"

"Try this: Carlisle has critical cash flow problems—except for this show."

"Which is a cash cow."

"Exactly, and the show is worth gold due to Kelli alone." Savick glanced around again with a disgusted look. "I mean, the pun gag is ancient, the game's a bore, the whole thing's as tired as his other stuff."

"But the folks tune in to watch Kelli."

"By the millions," eyes toward heaven, "bless their hearts. Without Kelli Dengham, Russ' cash cow is . . ." his eye caught the play dough in the safe ". . . just lotsa lettuce." He gestured at the magazine lying on the plastic top. "So what happens? He sees a nude photo spread of her and a few of the shots reveal she's a male."

Savick started pacing as he spoke. "So Russ thinks, right now *Oh-Pun Sesame*'s an asset worth millions. But if the folks find out their darling girl's a drag queen Russ'll have to bounce her off the show and that asset will drop to zero."

"Would they really react that strongly?"

"That's what Russell thought." He stopped and turned toward me. "Look at our demographics, Stoney. We're talking Flyover Frank and Corn Belt Clara here. Russ would think, *when they find out . . .*"

"*If* they found out."

"They *always* find out and Russ knows it. After all, he owns a tabloid that feeds them garbage just like this."

"But Carlisle pulled the plug on the *Insider* when they went after Kelli."

He walked back to the safe. "Look at the timing: they went after Kelli before he saw the pictures; he pulled the

plug *after* he saw them." He patted the air with a palm.
"Bear with me. So he has to unload his asset while it's still
worth millions, and that's when he thinks of me. I'm in the
market, I have the money, and he hates my guts."

"Why?"

"That's another sad story." Savick said this negligently,
but something ugly flashed across his face. "He knows I'd
be suspicious of any offer from him, so he does a big song
and dance about his dire fiscal straits—makes a big show
of hating to enrich his arch rival, but he's strapped and
where else can he go, and blah-blah-blah. And I bought
it." A self-derisive snort. "I must be getting old."

"So Carlisle sold you a worthless property."

Savick held up a lecturing finger, and the smile he put
on was not pleasant. "Ah, he did better than that. If I know
Russell's slimy mind—and I do—he thinks like this: sooner
or later Kelli will blow up in Savick's face. So why not
sooner?" With growing intensity, "Why not publish those
pictures, get great publicity from the scandal, maybe boost
circulation, and blow fucking Manny Savick into five thousand shreds, boom!" By the end of this, Savick's thick basso
was filling the sound stage and he looked more than ever
like a movie gangster.

I nodded regretfully. "I'm afraid it fits. He warned Parames and me away from Kelli's past . . ."

"*Before* the sale was finalized!" BANG! with his fist on
the Plexiglas safe. "Exactly!"

I said, "I'm sorry," as supportively as I could, but this
new Savick was suddenly not a nice person.

He waved me off, and his grin was even more unpleasant.
"Waste no tears, my boy. I have resources of my own."

"Could your attorneys prevent publication?"

He seemed to start off on a tangent: "I've made obscene amounts of money in this game by the time-honored Hollywood method. Not orginality or creativity, not business sense, not even crookedness. But I know what the folks, the viewers, want—I can always feel it. And before anybody else does, I know what they'll go for next." Using the safe as a lectern, he struck a dramatic speaker's pose. "Right now this sense of mine says Mother and Father America are ready for Kelli Dengham."

My insides curdled like milk going sour. "You're not going to stop Carlisle?"

By now the grin was positively evil. "No, just cut him off at the ankles. A week before *Raunch* comes out again I'll have Kelli on the cover of *People*, telling all." His eyes lit up at a sudden brainstorm: "I'll call up Larry Flynt at *Hustler*. He'll *show* all. And Carlisle's howitzer will turn into a popgun—as usual."

And Kelli will turn into a public freak. In a voice determinedly neutral, I said softly, "What about Kelli?"

Offhandedly, "I'm doing her a kindness. It'll make her career."

"I see."

Savick took a deep breath as if cleansed and invigorated. "So. Well, thanks for digging all this out, Stoney. It gives me the edge I need."

Mildly, "All part of the job."

"Okay, three shows to do tomorrow." My face made some acknowledgment or other and Savick started off the stage. "Be sure to tell Security when you leave." The door opened and then banged shut.

I stood there a moment in the San Quentin lighting, then addressed the phony money in the fake plastic safe: "All part of the job." Bugs Bunny wore a cynic's knowing smile.

I drove home in a clammy funk as viscous as cold oatmeal, killed the Beetle's rumble, and got out beside Sally's blue Supra. I stared at her car a long moment, making up what was left of my mind, then thought, *what the hell, get it over with*. Might as well crown this two-day farce with a suitable climax and coda. I turned and dragged up the steps to the deck as if mounting the hangman's scaffold.

Before I could reach the front door, it opened and Sally stood in the doorway. "I heard your car." Her tone was neutral.

I nodded.

Her face looked tense but not angry. "Had supper?"

I jerked a thumb vaguely toward my flat downstairs. "I've got some stuff." My voice sounded dead and dug up.

"Want to come inside?" When I hesitated, she backed up a step and pulled the door open wider.

Did I want to go inside? Was I *afraid* to go inside?

"Come on. You look tired."

"That I am." I trudged into the house.

I followed her into the living room, where, without warning, Sally swung around, strode up to me, and wrapped her arms around my waist. Instinctively I put my own arms around her shoulders, and we stood there awhile just hanging on. At first it was enough to smell her hair and feel her breathing in my neck, but then I started wondering what it meant. I stared blindly over Sally's shoulder at the sound system in the bookcase wall. Was this welcome home? Or did it say *we'll always be friends but goodbye and good luck?* Then my eyes focused on the CDs beside their player. Sally didn't own any CDs; those had to be mine—retrieved from the rain, cleaned up, and neatly shelved.

She said to my coat lapel, "Your clothes are washed and put away." Uncanny how the woman read my mind.

"Thank you." I didn't trust my voice beyond that.

"S'okay." Then her voice took on a funny tone: "Just answer *one* question, one very simple question, okay?"

I stiffened, cursing myself for jumping to hopeful conclusions. "Sure."

Then I held my breath.

"Why does your necktie smell like bird shit?"

I started laughing, and Sally squeezed me hard enough to crack a rib.

We sat an hour in the roiling spa, just holding hands and sipping Chenin Blanc and talking quietly, then thawed and cooked two lobsters that were as hard to eat as game hens but more fun.

I hoped for more fun still at bedtime, but when Sally finished fiddling in the bathroom, she found me on the bed still dressed but semicomatose. It had been a hard day at the office.

The next thing I heard was the bedside alarm's electronic yodel. Oh no, not yet! I fumbled out a hand and whopped it good. It went on singing. I pushed three other buttons, but the aria continued, as repetitive as Philip Glass.

It was the phone, not the alarm. "Yah?"

"Rise and shine, Bucky!"

"Ma?" The clock I'd been abusing read five-fifteen A.M.

"I need you chop chop, Winston."

"Wha?"

"Wake up, goddammit; today's taping's canceled."

"Hah?" Sally was now up on one elbow, looking at me.

"Kelli Dengham shot herself. Suicide."

My adrenal glands went on a war-production footing.
"Is . . . ?"

"I'm at her place. Get your ass out here."

CLICK.

31

*T*he streets were empty in the Sunday dawn, and since
the Beetle was now on steroids I made it out to Kelli's
house in half an hour. While I howled along Sunset Boulevard I wondered if Kelli'd killed herself, or if our faceless
murderer was back.

As I let myself into the front hall, Ma came down the
stairs like a wolf on the fold. "Christ almighty, Winston,
where ya been? You live in goddam Pomona?"

"What happened, Ma?"

She surged into the living room, produced a Marlboro,
fired it up, and waved the smoke away. "Kelli found out
about that goddam magazine. You might have told *me*, you
know."

"I . . ."

"So she runs upstairs, locks herself in the bedroom, and BLAU-EE!"

"Is she . . . ?"

"Dead? Hell no."

"How bad . . . ?"

Ma started to laugh: a raspy, nicotine gargle. "Between the itty-bitty purse gun and Kelli's general incompetence . . ." The sentence collapsed into chortles and coughs.

"Ma!"

"She shot her tit off! Blew—oh, this is choice!—she blew away a pound of silicone!"

I sagged with relief while Ma's control dissolved completely. She staggered over to the fireplace and hung on to the mantel, laughing, smoking, wheezing all at once until the tears piddled down her doughy cheeks.

As I looked at her, the disgust I felt evolved to understanding. Ma's response, however coarse, was not insensitive. This was her weird way of venting tension, worry, and, yes, pain.

After many helpless, sighing "aaaahhhs" and "haaaahhhs," interspersed with rattles and small hiccups, Ma finally pulled herself together. "Like they say, I needed that." She mopped at her streaming cheeks with both thick palms. "Truth is, she did chip a goddam rib, but that's the worst of it, thank God!"

"Where'd they take her?"

Ma resumed her normal look, which signaled that I was stupid. "Nowhere, Junior! You think I want her in some hospital? They'd find out she's a goddam drag queen and

how long would that take to leak out?" Ma stubbed out her
butt and lit another cigarette. "Speaking of which, why
didn't you tell me Kelli was a freak?"

"I just found out myself. But listen, Kelli needs care,
maybe surgery."

"She got the best, right here: stitched up, wrapped tight,
sedated, right upstairs. Got a nurse on, twenty-four hours."
Ma held up one arm, as if taking oath. "Okay, I did ex-
aggerate: she didn't shoot it off; just punched a little hole
in it—well, *two* holes." Ma's face started falling apart again.
"The silicone, though, is a total loss." She turned away,
her dumpy body shaking.

I left her to cackle at the mantelpiece and went upstairs.

The narrow second-floor hallway continued the Cape
Cod motif: flowery wallpaper, quaintsy prints, and slippery
yellow pine floor. The bath to the left was a museum of
pink ruffles, and the door beyond it was closed. I looked
through the open door on the right.

The little bedroom was bulging with computers, keyboards, screens, printers—PCs and Macintoshes, some
with covers off and green guts exposed, and all connected
by a maze of looping cables like a drunken spider's web.
The spider sat at the center, reading a Batman comic.

"Hi, Ron, how is she?"

He looked up and smiled wanly. "Better now. She's
sleeping."

"And how're *you* doing?"

He waved that off. "I'm sitting here thinking what's she
gonna do? What's she gonna do now?" His eyes behind his
glasses were enclosed in parentheses of worry, like Charlie
Brown's.

"Just have to cope—somehow." I remained in the door-way because there was no space in the room. "She has you to help, though."

A snort. "Some help! Hassan didn't work so good, did he?" He thought of something. "Did you tell them?"

I shook my head. "Did you send that letter?"

"Should be there tomorrow."

"Then I won't. We'll just let Hassan ride his camel into the sunset."

Tolkis nodded, then stared at a space three feet from his nose. "I'd do anything to help her, *anything*! But . . ." The sentence petered out in a sigh. He raised myopic eyes. "I'm scared, Winston. When those pictures come out she'll do it again—and do it better."

There was nothing I could say, so I nodded, contrived a reassuring smile, and went downstairs again.

When I reached the living room, I found that Ma had gone off somewhere and Manny Savick was now on line, dressed for Sunday brunch in turtleneck and fuzzy jacket. "Morning, Manny."

He nodded his gray curls. "Just the man I want to see." Savick leaned against the breakfront desk and crossed his tweedy arms. "Turns out you make a good sounding board, Stoney, so try this on, will you? So far, we've kept this nailed down tight. Her boyfriend had his head screwed on last night: called Drenko instead of 911. Drenko got a doctor and Marcia Barker. Marcia stayed all night; made sure nothing, but *nothing* got out."

Hollywood damage control at its best. I nodded.

Savick gazed out the window at the gray morning. "But now I wonder: maybe we can use this. Take her to the hospital, release the suicide story, and leak why she did it to the right people. Let it build up a few days while Kelli recovers and we negotiate with talk shows, magazines, and so forth. And then . . ." Savick turned toward me and stretched out his arms like a magician signaling the payoff of a trick ". . . ta-daaaa!" He dropped his arms. "What do you think?"

What I thought would get me fired on the spot, and what I felt like doing to Savick would get me jailed. I said carefully, "Tactically, it's great; but maybe we need to think about the strategy behind it." I paused to see how that went down.

"Keep talking."

"For one-shot publicity, it's fine. But if your objective is to save Kelli for the show—and that means save the show itself—it's not too swift."

Savick's look said people didn't tell him his ideas weren't too swift, but he only nodded.

"Kelli's dangerously unstable. Force her to expose herself like that and you risk a basket case—maybe even a *casket* case." I pointed at the ceiling.

Savick mulled this over with a serious expression, then shook his head. "*We're* not putting her at risk. She'll expose herself in four weeks anyway—in *Raunch*."

I shrugged. "Sufficient unto the day . . ."

Savick's pitying look said *dream on, pal*.

I picked the problem over in my head, but all I could hear was Tolkis saying, "*She'll do it again and do it better. . . . I'd do anything for her, anything.*" Hmh! But what could a propeller head like Tolkis do?

What Spidernerds do best!

I looked at Savick, thinking fast, then, "Suppose I killed that spread in *Raunch* and got the pictures back with a signed and witnessed unconditional release?"

"And just how are you going to do that?"

I shook my head and smiled. "You don't want to hear that, Manny, you don't want to know *how*."

He stared at me awhile as if sizing me up, then quoted Ma Barker in a musing tone: "You got a funny mind, Winston." Savick nodded. "Okay then, I'll keep the Kelli thing quiet if you do what you just said. Bad news is, you have only two days."

"That's hardly . . ."

"The clock is running, Winston. If you screw around too long, I won't have time to set up our preemptive strike."

Oh boy. "Give me until Wednesday, Manny."

A genial smile. "In a way, I almost hope you fail. My own idea is dynamite—and blowing Russ away with it would be amusing."

That was the danger in generals like Savick and Carlisle: their amusing little wars killed real civilians.

I hustled back upstairs to find Ron Tolkis exactly as I'd left him. I gestured at the computer junk yard. "Ronald, my man, would you call yourself a hacker?"

Tolkis looked puzzled. "Maybe. I guess."

"Good enough to crack a mainframe with a phone line?"

"I used to do it for laughs, but it got too risky."

"Too risky if you could help Kelli—maybe save her life?"

"What is this, Stoney?"

"*Raunch* is one of twenty publications, all on the same

mainframe. They all depend on it for library, editorial, layout, and production. If their brain goes down, they're out of business."

Ron said nothing, but his eyes narrowed in thought.

"And I have an access phone number: I.N.S.I.D.E.R."

Ron's face sagged again and he shook his head. "That would only delay those pictures 'til they fixed it. Besides, that stuff's a federal crime nowadays."

"We wouldn't crash the computer; just pretend to plant a bomb in it with a remote detonator. Then we show the publisher of *Raunch* the fake detonator with our finger on the button and ask, pretty please, for those pictures."

Though he looked more hopeful now, Tolkis still shook his head. "Just a phone number? Geez, that could take me weeks. If only I could get more information."

A six-foot light bulb blazed above my head. "Ronald, dear boy, it's time for you to meet *my* lady."

"Let's review this, Winston." Sally paced around our dining room in bare feet, short shorts, and T-shirt, while Tolkis tracked her like a radar gunsight, his weak eyes bulging with disbelief.

I said, "Roll your tongue up, Ron."

Sally ignored this byplay. "You want me to get gussied up in tight clothes with my killer bra . . ."

"The one that makes you look like a 'fifty-nine Cadillac bumper."

"And feel like an armored car. Then I dig out my old sales brochures and product books and go tell Carlisle I'm hustling mainframes."

"Which you did until two years ago. How much could

they change?" My plan was to have Sally conduct a "needs analysis," ostensibly to recommend a better computer system, but actually to get the information Ron needed to penetrate the one they had.

Sally was not tickled by this plan. "Basically, you want me to use sex to reach Carlisle. I don't like that."

Ten minutes of persuasion hadn't worked, so I took the risk of hitting her head on. "I think you're being disingenuous. For five years you moved a lot of product because you're a dynamite sales rep." Sally tried not to look pleased at that. "But half the time, you got in to begin with because the poor sexist buyers were too stunned by your appearance to notice your foot in the door."

"Well . . ."

"You knew that and you used it."

"I admit . . ."

"And you've said repeatedly that if males are victimized by their own glands, it's not your fault."

Sally was too honest to deny it. She nodded reluctantly. "Think it'll work?"

"Carlisle has an attitude toward women that went out with the Neanderthals: if it looks tasty, club it down and drag it home. It'll work."

Tolkis piped up, "*If* you can get past all the flunkies first."

Sally hit him with a smile like a skillet on the noggin. I could almost see the cartoon birdies orbiting Ron's head. He said in a suddenly sappy voice, "Well, maybe you can."

Once her mind was made up, Sally wasted no time. She swept a yellow pad off the sideboard, strode over to the dinner table where Tolkis was sitting, and yanked out a chair. "Let's go then."

As she parked her magnificence two feet away from him, Ron made an all too visible effort to focus. Then the two of them plunged into technicalities that left me miles behind.

Privately, I detested this stratagem as much as Sally did, but with only two days to stop Carlisle from destroying Kelli, I hadn't the time to be finicky.

32

Our little band of saboteurs rendezvoused on Monday. The place and time were the same, and Ron and I were as scruffy as we'd been the day before, but Sally was a different case entirely. She'd just returned from vamping Russ Carlisle and was more or less wearing a pale blue dress that was borderline illegal.

She kicked off the pumps that added two inches to her five-feet-nine and spread her notes on the dining table. "I got the goods." She pushed the notes toward Tolkis, but he just sat there frozen, stoned by the sight of her. "Ron!"

To give him time to pull himself together, I said, "Tell us how it went, Sally."

She shrugged. "About the usual. Security sent me to EDP, so I asked for the manager there. When they sent me to his office, I kept right on going to the service stairs and up to the penthouse." A chuckle. "Carlisle about dropped his teeth when I walked through his back door."

"How'd you hook him?"

Sally inhaled and did her puffer fish trick, strode up to me, and lit a smile that could have blown the Burbank power plant. "Russ, I'm Sally Helmer of R. T. Data Systems." She took my hand in one of her own and caressed its back with her other. "Sorry to bust in on you like this, but I'll do *anything* to sell you a system!"

I played Carlisle: "*Anything*, uh, Sally?"

She focused laser eyes on mine. "You try me."

I turned to Ron. "You see?" But Ron just sat there, so thoroughly hung that he'd have to be rebooted.

Sally exchanged her battle dress for sweats that covered her as shapelessly as any clothes can, and Tolkis settled down enough to focus on her notes.

Sally'd seen the EDP manager, all right, but not by walking through his door on a cold call. Instead, she was introduced by the big cheese in person. Carlisle had told his bemused subordinate to give this lady anything she needed, in a tone that implied that Carlisle knew what she really needed and he possessed an ample supply of it. What with the boss' carte blanche and the manager's own response to Sally, the man had answered her sneakier questions with information he wouldn't tell his mother.

After an hour of listening to these answers, Ron announced that he could do it, walked out with a last reluctant look at Sally, and rolled off in his white Ford Escort.

Then Sally and I prepared a script for getting the three of us in to see Carlisle. An actual needs analysis could take several days to write, but Sally said Carlisle was so computer ignorant that a few hours would be convincing enough. So just before five o'clock we rehearsed it one more time, and then she phoned him.

"Hi, Russell; this is Sally. Remember me? . . . Only parts? Which parts? . . . Oh, Russ, you're *terrible*. Listen: I . . . Hm? I'd love to but I'm all booked up tonight." Sally's face looked cold and grim, but her voice continued pouring honey. "I can't do that; he's another customer." Seductively, "I wish I could though, now that I've got such a better offer. Maybe tomorrow night, or you could buy me lunch after we meet. . . . Hm? About the needs analysis." A longish pause while Sally's look turned even blacker. "Now be a good boy, Russ. I meant your *system*. Business before pleasure." Quickly, "So how 'bout ten A.M.? I'll bring a field engineer and my top software guy. . . . Of *course* they need to come too; service is my motto. . . . Russ, be *good*." Sally heard the knife edge in her tone, took a deep breath, and cracked a ghastly smile. "But they don't have to come to lunch with us. Okay, ten o'clock." Her best leopard purr: "I'm looking forward to it."

She pushed the *clear* button before she slammed the handset down. "Like a pelvic exam!"

"Thank you, Sally."

"You *better* thank me, buddy." She wiped her palms together. "Yecchhh!"

"The man is pretty slimy."

"Carlisle, Tolkis, even you. What is it with you men?" Sally started for the dining room door. As she stomped through the doorway, she said, without pausing, "Times like this, I'm all for parthogenesis!"

I called Ron Tolkis to give him the appointment time

and place, and *we men* reviewed the situation. Kelli was still on sedatives, though mending adequately.

But they couldn't keep her permanently zonked, and how would she react when she descended from her cloud of dope? Ron's fake digital bomb just *had* to get us those pictures back.

I hung up and went off to make my peace with Sally. As I ambled toward the bedroom, I had a queasy thought: we were all so focused on suppressing Kelli's pictures that we'd forgotten the trivial matter of a killer still unknown and still at large. Well, take it one step at a time.

What else could we do?

For some peculiar reason, Tolkis needed to share the agony and ecstasy of hacking, which he did with almost hourly phone calls, long into the night. The trouble was that he couldn't seem to realize that I wasn't there to watch and wouldn't have understood him if I were.

On top of which, his speaker phone broadcast Ron's hourly bulletins from the innards of a metal storm drain: "Okay, I'm *there*. Clickety-click-click. BEEP! Damn! Try, uh . . . clickety-clack. BEEP! Shit! Okay, you mother! Clackety-click-clack, clunk! (Silence.) Aw-*riiight!*" I could see Ron high-fiving his VGA monitor.

When he woke me at two A.M., I finally told him to sod off, but when he called again at six and said the deed was done, I forgave him.

Ron had managed to tap the mainframe and download some harmless demonstration software. It couldn't do a thing to Carlisle's system, but he wouldn't know that. And if he thought we could destroy his entire operation, he might just give us those pictures.

Fully awake now, I said, "Outstanding, Ronald!"

"Duck Dodgerth, in the twenty-fourthth-and-a-half *THTHTHTHENTURY!!!*"

33

And so, at ten A.M. Sally presented her business card to the security man in Carlisle's lobby. She was equally stunning today, if less provocative, in a yellow cotton shirt and a calf-length skirt secured at the waist by a stainless-steel chain belt that resembled a dog leash but was fetching nevertheless. The guard stared at this tableau of Venus Attended by Nerds as he phoned upstairs, then unlocked the private elevator and launched us toward the penthouse. While we rode up, I noted Ron's attempt at corporate dress: a suit incompletely rescued from mildew and a tie nearly half an inch wide. No matter; the charade would be over soon enough, and at least he was well rehearsed in his role. In the penthouse foyer the receptionist pushed a button with an inch-long nail, and the door to the sanctum hissed open.

Our little cohort marched across the Oriental rugs to the desk, where Carlisle was again turned away to watch a tape on the screen behind him: an X-rated show of the usual dreary sort. Another performance for the benefit of visitors. He clicked it off and swung his chair around.

"Good morn . . ." His eyes widened and his hearty tone died. "What the hell's all this?"

"Good morning, Russ." I waved at Ron and Sally. "All this is a trade delegation."

"What?"

"Sally, you know, I think. May I present Ronald N. Tolkis, a computer programming expert."

Impatiently, "I don't have time for games." Carlisle reached toward his intercom.

Sally moved to one side. "I wouldn't, Russ, until you've heard what we're here to trade."

"Trade" was provocative enough to stop him. He turned to look at her. "What, then?"

I turned him back: "Pictures, Russell; pictures of Kelli Dengham."

Carlisle just stared a moment, then the light dawned. "Savick sent you." He looked at each of us in turn and then guffawed. "Jeez, he must be desperate."

Sally hit him with her laser eyes and cooed, "Not as desperate as your cash flow when every publication you own freezes solid."

Still chortling, "When you wave your magic wand, sure!"

I held up an index finger. "Not a magic wand, a magic *digit*." To Tolkis, "Take it away, Professor."

Ron leaned over the workstation on the desk return, and before Carlisle could stop him, stabbed some keys.

"Hey!"

The magazine page layout on the twenty-one-inch color

monitor exploded, the tiny speaker tinkled out the "Merry-Go-Round Broke Down" cartoon theme, and Yosemite Sam appeared in living color, brandishing two six-guns. "I got the drop on ya now, ya pesky varmint!" the speaker said.

Carlisle stared at the image blankly, then looked up and said very slowly, "What, the hell, is that?"

I said, "Ever heard of a computer virus?"

Contemptuously, "What, *that*?"

Sally said, "That's just our calling card."

Ron snatched up the keyboard on its coiled umbilical, typed something, and the magazine layout reappeared. "We hid a bomb in your CPU, and I can explode it whenever I like." He played an arpeggio on the keyboard.

Carlisle looked at the screen again and then gaped. The layout didn't explode this time. Instead it browned and bubbled like burning film and oozed down off the screen. Carlisle sat back in his chair and stared at it thoughtfully.

Sally leaned across his desk and murmured, "That page is now gone for good, Russ, and we can do the same thing to every publication on the system: all the database, all the working files, all the layout and production software, all the communications turned to garbage."

Ron said proudly, "This little baby'll do everything but melt your cables." He patted the keyboard.

I kept Carlisle's head swiveling: "And if you load backups the same thing will happen."

Sally's turn: "Even if you shut down now, it'll take a month to find the bomb, clear it out, test all your files and software—while everything you publish lies dead in the water."

Me: "And so does your bank account."

Sally: "Or you can just wait for it to detonate."

Carlisle studied each of us in turn, stared at the screen again, then gave me an unreadable look. "So what's the deal?"

"You give us Kelli's slides: every frame, every copy, every separation." I pulled the sheets prepared by Sally from a pocket. "You sign an unconditional release that you surrender all rights to use them in any way whatever, *whenever*." I put the release on the desk before him.

He read it, then looked up again. "And what do you give me?"

"Our word as gentle persons that we won't push the button."

His eyes widened. "You gonna *leave* it in there?"

"For insurance, yes." Sally said it as confidently as if she weren't just bluffing.

Carlisle stared at the release again. "I'll have to think about it."

Ron sang out, "Hey Stoney, look what I found!" The monitor suddenly displayed the front page of *The National Insider*.

I smiled. "I wouldn't think too long, Russ. Not with his creative juices flowing."

Carlisle yelled, "Knock that off, okay?" To Sally: "This on the level?"

She turned on the look that'd made customers believe anything she told them. "I sold systems just like this for five years, Russ, and I know how they work. Ron can do everything he says."

He thought another moment while his features slowly petrified. Finally, he sighed. "All right, I'll sign the damn release." Sally handed him her ballpoint pen. He signed and gave the pen back. "Satisfied?"

"And produce the slides."

Tightly, "You'll get the pictures."

"Before we leave."

He nodded almost absently, then shrugged. "So Savick won a round. Big deal." For these detached commanders, this was just one skirmish in an endless war.

Carlisle keyed his intercom again. "Clipper? Come on in, honey."

The speaker chirped, "Be just a minute, Russ."

"I'll have her get the film." Carlisle leaned back as if just a minute meant a while.

To fill the silence I said, "Manny wouldn't have won without that teaser shot of Kelli. The warning gave us time to hit back."

Carlisle sneered. "The art director's bright idea." But the look on his face said the idea had been his own.

"If you wanted to blind-side Manny, why didn't you just run *all* the pictures?"

Defensively, "I didn't have time. We got a two-month editorial production cycle, and I only got those shots four weeks ago. Busted my ass just getting that teaser in."

I nodded. "So the photographer didn't submit them with the original package." Hm: then four weeks ago, for some reason, Warren Arnesen sold Carlisle those pictures . . .

And was soon found beaten to death. A week later, so was Amber.

Unfortunately, Carlisle realized what he'd just revealed. Without warning, he stabbed the intercom button, snapped, "Special duty, Clipper," and pressed another but-

ton on his desk. The office door gave out a metallic SNACK
that sounded only too much like a deadbolt.

Carlisle appealed to heaven for patience. "Jeez, when's
this gonna stop?"

I shook my head. "Ron still has his finger on that trigger,
Russ."

He looked me at with tired disgust. "I got a bigger problem now, don't I?"

Sally'd picked up the change in tone. "What's going on?"

I sighed. "To get those pictures, Carlisle killed Warren
Arnesen and Amber Sung Li. His problem is that the three
of us just heard him admit it." Sally's face tightened and
Tolkis goggled at me.

Then the back office door opened and Clipper strolled
through it in a gray jumpsuit that made her look like the
Michelin tire man.

Carlisle nodded at her with grim satisfaction, then said,
"Wrong on both counts, smartass. Arnesen *sold* me those
pictures." He waved an arm, as if at the past. "Months ago,
he cooks up the idea of getting his girlfriend on the show
and using the pictures to squeeze answers outta Kelli Dengham. But Amber thinks, why should she share the wealth,
and she moves out of his place and cuts him off. When he
finds out he's been screwed, he gets so pissed he brings
the shots to me—at least make *some* money off 'em, right?"
Carlisle shook his head wearily. "Asshole didn't even know
I owned the show."

"You said I was wrong on *both* counts."

A sour smile. "*I* didn't take those two out, did I, Clipper?"

"Nope." She pulled her hands out of the jumpsuit pockets

and held them waist high. Her face and tone were as cheerful as a child's, but her left hand carried a sap. "I got carried
away," she chirped. Then she giggled.

"You saw a sample of her work, Winston. You want another?"

I looked around the giant room. "Clipper may be the
Karate Kid, but she can't hold three of us at once if we're
headed in different directions. Even with that sap."

"That sap has a friend." He nodded at Clipper and she
pulled an automatic out of her right pocket.

Carlisle leaned toward his intercom and punched a different button: "Listen, baby, take your lunch break, willya?"

The receptionist's voice said, "At ten-thirty, Mr. Carlisle?"

Confidentially, "Well, I got a lady in here, and . . ."

"Oh! Right away, Mr. Carlisle."

He released the 'com button and sat back. "Give her
some time to get lost, then we'll go downstairs, you and
us and Clipper's friends."

I said, "If you got the shots from Arnesen, why kill him?"

His exasperation doubled. "Try and see my point of view.
Here's a guy selling outtakes that don't belong to him, and
he already planned to take my show for a million bucks."
In a tone of virtuous surprise, "This is not an honest man!
What if he made copies? What if he sells them somewhere
else? If Kelli goes down in flames, my show goes with her,
and that show is my only profit center. Without that show,
I can't pay my interest. And if I can't pay, I'm history." He
shrugged dismissively. "So I sent Clipper to hit him upside
the head—scare him some."

"She hit him upside the head, all right."

Another martyred sigh. "Yeah, she screwed up. She does that—overreacts."

Overreacts?

"But what could I do? Go tell the cops it was a mistake?"

"And Amber?"

Carlisle's disgust was even deeper. "The same thing starts all over again! Before I turn around, *she* calls me up and now *she's* all pissed off and selling dupes of the same pictures."

"Because we threw her off the show."

"Just when I thought I was outta the woods. So I sent Clipper to her apartment to check out the pictures. Shoulda known better."

And the apartment manager noticed "a cute chick" with a bucket of chicken takeout, but not the fact that she was shaped like a Neolithic fertility statue. Thank you, Sherlock Coogle!

Sally shook her head in disbelief. "To protect a dumb quiz show you had two people murdered?"

"No, I *didn't*! The photographer was an accident. The girl—well—Clipper's so dumb she thought I meant go do the same thing again." He turned. "No offense, honey."

Clipper smiled as brightly as if he'd praised her.

Carlisle said in a reasonable tone, "It was just one thing after another. Well, then I got to thinking: how long can a ditz like Kelli Dingbat keep her secret—six months? Three? Sooner or later, that show's in the toilet."

"And so are you," Sally said. She stared distastefully at the pen in her hand.

Carlisle didn't notice. "So I unloaded the show and

cleaned up on the deal. Hey, let Savick take the bath instead of me."

I nodded. "And you kept us away from Kelli's past until the sale closed."

"I thought I finally had the problem wrapped."

"But even after you sold the show, you told me you got Kelli pregnant. Why?"

A sour smile. "I wanted the new spread on Kelli to be a surprise for my old pal Savick." The tone of a man much put upon returned. "But you and your cute computer games! Now I got one *more* thing to clean up."

"Nobody knows the trouble Carlisle has seen."

He actually took me seriously. "This is not my style, believe me!" With a sigh that said there was no rest for the wicked, he keyed the door lock button and stood up. "Okay, Clipper, hold 'em 'til I get the elevator. We'll go straight to the garage."

She smiled at him brightly. "Okay." Her innocent, empty face looked as pleased as if her daddy had just offered to buy her an ice cream.

The scariest thing about Clipper was her cheerful blankness, as if her moral circuits were simply disconnected. She wasn't even a proper psychopath because she hadn't enough mind to lose. As I looked at her happy, stupid face I felt that she would kill us as absently as she picked her nose.

Not that Carlisle was much higher up the food chain. He seemed opaque to the fact that he'd had two people killed and was holding three more at gunpoint. To him we weren't really people—just tiresome details of business to be cleaned up.

Carlisle said wearily, "Let's move it." He took Sally's arm and started toward the door.

"Not so fast, Carlisle," she said, "I can't run a marathon in this skirt." She grabbed the waistband in two hands and hitched it up.

Tolkis had been trembling visibly throughout the conversation, and now he started shaking in earnest and saying, "Hey, hey, hey, hey," in a half-audible bleat. Suddenly he stopped. "No way I'm going out that door!" he yelled, and then burst into sobs. Clipper swung around and started for him.

Carlisle sighed, "Aw, shit . . ."

And then Sally went nova. The hands at her waist separated and her right arm flashed through a backswing that zipped her dog leash belt out of its loops. She slashed it forward, and the steel chain spun around Carlisle's thick neck like a bola.

"Clipper!" The pneumatic Ninja whirled around.

"Helllllp!" Ron bellowed in Clipper's ear and she swung back as if two stimuli at once were one too many. I started toward them, but before I made it Clipper's reptile brain decided that her boss was more important. She wheeled and trained the gun and I stopped dead six feet away from her.

"*Clipper!!*" Carlisle's voice was now half strangled, and no wonder: Sally stood behind him with the two ends of the chain around his neck in one big fist. She jabbed her other hand into his back, and Carlisle squealed with pain.

Sally leaned toward his ear. "My anti-mugger knife, Carlisle, the very best from L. L. Bean. You want the rest of it?" He shook his head. "Then tell Clipper."

Carlisle said, "I . . ." then gargled as Sally yanked his chain. "Can't breathe!"

When Sally relaxed the chain a bit, Carlisle swung suddenly to the left, pulling her around with him.

Clipper fired.

Sally yelled and went down and the ballpoint pen she'd been shoving in his back rattled on the hardwood floor.

I launched myself toward Clipper, not caring if she shot me too, but before I reached her, three sharp CRACKs ricocheted around the room and glass shattered behind me. Clipper lowered her gun arm and snatched at her giant right breast.

"That hurts," she said in a small, amazed voice.

I grabbed her hand and gun and smashed them against the paneled wall, three, four, five times; then pried the weapon from her ruined fingers and let her flop to the floor.

But I needn't have hurried. Carlisle stood with the chain belt dangling from his neck while Ron Tolkis, still sobbing, covered him with Kelli's toy purse gun.

I raced around Carlisle and knelt by Sally, who was sprawled on one side, her eyes closed. "Sally!"

She opened her eyes. "I'll live, Stoney. She shot me in my big fat behind." I held her head and kissed her forehead. She grunted, "Lucky I was turned away."

I cradled her head. "How many times do I have to tell you you're not fat?"

Then my eyes happened to focus on Clipper, who was sitting propped against the wall where I'd left her, and a bizarre thought flashed through my head: her stained jumpsuit revealed that her breast was, after all, leaking blood, not air.

34

*T*he law was patient and professional, though skeptical at first. But Ron was there to bear me out, and Sally was able to give a statement in the hospital. When Savick and Ma Barker arrived they vouched for me, and I was finally allowed to walk out of the station, leaving Carlisle in the slammer and Clipper in the prison ward at County General, in guarded but stable condition. Two of Ron's shots out of three had gone wild, and the third round from Kelli's popgun had proved just as ineffective on Clipper. Come to think of it, it'd been a lethal week for silicone.

And now, ten endless hours later, I was slogging down a hall in the UCLA Medical Center toward the room where Sally lay plugged and stitched and patched and bandaged.

At the nurses' station I was stopped by a slight young woman with long blond hair and a lab coat. "Mr. Winston? I'm Dr. Sloan." I nodded a greeting. "You're listed as Ms. Helmer's . . ."

"Don't say 'next of kin.' "

She smiled with a look of candid intelligence. "Of course not. In fact, she'll be fine."

"May I have the details, please?"

"Mm. The gist of it is, the bullet lodged in the fleshy part of her upper left thigh." She consulted the chart she was holding. "No permanent muscle damage . . . um . . .

probably only *very* slight scarring. In other words, a piece of cake."

"That's very good to hear."

"The only little problem we had was finding the slug without X rays."

What? "Why no X rays?"

Her small, handsome face turned serious. "Well, naturally, that close to the abdomen when the patient's pregnant."

Hello!

"Especially at the end of the first trimester." She closed the chart and smiled again. "I guess you'd like to see her now."

Suddenly that was an understatement.

But then a thought struck me and I said, "Would a few minutes make a difference?" The doctor looked puzzled. "I've been in a precinct station for eight hours without any food. I'll be in better shape to, uh, cheer Sally up if I can stop in the cafeteria first."

Dr. Sloan smiled warmly and nodded.

So I sat for twenty minutes with coffee in a Styrofoam cup and a sandwich made with Styrofoam bread and thought about a lot of things, all of them linked to Sally.

Then I pulled myself together and marched back to her room. Whether it was the shock of today's traumas or just the culmination of a long subconscious process, I was finally ready to stand and deliver.

I knocked on the door and edged in, feeling the unease of all hospital visitors, then sat on a hard chair beside her bed, leaned over, and kissed her. "How you doing?"

A wan smile. "Just dandy, except for my Swiss cheese butt." She lay on her stomach with her face turned toward me far enough to reveal just one blue eye.

I smiled back. "It's not fair to get an injury that's funny."

Sally sighed and nodded.

"Well, I hope your backside heals quickly."

Faintly, "Me too."

"Because you won't be able to lie on your stomach much longer."

A very long pause while Sally's one visible eye stared blindly at the sheet below it.

"Will you, Sally?"

"No." The eye squeezed shut. "Damn!"

"Oh, the doctor didn't think she was spilling any beans. She naturally assumed I knew." I couldn't keep all the hurt out of my tone.

Sally's eye opened and found mine, then lowered again.

"So I sat and mulled it over. At first I thought I understood why you hadn't told me. For weeks now you've been edging toward some personal decision and then veering off again."

Sally mumbled, "I haven't been a million laughs, I know."

I ignored that. "But then I realized I was wrong. You made *some* kind of choice as long as half a year ago."

"How would *you* know?"

"You know my methods, Watson. You've been on the Pill, which is almost perfectly effective when you take it as religiously as you did."

"*Did?*"

"To get pregnant, you had to stop it."

"It doesn't *always* work." But her tone sounded defensive.

"What's more, you can't go off the Pill and just get pregnant in a week. It takes your system two, maybe three months to reconvert."

Stubborn silence.

"Since you're already three months pregnant, you decided to have a baby *at least* five months ago."

More silence, then, "What do you want from me, Winston?"

By now I couldn't keep my anger down. "I want you to put up or shut up. I have loved you for years, and now I love the idea of the baby—once I get over the shock. More than anything else, I've wanted us to marry, and if that puts heavy pressure on you, *too damn bad!*"

"You got quite a bedside manner there."

"And you have a genius for deflecting uncomfortable thoughts. So whatever your decision was, and for whatever reasons, I deserve to know it *now*."

Sally finally moved her head so that both eyes were visible. She surveyed my face, one feature at a time, her own face unreadable.

I stood up. "Do I buy a ring or start packing?"

Sally swiveled her head to look up at me, but stayed obdurately silent.

Finally, I nodded grimly. "So be it. I'll be out of the upstairs tomorrow. Give me a week to find a new apartment." I started for the door. "And in future, cover your ass."

"Stoney?"

When I turned around she was smiling.

"You finally did it. You *finally* stood up on your two hind legs and barked. Go buy the ring." Tears welled up in her eyes and spilled down her cheeks.

But she went right on smiling.

35

*T*he following Saturday was five weeks to the day since all the fun had begun, and as I sat through the end of the second taping, it seemed as if nothing had changed. The big plastic safe was on stage in its spotlights, Kilparrow's toupee was as splendid as ever, and three new perky contestants giggled and furrowed their brows.

The only change was in Kelli's gown, a cascade of chiffon with padded shoulders that hid the gauze binding on her damaged breast. She was in good form today and the audience howled at her ad libs and *shtick*.

Even I was back where I started, at the foot of the writers' table. As a grudging reward for my efforts this week, Ma had undemoted me. "I guess you can learn on the goddam job," was her gracious explanation.

But the goddam job wasn't fun anymore. Those past five weeks had changed it—or possibly me. Five weeks ago Amber had been on that stage. Now she and Arnesen were dead and Carlisle and his Kung Fu Honey were both in

the jug. They'd been easy to hold because Clipper'd confessed with an eerie good humor that said she hadn't the
dimmest idea of what her actions had meant.

I registered on Kilparrow's hearty bray. "Over to you
then, Kelli. Finance: Whaddya call a Russian country
bumpkin?"

"A ruble!" (Laughs, groans, and thunderous applause.)

Even the questions were off the bottom of the barrel. I
stared sourly at the answer printed in Chyron characters
on my monitor. Ron Tolkis was back at work too. Hassan's
farewell letter had done its job, and Parames had packed
up his coffee beans and folders and left in his square sedan.

Lost in my sullen fog I missed the ending of the show,
and when I registered again, the audience was milling
around the doors and the crew was battening down for the
night. Without much purpose, I wandered away toward the
Green Room.

There, the contestants were taking off their makeup and
telling one another how real neat it had been, while Arlo
Bracken mooched about in her black vinyl duds and Bart
Simpson haircut.

I was about to move toward her when the door opened
behind me and Kelli Dengham swept in on the arm of
Manny Savick. "Hi, Stoney!" She tripped over and kissed
me on the cheek. "No huggies today. My chest is still killing
me!" She was bubbling brighter than ever.

I couldn't help smiling. "But it looks like your mood is
sparkling champagne."

A beat while she pushed that through her processor, then
Kelli lit up like a pinball machine. "I'm so excited I can't

stand it! Guess what: Manny got me a *People* cover!" She clapped her hands like a little girl.

Savick beamed with avuncular pride. "Week after next."

Kelli leaned close and lowered her voice. "I didn't want to at first—I mean, how will people take it?" Her right hand made a little gesture toward her crotch. "But Manny said it'll be *fabulous* publicity."

I kept my smile stuck on, but my face felt like sun-baked mud. "Trust Manny about publicity."

She grabbed his arm. "Do I ever! He made me see my personal problems aren't, like, real important." With childish solemnity, "After all, my career comes first."

Ah yes: careers.

"Well, we gotta run. Manny's taking me to a big deal in Bel Air tonight." Kelli turned away, then immediately turned back. "Oh, Stoney?" Her tight-wound smile relaxed and her blue saucer eyes widened. "Thank you." She paused as if trying come up with more, then shrugged helplessly and repeated, "Thank you."

They strolled off with a genial wave from Savick, and I made for the standup desk where Arlo presided. "Yo, Arlo."

She didn't look up from her clipboard. "Winston."

To make conversation I said, "Kelli just told me she got a *People* cover."

Arlo put down her clipboard and sighed. "Big deal." She waved a hand spotted with bright green nails at the door through which Kelli had left. "So pretty soon everyone'll be saying, 'Now there goes a lady with *balls*.' "

"What?" I'd thought that the news wasn't out yet.

"Kelli told me today." A snort. "I knew it months ago anyway."

"You . . . ?"

"I handle her wardrobe during the week, and I'm not exactly dumb." She looked at me with something like hostility. "But it wasn't really anybody's business, *was* it?"

Was it? Even now, I couldn't decide. I changed the subject: "Want to go grab a quick beer, Arlo?"

She checked out my jeans and sneakers. "I dunno, Winston. Dressed like that you could ruin my reputation." Then a smile softened her tough expression. "I'll chance it."

I smiled back. "Give me five minutes. I need to write a note to Ma."

Arlo sneered. "A groveling thank-you for getting your writing job back?"

I shook my head. "A letter of resignation."

Arlo's raggedy eyebrows rose, but she was far too cool to comment.